Tears of Blood
(The Veronian Archives)

BY DANIEL L WELCH

DEDICATION

To my mother, Cindy Story, who once told me that I was a good man. I strive to live up to that compliment every day.

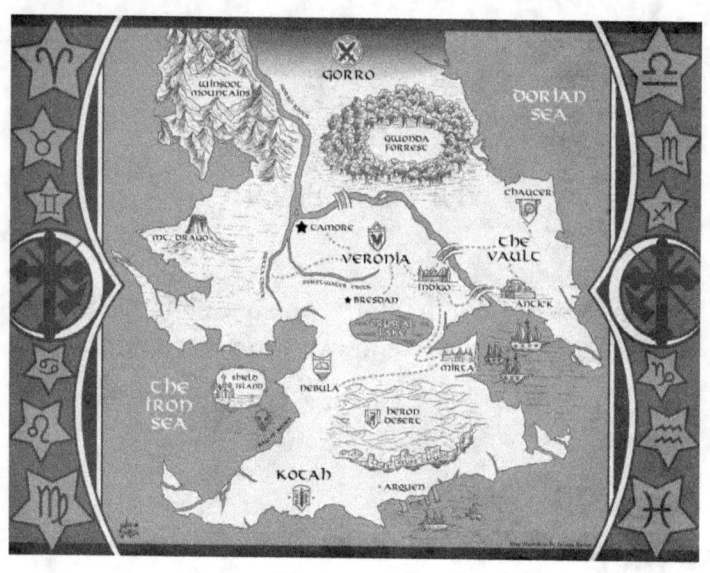

DEDICATION

To my mother, Cindy Story, who once told me that I
was a good man. I strive to live up to that compliment
every day.

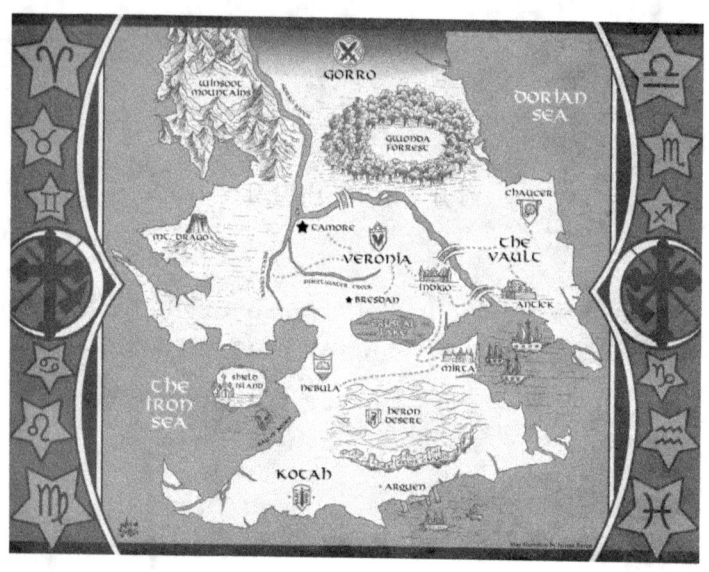

CONTENTS

Acknowledgments   i

Chapter 1   Pg 1

Chapter 2   Pg 32

Chapter 3   Pg 59

Chapter 4   Pg 77

Chapter 5   Pg 103

Chapter 6   Pg 122

Chapter 7   Pg 136

Chapter 8   Pg 156

Chapter 9   Pg 189

Chapter 10   Pg 215

Chapter 11   Pg 237

Chapter 12   Pg 265

About the Author   Pg 306

ACKNOWLEDGMENTS

I wish to thank the following people for their contributions to my inspiration, knowledge, and other help in creating this book:

Chris Jones, for handing me a book that sparked my passion for reading and writing.

My editor, Michelle Josette, for her professionalism, attention to detail, and encouragement.

And to my late friend Juan Legarreta. When the Bible mentions God-fearing, mighty men of valor, men of strength and renown, I think of you.

CHAPTER

1

Leo watched as sparks from Bruce's flint and steel showered the damp kindling below, igniting a fire that kept their limbs alive. The surviving officers of the Veronian Army huddled tightly around its warmth, while the enlisted men sought whatever refuge they could find outside the cave-turned-command post.

Many of them burrowed beneath the snow and into the earth to lick their wounds and shield themselves from the deadly, bone-cold winds. Others attempted to stoke and revive brittle fires left behind that morning, but dry wood was almost as scarce as food.

It was their eighth day in what the enlisted men dubbed the Frostbite, an icy campaign to repel the invading Gorronian Barbarians. They had not yet been resupplied as was promised, nor reinforced as discussed before their departure from Tamore to the mountains. Leo was keenly aware of their abandoned state; desertion weighed heavily on the minds of the surviving soldiers.

Lieutenant Juan Soberal groaned like a hungry bear tearing a tattered bandage from his forearm. "How long are we going to defend these mountains without reinforcements? It's been eight days and the cold's killing more of us than the Gorronians. Feel like I'm trapped inside a snowball."

"Ahhh. Fetch me another bottle," General Vrago wailed as the fire began to warm and burn his frostbitten legs and feet. Sergeant Birdsong retrieved another bottle of hard liquor and handed it to the lame general. It didn't take him long to race to the bottom, choking and hacking as he drank.

With Vrago suffering the chill on his deathbed, or rock rather, Juan had assumed second-in-command behind Captain Leo Rosewood. There were senior officers at hand, but soldiers look for men of valor, not seniority, to lead them in battle. Leo wouldn't allow another pussyfooted, king-appointed noble to lead them to defeat.

Lieutenant Natalie Collins was the only woman in the regiment sent to defend the mountain range. A tight auburn braid hung down the length of her neck. Bright green eyes lay concealed within a "don't fuck with me" scowl, the kind readily available to her women-deprived brethren. With each arrow she loosed, savage corpses piled higher and higher, quickly overcoming any stereotypes that women best belonged in the kitchen.

She shed her snow-dampened boots and sat barefoot, toes flexing close to the fire. "I'll second that. What good are these damn mountains anyways? Sure they look pretty and all from a distance but they sure as hell aren't worth dying for and that's all we're doing up here. If King Lawrence wanted to hold on to them so bad, why would he only send one regiment to defend it, and with no reinforcements besides?"

"I don't think the king realizes the severity of the situation," Captain Drew Strickland said. "He's known no fighting during his reign and he'll gain no knowledge of it sitting on his throne in the Capitol. The fact that he wouldn't allow Prince Marion to lead the campaign alongside General Vrago is also worth some deliberation."

That was an understatement. Every soldier in the Frostbite had quietly speculated why the king wouldn't allow the prince to accompany the campaign, despite Marion's very public displeasure. Many were less quiet than others after several days in the mountains.

The discussion continued back and forth as Leo leaned against the rock cave like a fly on the wall, his attention drawn to the queer-looking mineral deposits Sergeant Birdsong called stalagmites. Leo broke the tip off one, turning it over in his hand. He could think of only one use for the rough-edged rock, and set to honing the edge of his blade with it.

Leo had grown tired of discussing the same details day after day and was well aware of their situation, yet cared less about the king's intentions or motivations. Leo wore the customary Officer's Armor, lightweight chainmail under a metal breastplate and gauntlets. A purple belted tunic made up his outermost layer, the Veronian V woven onto the chest.

The enlisted soldiers wore chainmail under belted tunics and metal helms. Sergeants like Bruce Donnell saw the advantage a sound set of armor provided in a swordfight and lived a frugal life to pay for armor upgrades. Others made do with what was issued, or scavenged what they could from the fallen whose armor would be of no use in the afterlife.

Leo was content dressed as he was. His short-cropped blond hair was matted with Gorronian blood. Specks of it dried to his face and armor; after the third day he stopped trying to wash it away from his flesh. He was born for combat, a trait passed down from his father. While others sought an end to the carnage, Leo looked forward to the next battle.

Whether it was bloodlust that consumed him or the primal high one gets from a brush with death he could not say, but he longed for the next opportunity to test his mortal strength, a welcomed distraction from garrison life and awkward socialization among the nobility.

The deliberating continued until Drew's patience seemed to run thin. "What say you, Leo?" he barked over the other voices. "Or should I say Captain of the Frozen Army?"

The gathering drew quiet, their attention resting on their leader. However callous Leo was thought to be, there wasn't a man in the army, perhaps the world, who could stand against him with sword and shield. It was no secret why they had survived eight days in their present condition.

It hadn't taken Vrago long to make his first mistake as Commanding Officer. The first day in the mountains, the general led the army to an open piece of rocky land alongside a slow-moving, half-frozen stream between two snowcapped mountains. It was there Vrago lost his footing while pissing into the stream. He sank waist-deep before Sergeant Birdsong had fished him out.

Birdsong was half Gorronian, half Tribesman, and thought to be full of shit on account of his many superstitious beliefs. He was handpicked by Prince Marion to act as Translator, should they need one, but in the end did more babysitting than anything else. "The mountains watch over its mountain men," Birdsong said, peering into the distance. Vrago flopped like a fish out of water at his feet.

"What mountain men? Ain't never seen one of

'em," Bruce added, a bit concerned now.

"Me either. But I'll aim for the dirt next time nature calls."

They had no protection from the fierce north wind and the Gorronians sprang their trap, splitting their army into three masses. Attacking the Veronians on three fronts allowed Vrago's army only one option—retreat. Vrago, lame as he was, wouldn't hear of it. Instead he called for a mount to take him where his legs could not, to break the enemy lines.

"You want a mount, take mine," Leo spat, handing Vrago the reins.

Birdsong moved forward to lift the general onto the mount.

"Get back," Leo barked, pushing Birdsong aside with naked steel. "I've had enough of this amateur hour." Leo squatted, eye level with Vrago so nothing got lost in translation. "Only reason I ain't cut your feckin' throat is 'cause I look forward to watching the chill take you inch by inch. You get in my way and I'll dunk the rest of your sorry hide in the stream and let the wolves have what's left. Get him out of here, Birdsong. Everyone else, fall back!"

Juan lingered as the rest scurried off. "What the hell?" he said, palming his face. "The king will have your head for that. You know he will."

"Far as I could tell, Vrago's polar plunge rendered him incapable of leading," Leo said. "The fever clogged his judgment; the chill took his legs and turned him mad. You see anything different, Bruce?"

"The chill turned his brain to mush. Started eating his own shit, I'll say," Bruce replied, taking his leave.

"What about you, Birdsong?" Leo asked.

Birdsong pulled Vrago and horse up the hill. "We make it off this mountain alive, I'll dance to any song you sing."

The earth trembled as the Gorronian army closed in, the east flank having already made contact.

"Unbelievable," Juan said, shaking his head. "After you then, Commander."

At Leo's order, the regiment fell back to higher ground. Huge mountains on either side protected their new east and west flanks. From atop the hill Gorronians had no idea how few Veronian soldiers actually manned the lines. This bought them the eight days they had survived and left the Gorronians frustrated and tired of attacking uphill.

Rock on steel became the only noise to be heard in the command post. Leo slowly realized someone had asked him a question he hadn't heard. He stood, sheathing his sword and slinging it across his back. Fire danced from each of their eyes like predators stalking prey in the night.

Leo had been in charge only a few days but the strain of command was ever present and quite demanding. "Two more days is all I ask. If we don't get reinforced or send those bloody Gorronians running back north by the tenth day, then we'll fall back to the

Capitol."

"Some of the men think the king sent us up here for you to be killed off," Drew challenged. "That he feels threatened by your presence much like he was of your father's."

"I'm well aware of what's going on here. Whether I die here or return to the Capitol leading a defeated army, the end result is much of the same. You guys are more than welcome to head home when you see fit. Feel free to tell everyone it was at my command if it pleases you. Call it what you will but I'd rather be gutted by a Gorronian than stabbed in the back by my own king."

The group took their cue and left to pass the orders back to their men. Two more days. Juan lingered behind, along with Birdsong who tended to Vrago. He sat down in the cave next to Leo and rested his bastard sword in his lap.

"You're fighting twice as hard as the rest of us lugging that behemoth around, you know," Leo said. "Lucky you don't have to feed the damn thing or we'd all starve."

"Glad to see neither death nor disgrace rattles your sense of humor," Juan said.

"Death comes to us all. Honor and disgrace is in the eye of the beholder. Do you really think the king would sacrifice a whole regiment to get rid of me?" Leo asked, though he knew the answer already.

"If he felt it would prolong his or the prince's reign,

yes, I'm afraid he would. Whether you want to acknowledge it or not, Veronians love the Rosewoods despite you being among them. Your father was the most decorated general the army has ever seen. Your brother Jewel sits on the High Priest's Council and your sister Page is the most sought-after bride in the empire. I should know."

"And you've won a Guardian Dagger and Sword," Juan added. "If you come back a war hero too, you'll be one of the most powerful men in the kingdom. Of course the king sees that as a potential threat."

"I'm a soldier. I've no desire to compete with the king for power. He can choke on it for all I care. You think the fool would know that by now."

"And that's precisely why the people like you so much. No doubt you're rough around the edges but you are your father's son after all. Unfortunately you also possess a burning desire to forfeit your life as quickly as you can. That recklessness unnerves the common folk and nobility alike."

"Bullshit," Leo said. "You and I aren't much different, you know. We've shared much of the same course through life."

"Except you've always been a half step ahead. You've a way with the sword I've never seen before, but you're a regular recluse so I'm forced to follow you along and translate as best I can. You shouldn't race so hastily to the grave though, I'm not eager to follow you there just yet." A hint of a smile crossed Juan's face.

There was a brief pause as the two sat in silence looking into the fire. Leo figured most of the soldiers' thoughts wandered towards their loved ones at home. No mind-reader was Leo, but he'd too often caught Juan in a hot mess of nerves around his sister Page. *Is it her he thinks of now? Yes. Always her.*

Leo stood. "You're the only man I trust with her but you'll do no good to any of us dead. Don't do anything stupid like getting yourself killed," he said, walking out of the cave.

The next morning Leo peeled himself up from a rock-piled shelter. It had been another cold and restless night. Water came in the form of melted snow. He'd filled his water skin with stream water but it had frozen solid over night. Their food wagons had run out on the sixth day, forcing them to send hunting expeditions south to hunt and gather. Given the chance, many of the men did not return. Those who did brought back little game.

Spirits were high as the news of departure in two days spread throughout camp. A hot meal and the comfort of dry ground appealed even to Leo, who one way or another would have a reckoning with the king upon returning home to Veronia's capital city of Tamore.

"If you snuggled that water skin half as hard as the men snuggle the camp whores, that skin wouldn't have frozen on you," Natalie said, taking a pull of her own. "Mmmm. It tastes good as it looks. You look lively enough but you smell like you've turned to cuddling the dead for warmth. Of course warmth is a rather presumptuous assumption but I'll give you the benefit of the doubt."

"Waited long as I could by the stream for a scrubbing but you never turned up. As for the whores, if you see any about chase 'em off."

Her head tilted in curiosity. "You don't seem the type to deprive a man of such a primal pleasure."

"Their pleasure doesn't concern me," Leo said. "They can fuck holes in every wall we pass on the way home, but I'll not risk the Gorronians slipping a few diseased whores through our lines like the Norsemen did my father's army. Gave half his men the crotch rot."

Natalie laughed. "Expel the whores. Got it."

Leo watched his men finish what little chow they had before manning the lines. There's no job too small on the frontlines of a war. At home a man might complain about burning and burying a latrine. Ain't no honor in the shit watch but the beasts of the Winsoot grow larger than man and the smell of piss and shit is just as enticing as wounded and rotting flesh.

"Figured you weren't the type to give a heroic speech and rally the men to hold on for two more days, so Drew and Bruce took the liberty of spreading the word," Natalie told him.

"Ain't a whole lot needs to be said anyways. Best we just get on with it."

"Simple words for a simple man," she mused.

"We've already ordered the men to man the lines. If they send another wave at us, we'll be ready. I'll bother you no longer, Lord Commander. I know how terribly taxing these briefs can be on you."

"Natalie," he said, catching her attention as she turned and strode off. She'd unslung her crossbow, bolt in one hand, bow in the other. He said nothing further. Sometimes a look can say what your mouth cannot.

Natalie gave a swift nod and went about her business, assembling her archers as she went. "Archers up!"

It didn't take long after daybreak for the Gorronians to send their first wave of attackers up the hill. Endless as their numbers seemed to be, each uphill assault took its toll and each day fewer and fewer war cries were heard as they ascended. The Frostbite didn't discriminate against either army, it seemed.

General Vrago led ten thousand soldiers to the Winsoot Mountains. The Gorronians claimed a couple thousand of them. The Frostbite claimed hundreds more. Only a thousand or so Veronians could stand the line at once without cluttering the peak of the hill. This was a blessing in disguise for the soldiers. It meant they could break up into seven companies that rotated the flanks and front line.

Despite a body full of cuts, aches and bruises, Leo tended only the front line. His father had done it no other way and he was indeed his father's son. *Order your men to fight and they'll kill for you. Lead them in the front and they'll die for you*, his father had always told him.

Juan, strong and stubborn as he was, stood at Leo's side each attack. However, on the third day he received a deep slashing cut on the forearm that slowed him ever so slightly. He initially refused to stand down, arguing with Leo long enough to fight every other wave until his wound fully healed. With two days left, regardless of the outcome, Juan staunchly refused to sit through any attacks and Leo saw no use in arguing otherwise.

Up the hill ran the battle-hardened Gorronians. They wore thick furs that doubled as armor to protect from the harsh climate. Most of them carried crudely-made hatchets, stone-ended blunt weapons, and dense wooden sticks. Some of them had even acquired swords and shields from fallen Veronian soldiers.

Natalie's archers stood close behind the front lines as they had on each attack. She looked forward to Juan and Leo, awaiting the signal to loose.

Leo paced back and forth, up and down the line with sword and shield in hand. Like a crazed animal he beat the pommel of his sword against his shield, creating a *boom........boom.......boom.*

"Are you with me?" he yelled.

The rest of the army—those at the front line and the thousands behind—pounded the pommel of their own swords and shields in unison, creating a deafening sound. *BOOM........BOOM.......BOOM.*

BOOM...."Kill 'em all!"*...........BOOM.......*"Kill 'em

all!".........*BOOM*......."Kill   'em all!"............*BOOM*..........."Kill 'em all!"

Leo turned from his army to face the enemy. With sword and shield raised, he belted a war cry and lowered his arms to signal the archers. The captain watched as the arrows flew up into the sky. They hummed through the air like a wartime melody, cries of pain and triumph its song.

He watched the piercing rain pelt down and through the charging enemy. Dozens fell as others hurdled over stricken casualties to reach the summit. Leo locked eyes with his selected target. The big bastard chewed up ground like he was running downhill, hatchet in hand and ready for work.

Leo blocked a hatchet slash and buried his sword through the left side of the man's neck. He spun off the falling corpse to deflect another hatchet blow that threw the attacker off balance. Not bothering to slash or stab this foe, he ran his hand guard through cheek and bone, crunching the life from his pursuer.

Two more attackers ran towards Leo as he looked up. From the corner of his right eye Juan appeared, bastard sword raised high, delivering a blow that nearly cut a Gorronian in two.

A man appeared to Leo's left in a flash. He raised his shield a moment before impact. The sickening *woosh* of an arrow, too close for comfort, flew over his shoulder, taking the attacking Gorronian center mass. The savage bounced off Leo's shield, landing upon his back with only the frozen earth to hold him. It provided no such comfort as his bloody hands protectively clutched the bolt that protruded from his chest.

Leo took a brief second to glance back and found Natalie reloading her crossbow. She gave him a wink before loosing towards her next target.

He turned back to business as a sea of purple Veronian soldiers stepped forward to hold the line. It took only a few minutes to repel the first wave of that ninth day, and they would repel two more before day's end.

***

For the first time since they had arrived in the Winsoot Mountains, the morale of the men was somewhat high. Juan imagined most of them didn't care whether they won the battle tomorrow or not, focusing instead on staying alive long enough to make it home.

Inside the command post, the cave was eerily quiet without Vrago's sniveling. The general had passed away sometime during the day and Juan had ordered Birdsong and five men to carry the general back to the Capitol for a full ceremonial burial. They had been burying their dead as best they could in the snow but most lay above ground with only a few kind words of remembrance to send them off to the other side.

"We had fewer loses today than any other since we've been here," Drew said, peering onto the empty slab of rock their general left vacant. "The incentive to move out tomorrow increased their awareness or made them more cautions, one."

"No doubt about that. We need to discuss our........" The word 'retreat' stuck in Juan's throat like an apple core. A bitter one at that.

"Retreat." It was Bruce the Swordmaster from Indigo who spoke. He'd trained nearly half their men in sword and shield at one time or another. When the other lieutenants and captains started dying off, Natalie, who also called Indigo her home, had invited him to attend the command meetings.

"The way I see it, there's no shame in living to fight another day," Bruce continued. "Not sure whose bright idea it was to defend these fecking mountains but we can fight and die all the same on thawed Veronian soil. They want these mountains that bad, they can have them for all I care. Piss on anyone who says different."

"Nonetheless, 'regroup' sounds like a better choice of word for now," Juan said, a bit soured. "Once we return to the Capitol we can coordinate a more preferable location to intercept the Gorronians if they want another go at us. As far away from these damn mountains as possible, if you ask me."

Bruce rummaged through what was left of Vrago's death rock like a bull in a china closet. "Don't tell me Birdsong took all the damn liquor with him. Leave it to him to try and bury the general with a full cask to offer all the damned gods a drink."

Natalie shook her head. "When we get back we need to address the more obvious issues. Maybe the king stranding us in these damn mountains to die, for instance. And for what, to defend a deserted mountain range? To settle a score with the Rosewoods? No offense, Leo," she corrected, looking about the cave for the captain.

Juan continued unaware. "There are definitely more questions than answers right now. My father will no doubt be much more persuasive than any of us hope to be. The king cannot ignore public scrutiny from a commanding general. But the more pressing issues are when we pull out of here and under what circumstances."

Natalie, still seemingly distracted by her search, added, "If you ask me, we should be marching back right now. Why risk any more lives if we are leaving tomorrow anyways?"

Behind them, Bruce's search for drink continued. "I'll second that. Why put off for tomorrow what we can do today?" he said, peering into a bottle as if it had a false bottom.

Drew's gaze met Natalie who stood looking for something. "Leo never said whether we try negotiations with the Gorronians first or if we fight at all tomorrow. Speaking of Leo, where is he?"

There was a brief exchange of troubled glances shared among them before Juan sprang to his feet in alarm. "Shit! I wanted to believe he'd stroll back in here."

Natalie cursed the night, crossbow in hand. "We don't have much guessing to do this time around. The fool's probably headed to the Gorronian camp, if he's not there already."

"Said he'd rather be gutted by a Gorronian than stabbed in the back by his own king," Bruce whispered, realizing what Juan and Natalie were talking about.

Juan's head and shoulders slouched. "I should never have let him out of my sight. That crazy bastard. Set up watches around the camp and wait for his return. Make sure none of the men shoot him in the dark," he ordered.

Drew looked on incredulously. "His return? You think they'll let Leo walk right into their camp in the middle of the night and live to tell the story?"

Juan pushed past the others. "If anyone can do it, he can."

Outside the command post, word quickly spread of their captain's absence. A reinforced perimeter was quickly set up around camp. It didn't take long for one of the soldiers to spot Leo's armor just outside their perimeter, headed straight towards the Gorronian camp.

***

It was a cold dry night. The eve of the Veronian departure left their lookouts complacent and Leo slipped past them unseen. He knew his friends and family would curse his corpse a fool, but he had no choice but to play the hand he was dealt.

He shook off his armor, opting for a more quiet and lightweight, boiled leather jerkin. Carrying only his sword strapped to his back, he paused in prayer just outside the Gorronian perimeter.

"Blessed be the LORD, my Rock, Who trains my hands for war, and my fingers for battle," he whispered, descending the hill. A crimson moon loomed above, reddening the stars around it like a seeping wound. *A blood moon. How suiting.*

Only the crackling of fires could be heard as thousands of Gorronians lay sleeping next to them in roughly-spun shelters. Even at a distance Leo could smell their cooking pots boiling spiced venison. Where his army fought the elements just to eke out an existence, the Gorronians seemed to thrive.

So this was Lawrence's plan? To march an ill-prepared army into a lion's den to rid himself of competition? "By my last breath I'll have the king's head for this," Leo spat, unsheathing his sword. "His corpse will lay waste in the Capitol latrine."

Sneaking up on the first two Gorronian lookouts was easy enough. Leo flanked them from the east, slitting the throat of the first and breaking the neck of the second from behind. Any fear of death he might have had perished atop the hill. *A warrior fears not death but failure*, his father once told him.

He flanked two more lookouts, killing both with

his sword. The second let out a scream that was quickly muffled with Leo's hand but the shout set other curious Gorronians about to find the source. There was no time to hide bodies and no desire to do so. The more dead Gorronians he could pile up, the better. He wanted his presence felt, however short-lived it might be.

Like a shadow in the night, the Veronian captain wove in and out the darkness, killing those who straggled behind. Soon enough he'd sent ten men back to the earth in near-perfect silence. It wasn't long until one of the corpses was discovered, causing panic throughout the camp. They shouted among each other in their native Gorronian tongue. Leo couldn't decipher their meaning but the speed at which they armed themselves was translation enough.

As more and more of them piled out towards the south side of their camp, Leo swept around the east side until he found himself on the unguarded north side of it. Thousands of Gorronian soldiers ran back and forth through the night, torches in hand, trying to find the intruders.

Leo located what appeared to be the headquarters of the Gorronian camp—a large buckskin tent sown together and erected by wooden posts. His stomach churned, adrenaline consumed him like a feral cat. With sword in hand, he low-crawled under the tent flap. He couldn't defeat the Gorronians at the rate they were going so he'd opted for drastic measures. Like a mighty boa squeezing the life from its prey, the only hope of escape was to sever the head. Taking out the Gorronian general might release the stranglehold they maintained even at the bottom of the hill.

The frozen earth brushed his skin. It wasn't cold he felt, but his own body heat radiating off the ground. Once inside, he sprung to his feet, sword at the ready, but nothing in life had ever come easy for Leo. Only the chill of the night welcomed him inside the tent. A wooden nightstand suffered the brunt of his rage as Leo pummeled it to sawdust.

By the bones! Great plan, jackass. Leo had a moment there in that tent. A bit of self-reflection that didn't quite appeal. The cold began to fade as he made his peace. "Let's get on with it, then," he spat.

He strode out from the tent's entrance bold as you please and stood sword in hand. "Looking for me?" he growled, bearing his steel. Only death suited him now. Theirs, his, it made no matter.

The Gorronians trickled forward, blinking hard in disbelief. A few precious moments passed before realization sunk in. Incredulity birthed vengeance as one by one they surrounded Leo, spitting and cursing in a tongue drowned in hate. The circle closed like the proverbial snake he sought to behead.

Leo had often thought of dying in a blaze of glory. Gone over witty and clever last words to sting his enemy. Now that death closed in sure as the sun would rise, all those last lines eluded him. Not that it mattered now for he no longer felt the urge to speak. A smile spread as he awaited the storm of swords. *A death worth dying*, he thought, and lunged ahead.

Thousands gathered round, waiting and watching as Leo fought off attacker after attacker. Loud as lions they roared each time a blow landed, whether friend or foe. Their screams deafening, the world closed in. Each savage that fell was dragged from the circle, another challenger quickly taking his place. After every man he killed, Leo looked around, waiting for them to submerge him like a tidal wave that never came.

He had no idea how many savages he'd slain but more blood than sweat covered his skin. Each slash and stab that came his way stoked the fire inside to kill another. He'd found himself in the ultimate game of kill or be killed and sooner or later he would tire or they would get bored and finish him. But not yet.

His arms began to ache, his legs strained to carry his weight. A Gorronian lunged at him and Leo barely avoided the blade, much less raise his sword to land a blow. The barbarian shouldered forward, knocking him to one knee and sending his Guardian Sword to the cold, blood-stained earth. The crowd roared and although he didn't understand a lick of Gorronian, he could pretty damn well guess what they were saying. *Finish him.*

Behind his attacker loomed the crimson moon, hanging lower than Leo had ever seen. Like a blanket, the moon heated his blood-soaked skin like a warm lover in the cold night. Adjacent stars flickered like beating hearts in the sky.

The Gorronian circled round, taunting his kneeling unarmed opponent. Leo's boiled leather was a tattered mess. His arms and face were covered in scratches, cuts, and stabs. They should have hurt. His limbs should have ached, but no pain dwelled within him.

The barbarian strode behind him and stopped, sending a shiver up Leo's spine. Leo scowled forward into the crowd of Gorronians. "I'll be damned before dying on my knees," he said, standing. "Get on with it!"

The crowd fell silent. Leo knew his opponent was at his back and could sense the moment his sword raised to deliver the killing blow. As the sword came down to meet his neck, Leo stepped to the right and grabbed hold of the Gorronian's sword-wielding hand. He pulled the savage's head back by the hair, exposing a throat long enough to sink his teeth into the barbarian's jugular. Leo spat a mouthful of flesh onto the attacker who dropped to the ground, clutching the void in his neck.

He looked around at the crowd of Gorronians who stood staring in disbelief. He defied them once more, bellowing a war cry that depleted what little energy remained. The world spun and the ground rose to meet him. As darkness blanketed his thoughts, the biggest Gorronian he'd ever seen entered the circle and the crowd roared.

***

"What are they yelling?" Juan asked anxiously.

"*Bucha Enut*," Sergeant Wade Holloway answered. With Birdsong gone, Wade was the closest thing to a translator the Veronian Army had left, and he was far from fluent. "Blood plant?" he asked himself. "No. Blood Rose. Means Bloody Rose if I ain't mistaken."

It was midnight, as far as Juan could tell, and Leo had been gone for the better part of two hours. Shouts from the Gorronian camp could be heard for miles and everyone in the Veronian camp was on edge. None more so than Juan, who stood impatiently at the perimeter with Natalie and Bruce at his side. Every roar of the crowd was like a knife twisting in Juan's chest. Several times he flung himself headlong down the hill, only to be wrestled back to the line by the others.

"We can't risk giving up the high ground to save one man," Drew reasoned as Juan attempted to rally a rescue party.

Deep inside, Juan knew Drew was right. Didn't make listening to the roaring Gorronians any easier, though.

"It's him!" a voice cried.

"Who? Where?" Juan replied.

"It's Rosewood!" another shouted, pointing down the hill.

As the figure approached, soldiers gathered along the perimeter to receive what was left of their leader. The crimson moon turned pale, illuminating Leo who looked more beast than human. Red as a man tending the winepress, he clutched his sword with wild eyes that saw nothing and everything.

The perimeter parted to let Leo pass as he made his way to the command post. He turned to face his army at the cave's entrance. Their faces were covered with questions that none had the nerve to ask.

Juan could tell Leo was in no mood to be put to questions, and his bloody scowl emphasized the point. "One more fight. Those of you ain't got no killing left in you better leave tonight. Ain't no shame in it I reckon. Hell, I can't even remember why we're here to begin with, but I need hard-boiled warriors at my side tomorrow."

They stood speechless for a time. Uneasy breathing broke the cold silence, each man weighing the task at hand. Most couldn't give two shits about winning or losing at this point, they just wanted to make it home.

"You know I'll be your shoulder man," Juan said.

"And I," echoed Natalie and Bruce in unison.

More pledges to fight trickled in till the whole army had their swords raised in the night. Wasn't long before the chanting started to ring out.

Bloody Rose!...... Bloody Rose!....... Bloody Rose!

"They're calling me Bloody Rose now?" Leo asked as they entered the cave.

"It was either that or pretty flower, so Wade gave you the benefit of the doubt," Natalie japed. The fire's light began to reveal the full extent of Leo's injuries, and Natalie's smile reversed.

Try as he might, Juan couldn't restrain his disdain. "Call for a healer! What the hell were you thinking, Leo? Just what in the hell happened down there?"

Leo flashed a wolf grin and sprawled onto the bedrock. "Stories are supposed to be told after the war. I'm not done with mine yet."

***

Morning came faster than Leo had wanted. Muscles he didn't even know he had ached all over his body. Wounds had scabbed over and tightened; stretching was out of the question. He instantly longed for a soak in the clear waters of Crystal Lake. But it was not meant to be.

Natalie had tried to treat what wounds she could but Leo had waved her away, opting to get a few hours sleep instead. He'd slept in the command post for the first time and didn't feel the least bit guilty of it. *So this is what Vrago must have felt like, dying in a rock tomb.* He had stumbled to his feet when he had realized he was on the same rock.

Juan chuckled, obviously enjoying the sight of Leo's discomfort—perhaps a bit too much. "I'm sure you'll be a terror on the battlefield today. But how do you expect to fight when you can barely stand?"

"Laugh it up, jackass," Leo replied, looking for his gear. His skin was thick—in this line of work it had to be—their prodding just dust in the wind. "Where's my armor?"

Natalie clanked forward holding Leo's breastplate. "You deserve every ache and bruise you got. Remember that the next time you turn your armor into a lawn ornament."

Leo slid on a donated leather jerkin, then fought and lost the battle of securing his breastplate. "Where's a good little squire when you need one?"

Juan hefted the breastplate and slid it over Leo's shoulders. "You're going to need more than foolish pride to fight in the shape you're in. Can't have you dying a meaningless death on the last day of a pointless campaign, can we?"

Natalie reluctantly handed him his sword. Her nose turned ever so slightly when she looked at his wounds. "They left a few holes in you that need some mending. Even the smallest wound can fester and take the mightiest of men down and you're covered in them. Don't be a fool, Leo. Sit this one out and let us finish it. You've done more than your share thus far."

They tell those with a fear of heights to keep their eyes up. Never look down or the phobia will set its hooks in you like a glance towards Medusa. Works the same way with wounds, but Leo took a look down anyways. Dried blood covered much of the damage, but he'd have to keep it clean to let it mend, for that's when the real pain starts. *Perhaps they're right. Maybe I do need to rest, but I'll be damned before I stand aside a casualty.*

"I know you're worried about me but we don't have time for this. Save it for the eulogy," Leo said, shrugging to loosen the stiffness in his neck and shoulders.

The soreness was a weakness he wished to strangle just for the bloody inconvenience. "They should have killed me last night. Probably would have made it a lot easier on the lot of you. I don't mean to be ungrateful but in war you kill those who want to take all you got and letting me live is rather bothersome, like an itch I can't scratch. By the sword, they'll regret the day they spared me."

After a meager breakfast of dried venison and water so cold it nearly froze his pipes, Leo ran in place and called for Juan to spar before heading to the line.

Leo's lean, muscular frame had a slight height advantage over Juan, and on most days he was the better swordsman. However, the past nine days had finally started taking their toll. It was all he could do to backpedal and raise his shield up again and again as Juan delivered brute blow after brute blow with his bastard sword.

His knees shook and strained as they fought to keep him upright but resistance was futile and after a few more overhand blows, Leo found his ass-end buried in snow. Juan had taken nothing off his blows, an obvious effort to prove even the Bloody Rose bruised like the rest.

Juan lingered where he stood above Leo's seated form. Anyone else and Leo would have cut their damn ankles off. As it was, the cold snow began to chill his already tight muscles. It would have been almost comfortable if not for the peanut gallery of gawking soldiers who quickly had shit to do when he met their gazes.

Leo shook off his shield and lay on his back, staring up at the sky. It was another cold day on the mountain but at least the wind was calm. His eyes searched the clouded sky for familiar shapes until Juan's disapproving head came shaking into view.

Juan extended a helping hand, then quickly reeled it back in. "Just as I suspected. You'd be hard-pressed to fight gravity and make it to your feet in the condition you're in. Why don't you just stay there for a little while? Get a little beauty sleep; Lord knows you could use it. We can handle this without you. Afterwards, we leave."

Leo struggled to his feet, till Juan clasped his hand and effortlessly lifted him upright. "Next time I'll not cut corners to protect your pride," he said, garnering a few chuckles from Drew and Bruce.

Now on his feet, Leo realized it wasn't just Juan and Natalie gathered around to watch the sparring debacle. Seemed the majority of the army had a vested interest in their commander's welfare. A broken leader spreads doubt like cracking ice, and none knew that better than Leo.

His wounded pride caused his face and neck to heat, and the pain began to fade away. Leo tossed his shield and stood sword at the ready, eyes set more on killing than sparring. "Juan. Brother. Care for Round Two?"

"You look pretty well warmed up to me," Juan replied. You don't live long in the presence of a crazy fucker like Leo without knowing certain boundaries, and no dullard was he.

"Anyone else?" Leo barked. His shoulders set, beckoning a challenger. None came.

Wade approached, hands visibly empty to ease the tension. "We'll be close by should you need a helping hand. I would say a man can't take on a whole army by himself, but......."

Enough distractions. "We'll call on the archers early. Natalie, use what's left of the venom tips and fire. However many they send up the hill, make sure none of them make it down." Leo strode towards the front line. "The rest of you, on me."

He ordered all swords to man the line even though footing was scarce. The idea was to give the appearance of a reinforced army ready to finish the battle once and for all. Not necessarily a total bluff as he was getting tired of the monotony.

He paced the line, mind already doing a bit of killing like soldiers do. They stood there waiting for what seemed an eternity but the Gorronians never came. Nobody dared speak or reason why. A voice might upset the fragile balance of things, sending the savage bastards up the hill.

Time has a way of playing tricks on a man the moments before and during a battle. Whether they stood waiting a minute or an hour, Leo couldn't say. But after a while the Gorronians broke their battle formation and began marching away.

Veronian soldiers shouted in jubilation as the barbarians trekked northeast. Others hugged each other, plenty more began to cry at such a beautiful sight. Ten grueling days in the Frostbite and they had finally repelled the invasion.

Tired, starving, frostbitten and wounded, the remaining Veronian soldiers drank their fill of victory and toasted the Bloody Rose.

Juan clasped an armored hand on Leo's shoulder. "You were right, I can't believe it. We can go home!"

Leo resisted the urge to celebrate just yet, eyes still fixed on the barbarian horde, trying to make sense of it all. *Something's wrong. They're unbeaten but where the hell are they going?* "We go home as promised, but this, I fear, may only be the beginning. Unless the Gorronians have lost all sense of direction, they're not only marching away from our army, but away from their homeland. Right towards Gwonda."

CHAPTER

2

They followed the Gorro River south till they found a
manageable crossing at Britta Creek that led them to the
King's Road and back to the Capitol. The trek to the
mountains seemed days longer—perhaps that was
Vrago's intention, but why? Leo spent the whole
journey back in such calculated silence that not even
Juan chose to invoke.

Only a handful of mounts had survived the
mountains and they hauled the wounded, of which there
was no shortage. Bruce bit off a plug of chewing
tobacco and set to spitting as they walked along the dirt

and flat-rock road. "He hasn't said a word since we left the mountains. Haven't seen him eat or drink anything either."

"Maybe Bishop Jewel will be awaiting our arrival," Juan said with a sigh. "If anyone can talk some sense into Leo before he gets himself killed, it'll be his brother."

A smile spread across Natalie's face as distant villages came into view. "Let's hope so. We're home, boys!"

The Veronian Empire's capital city of Tamore sat southeast of the Winsoot Mountains, bordering the mighty Gorro River and the Britta and Sweetwater creeks. The location was carefully chosen many years before because of its rich fertile soil and natural river defense that also teemed with fish.

The castle itself was more than a century old, constructed mostly of large redwoods and oak trees from the sawmills of Crystal Lake. Its design catered more to the residential aspects of a king and his court rather than a defensive stronghold. Modest cottages sat inside the wooden walls, intertwined with trading wagons, storehouses, taverns, and the Capitol Watch barracks.

The castle keep housed King Lawrence and his court, but most of the king's business was conducted in either the open or closed council chambers. Depending on the weather, the king was oftentimes known to gather the open council outside in the courtyard where an elaborate stone and marble platform was erected to seat the king high above his people in order to hear and decide their business. The queen fancied the open air and was only seen outside her chambers at the courtyard.

The sight of the sprawling Capitol caused most of the men to break rank and run to whatever comforts and loved ones they could find. A loud trumpet sounded from the Capitol watchtowers, signaling their return. Each of the four outermost towers was manned by a handful of eagle eyes that had no doubt spotted the returning army much sooner, but blasted the horns again for dramatic effect.

Hundreds of people began to run out of the Capitol's walls, filling the streets to greet the returning soldiers. Townsfolk and soldiers alike ran back and forth, enquiring about the welfare of loved ones. For many soldiers it was a very welcomed reunion, having been reconnected with family thought to have been lost. Other townsfolk were less lucky, forced to sift through the corpse carts for recognizable features of the dead. Most of which had been left on the mountain.

Juan struggled on his tiptoes, trying to look over the crowd for his father to help calm the storm that was to come. He pushed through to the main gate. The calling of his name stopped him short, his head on a swivel.

"Juan! Juan, up here!" came a woman's voice from above.

It was Page, yelling from atop the castle walls. Her blonde locks cascaded down the back of a crimson dress cinched tight at the waist, exposing a copious amount of curvature. Juan abandoned his mission and ascended the wooden rungs of a ladder to meet her. Atop the wall, they embraced.

She pulled away not too soon. "Where's my brother?" she asked, looking back over the wall into the crowd.

"Right," Juan said, regaining his composure. "Leo's alive and better than he deserves for now but there's a lot of catching up to do and your brother has never been a very patient man. I have a feeling he's about to try and kill the king. You or Jewel, one will have to get a hold of him fast and talk some sense into him. Lord knows I can't."

Page looked back at him quizzically. "Kill the king, you say?" She cupped her chin in thought. "I see how that could pose a problem for us."

"Where is Jewel?" Juan asked.

"I don't know. He'll probably be in the courtyard welcoming the regiment home with the rest of the High Priest's Council. They haven't left the Capitol since the army departed. I'll seek him out."

"Well, let's hope so. I'm going to warn my father."

Juan took off down the ladder and through the mass of people looking for his General father. Page took the long way, across the battlements and down the steps, waiving away Capitol watchmen who sought to lend a helping hand.

***

Leo was the last of the soldiers to reach the Capitol's bittersweet embrace. He bypassed the applauding crowd, voices full of praise shouting his name as he went. It was no surprise that Page's voice was drowned out from the crowd as she struggled to get to him.

In his peripheral vision, Leo saw Wade embracing the wife and daughter he'd spoken so often about in the mountains. He and Wade exchanged brief nods of respect like soldiers do.

Leo could see the courtyard ahead of him. It was midday, sun shining overhead the well-manicured lawns although winter had begun sucking color from the grass. Stone and marble sculptures of heroes, politicians, and artisan mastery of every kind surrounded the courtyard walkways. The same ones he'd swung and played around as a kid somehow calmed his nerves like old friends welcoming him home.

A robed figure suddenly blocked his path. Only one of such kind would be so bold.

"Never really had any doubts but I'm glad to see you've made it back in one piece, brother." Bishop Jewel stood before him, slightly shorter but stocky as they come. The priest teetered on the verge of a handshake and a hug but chose neither. "That murderous look in your eyes doesn't suit you here. Not uncommon after what you've been through, but you're home now."

Giving the king a tongue-lashing amidst his people was a task that took a lot of nerve and concentration. Leo was glad to see his brother, but now was not the time for a reunion.

"It's good to see you brother, but I've got a bone to pick with a certain king of ours. If you'll excuse me," he replied, stepping around the bishop.

"Leo!" Jewel yelled after him. Bishops are trained not to raise their voices as it doesn't reflect very well on the church, but it had the desired effect. Leo stopped in his tracks. "If it's revenge you seek, it's best left to the righteous wrath of God. The people are not oblivious to what happened to your regiment. If my reason is of no interest to you, perhaps seeking an audience with General Soberal would better suit you. I must caution against any rash decisions though, brother."

"Don't chastise me with scripture. Let me guess—you expect your hotheaded brother to charge into the king's court demanding answers and retribution? That sound about right, brother?"

Jewel rocked back and forth on his heels, selecting his next words with apparent care. "You're a hero now, Leo—or is it that red name, the Bloody Rose, you prefer? Veronia has not been deaf to the troubling stories of your frostbitten campaign. I've also heard of heroism that trumps even our father's in Kotah. You're perhaps Veronia's most beloved son at the moment, but challenging the king will only bring trouble. I daresay King Lawrence would welcome the opportunity to stain the Rosewood name. Don't give him the opportunity."

For a priest, you can be a real pain in the ass sometimes. "I appreciate your motherly concern, Jewel, but it's not revenge I seek. I'll have that in due course. The war you speak of ending has only just begun. The Gorronians are marching on Gwonda; we must sway the king to action."

It's not too often that Leo surprises his brother but Jewel stepped back, stroking his beard in dismay. "Gwonda, you say? Hmph. We both know the king will likely refuse any request of yours. Perhaps General Soberal should make the announcement."

Leo allowed a mischievous grin to spread across his ravaged face. "Who said anything about requesting?" And with the slightest bow of his head, as was the custom greeting or departing from a clergyman, Leo took his leave.

The crowd welcomed the war commander with applause as he strode to the courtyard, none the wiser that Leo had snatched the title from an incompetent, lame-footed general rather than being dully appointed. He deflected their fair-weather smiles with a resting war face as he made his way through the center of a cobblestone walkway towards the King's Pavilion.

King Lawrence sat upon his throne, dressed in royal battle armor—another custom for Veronian kings, regardless if they were near the action or safely behind enemy lines. Queen Mirtle was absent, which was not unusual as of late. No doubt clinging to life in her chambers, coughing blood in a mortal battle with the white plague.

That left Princess Gabrielle to sit next to her father, whilst her elder brother, Prince Marion, an honorary captain in the army, stood next to the king.

Chamberlain Magnus silenced the crowd with raised hands. "Welcome home!" he bellowed, inciting another round of applause from the crowd. Magnus rested his fleshy hands atop his pot bell, patiently waiting for the applause to die down.

"High Priest Frances, would you be so kind as to lead us in prayer, to pay homage to those brave soldiers returned and those lost in battle?" Magnus asked.

The High Priest's Council consisted of the High Priest and his five council members: Bishops Isabelle, Michael, Theodore, Jewel, and Malachi. Each of them wore white robes with a violet-colored *mozzetta*. Silver- and gold-struck council medallions rested in plain view over their hearts.

The High Priest gingerly walked up the pavilion, leaning heavily on his golden staff of office to address the crowd. He greeted Leo with warm eyes as their gaze met amongst the crowd. Leo was first to take a knee and bow his head for the High Priest's address, and the rest of the crowd followed suit.

"Wars are terrible to behold. They take away our

loved ones, and forever change those lucky enough to survive. Wars of riches, power, good and evil will continue to rage until the end of times, therefore, be prepared. We must celebrate the lives of our brave brethren who have made the ultimate sacrifice. We must also celebrate our survivors, whether they return in triumph or defeat."

Frances led the procession in the Lord's Prayer, then a moment of silence before blessing the crowd and the soldiers who had gathered in attendance. Magnus shuffled over to help the High Priest down the steps, but Frances shook off the half-assed attempt.

General Jaminez Soberal was then beckoned to address the crowd. He clanked up the staircase in polished armor, an unseen aura of command clouded around him. It reminded Leo of his father.

"Sons of Veronia, I salute you," the general said in flawless execution. Leo rushed to return the gesture, but Jaminez was already in mid-sentence. "Captain Rosewood, the kingdom is indebted to your relentless service and the hard-fought victory of your men. There will no doubt be many awards and promotions to be discussed this eve. Would you like to address the open council?"

The crowd fell silent; nervous tension filled the air. Leo noticed Bruce, Natalie, and Juan crowded at his back as if they were on the front lines again. Some habits die hard.

Leo chose to remain in the courtyard rather than

take to the podium. The urge to drive a dagger through the king's smug smile still burned strong.

"A battle we've won, yet the war rages on!" Confusion spread throughout. Leo let it marinate a while before continuing. "How we beat an army twice our size—and more provisioned besides—is a tribute to the steel will of our men, yet the Gorronians are anything but defeated. They're marching on the Tribes of Gwonda as we speak. Such a foothold, should they win it, will bring them dangerously close to our people."

Leo paused again, allowing confusion to birth panic. "I'm well aware that Gwonda is not part of our kingdom, therefore none of our concern, but we cannot sit idly by and watch them slaughtered or it will be our villages next. Give me the men and we'll leave behind a slaughter so red, the savages will fear even whispering of the Veronian warriors south of their border."

All eyes fell on the king who stirred uneasy in his seat. For the first time Leo could remember, Lawrence's iron-clad confidence began to falter. Not only had Leo returned alive, he returned victorious, requesting to fight again.

Lawrence shrugged off the request as if it was below him. "As you mentioned, the Tribes of Gwonda are not part of our kingdom, therefore, I see no legitimate reason to shed any Veronian blood for their sake. We owe General Vrago and the rest of the army a great deal of gratitude for defending our borders, but

Gorronian encroachment into Gwonda, as you've pointed out, is none of our concern."

Lawrence's praise of Vrago's corpse rather than Leo didn't go unnoticed. In fact, Leo had expected it. Yet it still set him in a mind to do a bit of killing.

"If they conquer the Tribesmen, they'll move south onto our land by next winter." Leo turned his back on the king to address the crowd that had gathered round the courtyard. A sleight that visible would not go unpunished. He could sense Lawrence's cold stare burning holes into his back.

"They want our land, and what's yours and mine. If we sit back and let them, they'll sure as hell take it. Give me an army and I'll cut their bloody hearts out to spoon-feed their wounded." As Leo had intended, the proposal struck all the right nerves in the crowd as soldiers and common folk alike began pledging their swords to the cause.

"The king has spoken!" Magnus shouted. A futile attempt to regain a turning crowd. An apple core struck his head and sent his jiggling jowls scrambling for safety.

Even Prince Marion gave a go at restoring order, but his resolve was untested, his voice lost in the crowd. The king stood in fury, directing his Capitol Watch to root out the unruly with brute force. They descended on the crowd; their head-cracking cudgels dulled the noise.

"I wish the Tribesmen the best of luck against the Gorronians," Lawrence said. "We will send supplies to aid their defensive efforts, but you will lead no army of mine to their aid and that is final." Lawrence turned to Magnus. "Chamberlain, we are done here."

Magnus tried once again to bring an end to the madness and took another piece of fruit to the shoulder. He said nothing further, opting to take what little pride remained with him into the keep.

Leo ascended the vacated platform. "Silence!" he bellowed. "The king's made his decision and I'll make mine. Tomorrow morning I'm going to Gwonda. Who's coming with me?"

The crowd roared yet again as the pledging of swords continued. Leo hopped down and walked out of the courtyard. The Capitol Watch followed close behind, no doubt ordered by the king to seize Leo and put the crowd to rest. A dozen of them in close order pursued Leo but were cut off by a shielded wall of Veronian soldiers.

"Out of the way or you'll be joining him," said one of the watchmen. "You heard the king. We've orders to take Leo to the dungeon. He'll face the council on the morrow."

Bruce stood unyielding. "If you got the grit to move me, give it a try. Otherwise go eat a bowl of dicks." He punctuated the insult by spitting on the watchman's tunic.

The watchman wavered, but held his ground. That was until Juan barreled through the crowd, grabbing the soiled watch leader by the neck and tossing him at his comrades like a battering ram. "After you pick your sorry ass off the ground and slither back to your barracks, you'll realize I just did you a favor. We've got a war to prepare for and no time to deal with you lack-wits."

Natalie entered the mix, her crossbow pointed at the nearest watchman's manhood. Behind Wade, a dozen more soldiers readied their steel. The watchmen raised their hands in surrender and backed away.

**

Two thousand volunteers marched their way over the Netche Bridge into the Gwonda Forest. Their faces turned sullen the closer they got to the forest as realization of another battle sunk in. Wasn't just the temperature giving many of them cold feet.

The forest was a foreign thing, green all around, and Leo found himself missing Birdsong's superstitious ass for the first time. They passed several small desolate villages the further north they traveled. From what Leo could gather, all the capable men were up north fighting, leaving behind the elders, women, children, and the lame.

Villagers addressed them with hard looks. The kind that asked all sorts of questions like *Who the fuck are you?* and *What are you doing here?* without having to voice a word. Wade's tribal dialect didn't render much effect to ease their hearts and minds, so after a while

Leo marched on without trying.

That was until a boy Leo guessed was no older than ten summers surprised them all by walking right up to Natalie and introducing himself in broken English.

"Hulo, I'm Quelu, son of Tekrano of the Antuchawhah tribe. Why are you paleskins here?" The boy wore buckskin pants with red armbands on each bicep. Despite his youth, his face was painted for war and he carried a hatchet with the swagger of a veteran soldier.

Leo spotted one of the village elders standing nearby, eavesdropping on the conversation. When Quelu addressed them as paleskins, the elder's face paled.

Leo chuckled. "Straight to the point, I see. Well met, Quelu, son of Tekrano. I'm nobody special. Names aren't as important as a man's intentions. We've just repelled a Gorronian attack in the Winsoot Mountains. Even though it's your land the savages march on now, we don't like to leave a job half-finished. Can you take us to the battle?"

Quelu's head tilted like a dog struggling to understand. "Why you want to help us, Nobody Special?"

I'm starting to like this kid. "Not interested in helping so much as your people being on the right side of our bad intentions. We mean your tribes no harm. Show us the way or step aside. Bad a tracker as Wade is I'm sure even he could stumble upon an active battlefield."

Quelu turned to the village elder, who sat listening nearby. Someone had to teach Quelo English and Leo's guess was the old man. The elder said nothing but seemed to follow the conversation easily enough. A nod signaled his blessing.

The son of Tekrano led them deep into the forest. Leo continued to look for tracks the Tribesmen should have left behind, but found none. It was no wonder, looking at Quelu, who moved nimble as a panther quietly stalking its prey, his bare feet patting along the forest floor, leaving no signs of his presence in his wake.

Before long, the sounds of battle rang out. Quelu led Leo and Juan onto a small game trail, through the forest's dense trees. They came out on the east side of the battlefield in what Leo observed to be the perfect flanking position. Leo looked at Quelu in wonder. *I doubt the kid led us to the flank by accident. Did the old man teach him the art of war, or was it his father Tekrano?*

The Veronian volunteers were neatly concealed in the forest until they chose to strike. As they surveyed the battlefield it was no surprise the Gorronians outnumbered the Tribesmen. They may have even added to their ranks since the Winsoot. Say one thing about Gorronians, they're a fertile lot.

The Tribesmen were broken up into three formations. Leo and Juan tried to make sense of the strategy but came up short. Quelu took the opportunity to enlighten them.

"Three tribes in Gwonda," the son of Tekrano said, holding up two fingers. Apparently numbers weren't Quelu's strong suit.

Quelu pointed to the formation closest to them on the east side of the battlefield. "My people, the Antucha-whahs." They were Tribesmen dressed exactly as Quelu with buckskins and bright colored armbands. They had painted faces and each carried a hatchet like the son of Tekrano.

He pointed to the second formation of Tribesmen. "The Netches." They were dressed similar to the Antucha-whahs but instead of hatchets, they wielded an assortment of more practical weaponry, short and long swords, spears and so forth. Unlike the Antucha-whahs, the Netches only painted half their faces.

Quelu pointed to the last formation and identified them as "the Vrattas." Although their faces were bare, they looked a savage enough lot, each wearing bones for armor—some human, some animal. Their blades were dark as night which indicated they were poison-tipped, if Leo remembered his lessons in tribal warfare correctly. They flung fiery, smoke-filled objects into their enemy's mass formation. The smell of charred hair and flesh turned Leo's stomach; the stench burned his nose and watered his eyes.

The cries of a burning man are quite frightening. The sorrow-filled wails pierce deep into a man's soul, lingering like a cancer you can't rid yourself of. Despite being outnumbered, the Tribesmen were holding their own. The Gorronians wanted no part of the Vrattas' vile black magic tactics, and began directing their full attention towards the Antucha-whahs and Netches.

Leo had seen enough. "We'll attack from here straight into the Gorronian flank. No mad dashing, tell the men to hold the line nice and steady. Slow is smooth, smooth is fast. We'll get there soon enough."

Juan took another look at the fight they were about to join. Sometimes a man needs a moment of calm before the storm. "Right, I'll ready the men," he said, soldiering on.

Killing's an unnatural thing that requires a hardened heart to be any good at it. Leo clenched his murderous hands, exhaling slowly to steady his wits and calm his nerves. *When did it become so easy for me?* He got up to go and found Quelu's curious brown eyes at study.

"In a fight you have to train yourself to breathe steady," Leo told him. "You get so preoccupied with the chaos around you that many hold their breath—until you feel the blade of your sword start weighing you down. Sweat starts to bead on your forehead and your grip starts to weaken. The heart races for oxygen and the world starts to spin around you.

"When that happens in battle, you usually don't live through it. Least not in one piece like you were before. You can avoid all that shit by simply controlling your breathing." Leo put a hand on Quelu's shoulder. The boy was too intrigued to pull away, busy translating Leo's words into his own language. "It also calms the nerves. There's no shame in a few of those before a fight. You'd best get back to your village, son of Tekrano."

Quelu stole one more glance at the battlefield where his fellow Tribesmen fought for their lives, then back to Leo. His mouth opened as if he were about to say something but closed just as fast as he slipped away into the trees like a startled rabbit.

"You got battle shits or something?" Natalie asked from behind. "The men are ready. Looks like we better get moving before we miss all the action."

Her brown locks were tied back as usual except for a small strand that fell loose, dangling over her left eye. A sword hung at her hip, arms cradling a crossbow. Leo never tired of seeing her, no man ever would. She was often the only beautiful thing in this suffocating world full of evil, treachery, and chaos.

He closed the gap between them until they stood intimately close. "Tell me something, Natalie of Indigo." To her credit, she stood her ground, eyes holding his until it was he who felt small and broke his stare. "Why did you come here? To trek knee-deep through the bowels of Earth when you could drop your bow and take from life whatever you wanted?"

She moved close to whisper in his ear. Even in the forest her hair smelled like flowers, though he couldn't tell which kind. "I'm right where I want to be. Aren't you?" She departed with a wink that left him weak in the knees.

He stood frozen, a pervert cast in stone, fixated on her hips and ass as she swayed to formation. A snicker of laughter from the trees broke his trance. Leo looked around and saw nothing.

"Lesson two," Leo said, holding up two fingers with a mocking smile. "Stay focused on the task at hand." His fingers clenched to fist and he joined his men at the front.

They set onto the battlefield from the east tree line as was planned. There were no battle gimmicks, no complex strategy. Just closing a gap to do some killing. War isn't all that difficult, really.

Their army was spread out a few hundred yards wide after they had filtered through the trees onto the battlefield. Bruce and Natalie took to the opposite ends of the line to ensure it was held straight and true.

"Steady! Steady!" Leo shouted to steady the men from its center.

"Looks like they didn't expect us," Juan said as Gorronian and tribal heads alike began to turn their direction.

The Gorronians' attack seemed to implode at the sight of the flanking Veronians. The Tribesmen squinted curiously, not quite sure who the Veronians were going to attack.

They stood fewer than fifty yards away when Leo

selected his first target. The savage had long hair and a grizzly beard, which came up short in concealing the fear in his eyes as Leo approached.

"The Bloody Rose!" the savage shouted. "The Bloody Rose," he said once more, backpedaling and tripping over his comrades to escape. Others began to run as the name was repeated like an echo through a canyon.

It went without saying, but Leo said it anyways. "Attack!" He barreled ahead into the Gorronian horde. His first target had fled but others were not so lucky and Leo cut down two of them before they could scamper away.

To the right, Juan was busy at work, delivering a bone-crunching head-butt to an unlucky foe who had attempted to take the reach advantage away from Juan's bastard sword. Not all ideals are good ones. Some you overcome, others get you killed.

On the south end of the line Bruce stood shoulder-to-shoulder with the Antucha-whahs. He ducked under an incoming slash, pushed off the Gorronian's stomach to tilt the balance, and delivered a vicious backhanded slash that tore through flesh and cheekbone.

Bruce turned to see a much larger Gorronian on top of a Tribesman who had been his shoulder man a few seconds before. The two men fought and clawed weaponless at one another. Bruce clutched two handfuls of hair and jerked the savage's head back with enough force to snap his neck. Unluckily for the Gorronian, his neck didn't snap but relief was short-lived as Bruce rammed the point of his sword under the man's chin. The eye stuck to the tip of the sword as it pierced through the skull and exited through the socket.

At the north end of the line Natalie was on no holiday. She opted for a sword-and-dagger approach given the close proximity. It was not so difficult a task because most of the Gorronians were trying to get the hell out of there and Natalie had no qualms in slowing them down as they ran past.

Leo and Juan cut their way deeper and deeper into the Gorronians' line. Before too long they were detached from their own and found themselves surrounded. They turned their backs to one another and went to work.

Juan labored to catch his breath but had plenty of strength to heft his bastard sword over his shoulder to swing. "Slow and steady. Hold the line, you said," Juan mocked, punching a would-be attacker in the chin. The Gorronian dropped to ground, and Juan kicked the sword from his hands and let him crawl away.

"Oops," Leo replied, spitting a mouthful of blood to the earth.

"What's the plan now, Sun Tzu?"

"Oh relax, Juan. We're just a couple of guys standing around cheating death is all. Don't know about you, but there's no place I'd rather be."

Leo and Juan were surrounded. "Shit," Drew fumed, shaking his head. Juan had been pushed to the ground from behind, fighting two of the bastards at once. Leo wasn't in much better shape surrounded by three, each taking turns trying to land a blow. But Captain turned Commander was only able to block so many blows at a time. More and more of them were hitting pay dirt, and blood cascaded down Leo's right shoulder.

Drew ran to them and cut down one of Leo's attackers from behind. He shuffled over the fallen foe to stand at Leo's side.

"Drew Stickland, ladies and gentlemen," Leo said, using his best Chamberlain Magnus voiceover.

"Looks like Juan could use a hand as well but I got only the one sword," Drew said hurriedly.

Leo risked a brief glance to his right to find the source of Drew's discomfort. Juan sat straddling a Gorronian, forearm pressed against the bastard's windpipe, too tired to deliver any more blows. Another Gorronian was on Juan's back, struggling to choke him out but Juan had more shoulder than neck.

Leo diverted his eyes from his opponents and rushed to the man at Juan's back, cracking his head clean open. The strike of a sword is quick as the blink of an eye. Such a short span shouldn't tear such a whole, but time is often colder than a winter's storm.

He turned back to his opponents who were both charging in unison. One at Wade, the other at him. A beam of light danced off Drew's polished blade when it reached out to deflect the blow meant for Leo. Sparks burst from the colliding blades, a vision that would linger a lifetime.

The clash of steel jarred Leo from the tunnel vision prison just a moment too late. The other savage drove the length of his sword through Drew's chest. The charging momentum carried the blade through bone and armor. The sight of a blade peering through Wade's back released the murderous demon caged within Leo, hailed as the Bloody Rose.

We are all plagued with inner demons continually antagonizing us to commit life's most despicable fallacies. Containing them is a constant struggle that separates good men from the bad. Leo's demon was a killer, a master of the art.

The Gorronian couldn't free his sword from Drew's chest. Not that it would have helped him anyways. Leo reared back as far as he could and drove through the bastard, separating the savage's upper and lower halves at the waist.

He cut off the raised sword arm of the other barbarian, leaving him to stare at a spouting crimson fountain where his arm used to be. A right hook sent the man to the ground. Leo followed him there, blow after blow until no facial bones resisted him and brains where more outside than in.

The Bloody Rose stood among men like death at a massacre. His mighty roar chilled the air with a terrifying sorrow that chased men ripe in fear from the battlefield.

He pressed on, carving through flesh and splintering the bones of anyone standing before him, leaving a trail of broken bodies in his wake. Veronians and Tribesmen alike stood in astonishment as the savage army was chased away by one man.

***

Leo sat back, numb to the world where he and Juan and Quelu had surveyed the battlefield just hours ago. Now he watched his soldiers and Tribesmen sifting through and carrying away the dead. He'd seen this part of war play out before in the Frostbite but it didn't get any easier. And this time the Veronian blood was on his hands.

The volunteers were long past ready to march home and Leo felt himself stalling. Natalie and Juan approached, behind them soldiers were saying their goodbyes to the Tribesmen. Many of their words were lost in translation, but appreciation is a universal language.

Juan looked like hell. They all did, but he was a bigger target than most and it showed. "You're not coming home with us, are you?"

"You know I can't," Leo replied without looking up to acknowledge them. It was easier that way.

"You can't blame yourself for this shit, Leo," Natalie insisted. "Not for the Frostbite, not for Gwonda, and not for Drew and the others. It won't bring any of them back."

Drew's death didn't seem real until Leo closed his eyes and the spark of swords lit the darkness and the blade meant for him killed Drew.

Leo winced at the memory. "I defied a king, jackass that he is, and good men died because of it. Lawrence will want nothing more than to parade my head on a spike around the Capitol. He wants my head, I aim to make him work for it."

"So exile, then?" Natalie asked. "You'd rather be exiled to this damn forest? Come back with us, Leo. To hell with the king; Veronia stands behind you and so do we."

Which is why he wants my head. Leo met her eyes. "It's not just the king, Natalie. I'm tired. The kind of tired you can't sleep off. I need some time away."

She opened her mouth to speak, but no words came. In the end she just walked away shaking her head.

Juan clanked down next to Leo. "She likes you, but you're damn close to losing her and once you do she'll be gone for good," he said, watching her go. "What's our next move, then?"

"We caused a bit of a scene before leaving the Capitol. No doubt there will be consequences. I want you to take the army back and deliver this letter to the open council." He handed Juan a rolled parchment, sealed with the Veronian Army's coat of arms, tightly bound with leather straps.

Juan turned it over in his hands. "You planned this all along? Where'd you get the seal?"

"From your father. He helped me write it before we left. Said my chicken scratch wouldn't do and that it had to be official or the king would wipe his ass with it. Not that he won't try regardless. It says I take full responsibility for the actions of my men and that they were only following my orders from a senior ranking officer. The king should be happy to receive it since killing a whole army is messy work. I just gave him my head, but he'll have to come take it."

The parchment seemed to drain all the fight from Juan. Either that or he realized this was the most sensible course of action. "We'll plead your case for exile instead of the chopping block. In time we'll seek a pardon. What will I tell Page and Jewel?"

Leo thought of Page—the younger version, of course. The little girl who had driven her septa mad, following him to sword practice every day as kids. In his mind, Page would always be young and pure. White dress, spotted in dirt to match her knees and elbows. A common side-effect of playing Blind Man's Bluff with the other boys.

Now she dutifully occupied the Rosewood Manor just west of Crystal Lake. But with the war going on, Page spent the last few weeks in a meager Capitol cottage, hounding General Soberal for the latest frontline news, eagerly awaiting her brother's return.

Guilt gripped him not for the first time. *Tell them*

I'd tear the world apart to save them from a single moment of pain, but a brotherly embrace terrifies me. Tell them I love them. "Tell them what a good brother would say. My words often miss the mark."

"And when we come looking for you?" Juan asked.

Leo smiled for the first time since Jewel had earned his priest medallion, gesturing behind where two Tribesmen sat in perfect silence like flies on the wall. The first Juan recognized as Quelu. The other was a bigger, more dangerous-looking version. "Look for Quelu, son of Tekrano," Leo told him. "He'll know where to find me."

CHAPTER

3

Liz's gloved hands gripped the splintered rail of the rocking ship, eyes straining inland towards the rickety Heron port town of Arquen. She hadn't expected anyone to see her ashore, except maybe Kano. He could teleport anywhere, but she didn't sense or see his half-sized figure amongst the crowd. As the boat sailed closer to shore, her twelve-pointed star of a heart sensed two other starborn.

"What would Prothica be doing this close to Zeus's Canyon?" she thought aloud. Such unannounced encroachment put Liz on edge and soured her homebound mood.

The ship touched down on a sea-weathered, sun-scorched dock that appeared to be missing more planks than it had. Liz waited as long as she could to depart, trying to spot them before they spotted her. It didn't take long before the second mate began nudging her along.

"Move along now, m'lady. We've got a schedule, that we do. Less you wanna keep me bed warm on the way to Chaucer that is. Sailing's not the only thing old Crester's good at."

Crester's teeth were in worse shape than the dock. The few that remained were rotted down to green and black stumps. That didn't stop him from putting another chew between cheek and gum while he awaited her response, though.

"I'd rather snatch my dinner from the latrine," she said, pushing past him.

Liz tried to lose herself in the crowd. That proved a difficult task since there were only a baker's dozen or so men awaiting the ships, landing with little else but rock and sand in the distance.

It seemed her double-trouble intuition was correct. She spotted Borin leaning against a nearby cargo wagon. The rebel starborn wore a form-fitting grey surcoat, not bothering to conceal the star markings on each of his hands, like visible fighting words proudly on display. He carried himself with the discipline of a veteran soldier, but unfortunately that bearing was overshadowed by a cocky, arrogant aura of nobility.

Borin's brother Lucian was his spitting image, down to the dark flowing hair. Liz suspected he was the other Prothica member she'd sensed, however, Lucian's ability allowed him the luxury of invisibility.

"To hell with this," she muttered to herself. She made right for Borin to see what this was all about. She'd not give them the pleasure of watching her run.

"What's your problem, Borin?" Liz demanded through clenched teeth. "You've got some rocks showing up here like this amongst all these people flaunting your star burns. And Lucian using his ability in my presence is a direct violation of the accords."

Borin lifted himself from the cart and addressed her with that vile, knowing smile of his. She wanted to slap it off his face but restrained herself.

As if reading her mind, he stepped within arm's reach. Another challenge, another threat. "The accords were just something we agreed upon to shut you pussy-footed Zodans up a century or two. We're over that now."

She didn't like where this was going. Part of her wanted to call the wind and fling his pompous ass into the ocean. Another part of her said he wouldn't take that too well and a lot of innocent bystanders would die as a result.

He pressed on, disgusted. "Look at you. Assessing the situation for minimal casualties as if these peasants would do the same for you. The mundane should fear our presence and pay tribute to maintain our peace. Instead we cover our markings and lurk in the shadows as if the Mozzaroth are a curse rather than a blessing. That time is over!" Borin spat the last words, a mist of spittle and hate.

A chill crept up her spine and spread through her limbs. The twins were clearly here to pick a fight. Her only chance was to strike first.

"If it's a dance you want, all you had to do was ask."

Her eyes came aglow. A bright, burning star emerged on her right hand bearing the Cancer Zodiac symbol at its center. Two smaller stars appeared on her left hand as what was left of her gloves burnt away. Borin's hands lit in defense just a second too late. A howling north wind burst forth, taking Borin with it, and cast him into the sea.

Liz hurled herself to the sand. The wagon Borin had leaned on just moments ago flew past, striking the boat and sending ole Crester and his crew overboard. Before Borin splashed into the sea, Lucian struck.

His invisible form ran towards Liz, dagger in hand as she lifted herself from the sand. Unable to locate him but sensing his presence, she called the wind again. It whipped her hair and whistled through her ears as people, horses, and carriages were sucked into a whirlwind.

Everyone on the bank was pulled into the twirling funnel that reached down into her right palm. Lucian's star-burned markings betrayed him, fluttering alight as he began to fight his way out of the twister. She singled him out with her left hand, moving him to the side in a twister of his own, and slowly dropped everyone and everything else to the ground with her right.

Liz gasped in effort. The two minor stars on her left hand began to dim. Soon they'd burn out, leaving her with only the strength of the major star on her right. She would have to start thinking of an escape route.

Borin fought against the tide which threatened to wash him further out to sea. His star burns were aglow, his eyes burned in fury. Struggling to swim and fight at once proved a difficult enough task, but he hurled whatever objects he could manipulate towards Liz with reckless abandon. Most of them missing the mark and consequently sucked up into the twisters.

The people who dropped from the first twister ran as fast as they could to whatever safe haven they could find. Some swam into the sea, figuring distance is distance. Others sat dumbfounded, staring at Liz as if she'd snatched their souls and left them paralyzed on the desert shore.

Lucian's form took shape inside the twister. No need to waste energy on invisibility when he could throw starfire. The first blast just missed her ducking head—a lucky throw given he was still twirling in her hands. His second blast singed her left leg and got her thinking of better ideas.

She cupped both hands together, spinning Lucian

faster and faster in a twister that grew darker with speed. Lucian screamed in agony as the wind sucked him higher and higher in the air, the force so strong it threatened to tear his body apart.

"Lucian!" Borin wailed, face twisted in panic. He patted his chest pockets then retrieved a miniature metal star. Flipping the star into the air like a lucky coin, Borin mustered whatever strength remained to launch it screaming through the air towards Liz.

The star bit through her cloak and into her back, knocking her off her feet. With her concentration broken, her twister vanished and Lucian fell to the ground. His wounded scream on the way down rang in the distance but did little to break his fall.

Liz was on her knees now, back arched, fingers searching to retrieve the metal between her shoulder blades. She grabbed hold of it and pulled, nearly collapsing onto the ground beside Lucian's splattered form. The sharp as sin metal nearly took her fingers off. It would have to remain where it was for now.

Beside her, Hamal, the brightest star in the Aries constellation, lifted up its namer. Lucian's limp body hovered in the air. His eyes and hands began to shine for the last time, burning brighter until bursting like a split atom. Nothing remained of Borin's brother.

She turned to the sea, ready for another of Borin's blades. Instead she found Borin slumped over a piece of driftwood. Liz wasn't sure how many objects he'd flung at her, but the last one must have left him burnt out.

Not having the energy to swim out and finish him off, she chose to flee. She stumbled as fast as her shaky legs would take her, wanting no part of Borin when he came to, and knowing full well that a brother's vengeance never wilts until the score is settled.

***

Leo stopped his mount just outside the fortified stone gates of Bresdan, the new Veronian Capitol. He'd discarded his armor two years before in Gwonda, trading a Netchan for a change of buckskins. Dirty-blond hair extended to his shoulders coupled with a finger-length beard that concealed nearly all recognizable features of the exiled former captain.

He was a simple man before, but his time with the Tribesmen had taught him an even simpler lifestyle which is why he carried only three things now: a water skin, his Guardian Sword slung over his back, and a tomahawk which was handcrafted by members of each of the three tribes as a token of their appreciation.

The Netches donated an ingot of Drago steel for the head and local Cavee wood for the handle. The Antucha-whahs forged the razor-sharp bearded edge, opting for a pointed backside rather than a hammer.

Chief Ansuk of the Vrattas took an unusual interest in the weapon's construction, making the necessary intricate wood and steel carvings himself to give it more of a ceremonial look. Tribal runes were carved into the wood and filled with red stones, then heat-treated and solidified. They appeared to blaze through the wood and steel like the orange coals of a fire threatening to consume it.

Leo knew his return would be a cold one. He'd expected the king to send men for his head in Gwonda but none came. After a few years on foreign soil, he manifested an urge to return home if for no other reason than to clear his name. Much as Leo said he didn't care, a man can only take being called a coward for so long before he seeks rectification.

What the hell? Leo thought, looking at the Capitol which appeared more a military compound than a royal court.

Lawrence had spared no expense on construction. A stone wall surrounded the keep taller than any man could climb. Watchtowers had been erected on each of its four corners. The keep itself towered over all of it like a stone mountain. Veronian banners streamed down the sides of the keep and could be seen from miles away. A gatehouse provided the only entrance, a large wooden gate heavily guarded on both sides.

Leo rode through the outskirts toward the main gate, drawing more than a few curious looks. Only Tribesmen wore such attire, and even they wouldn't dare to stand out so far from home. Some followed close behind, others cared less. As Leo reached the gate he was challenged by the Capitol Watch.

Two watchmen stood side-by-side, blocking the

gate. They wore bronze helms, thick leather gauntlets, and more chainmail than cloth. "What's your name and business, traveler?" the shorter cross-eyed one asked, but their faces showed they both wondered.

Leo had contemplated this very moment for the past two years. Each scenario never turned out to his advantage so he just settled on making peace with his maker and killing the first bastard that thought to goal him, and as many others as he could after that.

"My name depends on who you ask. Call me what you like, just get the fuck out of my way. I'm here to see the king."

The two watchmen exchanged glances before turning back to the traveler. They could see the hilt of a guardian sword peering over his shoulder, a hatchet secured to a leather belt around the waist. Long hair covered his eyes and downcast face.

The taller one with proper eyes spoke next. "We'll send word the council has a caller but first we'll have to take your weapons."

A reply Leo had anticipated, expected nothing less. He looked up at the two watchmen for the first time, combing hair from his face. Unease, panic, excitement, who really knows, but it crept into both of them as the slightest recollection of an exiled captain filled their thoughts.

Their unease caused Leo to grip the handle of his tomahawk, ready for work. They backed away, palms out in front of them. A silent understanding was met just then, no further words wasted. Leo trailed the two watchmen through the gate.

A bloody reputation prevents a lot of meaningless chatter. The brief standoff did, however, result in a rather large following. Capitol folk began pondering Leo's identity aloud. It was a short list of names—who else carried a Guardian Sword and would be seen in buckskins?

The courtyard came into view only a few dozen steps later. There, Leo waited as the Capitol Watch sent word to the king of Leo's arrival. He studied the crowd, looking for the hate-filled faces he always imagined, but found curiosity instead. That was until the king and his handlers took to the courtyard pavilion.

Magnus had gotten fatter, much fatter. His red face glistened with sweat, stomach so round he couldn't reach his belly button, still struggling to silent the murmuring crowd. At least this time he wasn't dodging food.

King Lawrence stood behind Magnus in a very animated discussion with two of his council members. The three of them paused only to steal looks at Leo, clearly not prepared for his unexpected arrival.

Magnus cleared his throat and gave it another go. "Here! Here! It's the Open Council's understanding that deserter Leo Rosewood has returned." Magnus looked down at the bearded figure standing before him, his beady eyes resting on the foreign hatchet. "State your name and business for the open council."

Leo fought the urge to heave his hatchet at the king. Would have been a difficult toss from where he stood but he'd practiced such a throw countless times with Tekrano. Still, it wouldn't do for the brother of a bishop to kill the king. Not yet anyways.

"You heard right." *And you know damn good and well why I'm here, fatass.*

Magnus entered the king's huddle for guidance. The crowd was growing; townsfolk filled the streets to view the spectacle of Leo's return.

Word reached General Soberal as quickly as his lookouts could run. Jaminez darted up the public stairwell to the king's pavilion, stealing a look at Leo as he went. The long hair and beard did nothing to conceal the identity of his son's best friend.

The general had aged, his once dark hair now filled with iron. For the first time Leo saw Jiminez worried, so much so that it looked as if he were swimming against a current too strong, climbing a hill too steep. Albeit the Soberals and Rosewoods shared no blood, there was no limit to the amount they would spill for one another. Blood births relatives, loyalty breeds family.

Leo struggled to eavesdrop on their conversation, but from where he stood he could read the general's lips well enough.

"Why wasn't I called to council?" Jaminez said, shouldering into the king's council.

Lawrence waved him off like an annoying dog

begging for scraps at the dinner table. When Magnus began to speak, Leo knew his fate was sealed. The king slouched onto his throne and sipped a cup of red. Jaminez hurriedly whispered orders to junior officers who scurried off to complete their tasks.

"Mr. Rosewood," Magnus said. "You stand charged with disobeying the king's orders. Consequently, your defiance also led to many deaths of Veronia's finest soldiers."

Twenty-five feet, Leo thought, estimating the throwing distance. *Wish Lawrence was as round as Magnus. If my throw is off course, burying the blade in his fat ass wouldn't be a total loss.*

"Rather than stand trial for such treason, the open council will decide your fate, having already taken into consideration the written confession you left behind. Have you anything to say before judgment?"

This is where the guilty plea for mercy. Even the strong wilt when self-preservation rears its ugly head— he'd seen it a dozen times.

Go fuck yourselves. "Get on with it."

Silence lingered while Magnus waited to bait a change of heart. "For the crimes committed against our king and country...... Thirty-nine lashes."

The townsfolk gasped in unison, sucking air like a choreographed orchestra. A man doesn't just walk away from thirty-nine lashes. Most die before the count is done, others from infection. For a moment Leo thought he caught a whiff of Vrago's rotten stench. The chopping block seemed more appealing.

"If you should survive the whipping pole, the dungeons await your embrace. A mercy obliged only because of your late father's service to Veronia and Bishop Jewel's request to spare your life."

Magnus continued babbling; only eating pleased him more. Leo held the king's gaze as the Capitol Watch moved to seize him. At some point he'd gripped his hatchet and sighted in.

"Leo, don't....... Leo!" General Soberal's hand grasped his throwing shoulder just before the axe took flight. "Easy son," Jaminez said, arms stretched wide in attempt to separate Leo from the goalers. The watchmen were thankful of the barrier. Nothing more dangerous than a dead man.

Leo shook free of the general's grasp. "To hell with this. They seek to flog and leave me rotting in a cell. Should have shot me down on the way in."

"Don't be a fool. You sealed your fate in that letter we wrote and damn well knew it. I don't like this shit sandwich any more than you but we both have to take a bite. You take your damn lashings and I'll work on getting you out of the dungeon. Do you hear me?"

One of Jaminez's hands rested on each of his shoulders now. A lesser man would have been clutching their broken mouth. Leo brushed the general's hands away for the last time.

"If the lashes don't kill me, Lawrence's dungeon goons will, and that ain't the way I'm going out, not like that. I'll choose my own death."

A sigh full of age escaped Jaminez. "I can't refute that. You're in a bad spot, that's for sure, but even it will soon pass. Sure, you'll be the one taking the lashes and serving the hard time, but don't think your friends and family aren't suffering alongside you. Throwing your life away now is just what the king wants. Let us help you get out of this mess."

Like his own father, Jaminez wouldn't sugarcoat the truth of things, and more times than not he was right. Leo's only consolation as far as he could tell was that his brother and sister were not there to bear witness. Jewel was no doubt back in Mirta doing the lord's work. Page visited him a few times during exile and took a liking to Nico, the son of Chief Dretchel. It was with the Antucha-whahs Leo left her none the wiser as to where he had gone.

Leo had kept his return to the Capitol a secret only he and Tekrano shared. He slipped out of the Antucha-whah camp under the cover of darkness to face the king. It didn't fool Tekrano who said he had been awoken by a frightening dream of a mighty lion forced into captivity. The Tribesmen offered to go with him but Leo would hear none of it. Whatever punishment lay ahead was his to bear.

He didn't ask Jiminez where Juan was. Stationed as far away as he could get from the king and his Capitol, most likely. With the Capitol Watch firmly under Lawrence's control, there wasn't much need for additional soldiers.

Leo unslung his sword and hatchet. He peered down at them, one in each hand, wondering if it were harder to say goodbye to flesh and blood. Bankers have their coin, a priest the word of God, a smith his hammer, and the warrior has his weapons with bloody memories besides.

He passed them to Jaminez's sure hands. The general couldn't meet his eyes and Leo was thankful for it as he walked past him and climbed onto the pavilion.

Like moths fixated with light, the crowd watched Leo walk to the wooden post that stood ten feet high in the middle of a cobbled circle. He wrapped his arms around the splintered oak, and the floggers secured his hands to the other side where a wooden peg protruded to lock his hands in place. They ripped his buckskin blouse from his torso and flung it into the crowd.

Two floggers were assigned to execute the lashings, alternating each time to stay fresh. They wore black cloaks with hoods that covered their faces to prevent retaliation. Leo would find them nonetheless, once this was finished. Taking their arms off at the shoulder seemed fair enough. After beating them senseless, of course.

The justices took their positions behind Leo, each wielding a cat o' nine tail made of knotted leather to inflict as much pain and misery as possible.

"Begin!" the king roared behind his golden chalice of red.

He felt the first lash before it was heard screaming through the air. That sound would stay with him. The impact jolted him forward, lips busting against oak. The pain took his breath away, the second lash was on him before he could get it back.

Leo thought he could feel each of the nine throngs tearing into his skin lash after lash. The fifth and sixth ones came in quick succession. Much as he tried, he couldn't help but wail through gritted teeth.

He promised himself he wouldn't give the king or the crowd the satisfaction of hearing his torment. But foolish pride won't shield you; won't ease the pain of a whip either. Now his only focus was bracing for the next lash. *How many have there been now?* After wetting himself he'd lost count.

Only the peg held him up now. His arms ached under the strain of his weight; he wished they'd just cut them off to ease the tension. Torture has a way of putting things into perspective, all your everyday wants and needs suddenly become miniscule. Getting it over with or making it stop is the only thing that matters, and it never comes soon enough.

His world spun. Fuzzy white blotches were all he could see though his eyes were clenched shut. At one point the shocking pain knocked him out cold, but the next lash woke him up. The twenty-sixth crack of the whip reached under his shoulder and tore away the soft tender flesh that was his armpit. Beneath him, blood pooled and spattered all around by the justices who began to take running starts.

Jaminez's knees buckled, his hands planted in a pool of Leo's blood. "That's enough! He can take no more!" he shouted, fighting loose from a soldier's grip who tried to help him up. Jaminez could take no more and made a move for the justices but the Capitol Watch cut him off.

"Stand down, General!" the king yelled. "Any more interference from you and you'll be next. Guards, escort the general back to his quarters. He appears to be feeling ill and needs to rest."

As watchmen took the general away, King Lawrence turned back to the flogging. The justices were now standing at parade rest, signaling their completion. Behind them, Leo's body had detached from the pole and lay mangled, flat on his stomach.

A lava wave of pain washed over him but at least the whipping had stopped. He had to dig deep, deeper than marrow, to find strength enough to stand. The thought of being dragged away seemed more unpleasant than a few more lashes.

His right palm found cobble and started the ascent. Slowly he began to rise and soon swayed upright. Leo's eyes were battered shut from the whipping pole. All the blood he saw scattered around should have been enough to kill him. All it did now was piss him off. He was too weak to speak, too tired to fight, but he stood defiant all the same.

"Unbreakable," one man muttered from the crowd.

"Got a demon in him," another said. "Should be dead, look at all the blood. And still standing. Damndest thing I ever saw."

"Take him away," Lawrence bellowed. "Get him out of my sight."

CHAPTER

4

Liquid Courage was the only tavern in the little mining village of Nebula. Nothing fancy about it, just a wooden two-story tavern with wide double doors at the entrance. Patrons sat at oak tables on three-legged stools atop the cobblestone flooring.

Empty wooden barrels were cut in half and slid around the tavern as a platform for gaming and whatnot. A lute player sat next to the hearth while a young beauty with jet-black hair in a dark blue dress sang along.

Getting a room on the second floor was

competitive unless you paid twice as much to share it with a mistress of the night. Chicken and deer stews were served from the kitchen. Cooks labored night after night as patrons sought refuge from dangerously high blood alcohol levels via mediocre stews to counteract stout liquors and watered-down ale.

At a corner table sat four Zodans, inconspicuously lost in the crowd. They found it easier to discuss the order's business in plain sight of the noisy tavern, rather than 'secret' hideouts that are always discovered anyway.

The Zodans were an ancient order of the Zodiac, not to be confused with their Prothica rivals, although both were starborn. Both groups collectively make up the Mozzaroth, which were comprised of gifted members dedicated to naming, mastering, and harnessing the power of the stars. They were considered folklore to most people, while others found them uncomfortable to speak of.

Kano's gloved hands concealed the miniature star-burned marking of Sadalsuud, the brightest and major star of Pisces on his right hand and four minors on his left. Inside each of the star patterns, the symbol of the Zodiac it represented was also burned into the flesh.

He was accompanied by his protégé Ambrose, a very ambitious third generation Zodan with aspirations of joining the twelve. That being said, he'd only named one minor star at present. A great accomplishment nonetheless, being there are only two dozen or so known to possess the power of the stars.

Across the table from Kano and Ambrose sat Hadrian and his own protégé, Torrez. Hadrian bore the mark of Zebeneschamali on his right and three lesser stars on his left.

As luck would have it—and Kano had little of it—he was once Hadrian's protégé. One night many years ago at the age of 17, he mounted his father's horse and wandered towards the source of a loud racket deep in the desolate Heron Desert.

At the top of a deep canyon he happened across an older man in a brown woolen cloak with greying hair. The old man was so caught up in the mastery of his major star that he hadn't noticed Kano's arrival. Kano stood in awe as Hadrian cast down bolt after bolt of lightning, shattering dozens of undeserving boulders that lay in the canyon's depths.

Unable to fabricate a believable story, Hadrian thought it best to tell Kano about the Children of the Stars. Atop that canyon, Hadrian tutored Kano for several years, teaching him to learn the names of the stars in each constellation, seeking to harness their energy and become starborn. The locals cursed the location as haunted, dubbing it Zeus's Canyon, and to this day they won't set foot there.

At a table near the inconspicuous Zodans sat a hunchbacked old man slurring and spitting through his story. "The Bloody Rose, they call him. Say he killed more'n a hundred men in the Frostbite and more besides in Gwonda. Heard the moon bathed in all the blood he shed."

The hunchback's much larger companion slammed a cup down. "They say a lot of shit in the north these days, ye drunk bastard. I'll believe it when I see it."

The third of the hunchback's party weighed in. "You won't see any of it sitting in this damn tavern all the time. I suppose you were too damned busy when ole Wade Holloway came recruiting, huh?"

The big man took offense to that, his face reddened in undignified restraint. "You hold your tongue, Charles. I'll take no lip from the likes a'you. Piss on the Frostbite and Rosewood besides. At least I ain't ever turned on my country for some wrong-skinned flatheads."

Hadrian cleared his throat, bringing Kano's attention back to their business. Beside Kano and Hadrian, Ambrose and Torrez engaged in small chat as their mentors continued discussing the order's business.

"Right," Kano said. "They're up to something, I can feel it. Rasalhague's been burning up the Sagittarius sky. I can't be the only one who felt Lucian's death. Liz is MIA, the Prothica missed the accords assembly, and I doubt this is all a coincidence."

Hadrian cringed as a lapse in the music carried Kano's voice further than intended. "Calm down, for Christ's sake, I don't think the barkeep quite heard you. It's not that uncommon for the Prothica to miss an accord meeting every once in a while just to spite us."

Kano absentmindedly rubbed the soreness from his left hand. "Yeah, well, that doesn't explain Lucian's death and Liz's disappearance. I knew I should have gone with her."

"You name another minor?" Hadrian asked, knowing full well how uncomfortable it can be when a star marks you.

Kano leaned in over the table, and Hadrian met him halfway. "Shh," he whispered, turning away from his protégé who was still caught up in his own conversation. "It was supposed to be Ambrose's. We spent months at Zeus' Canyon zeroed in. He shriveled to skin and bones, sacrificing meals and sleep while trying to wrestle the stars into submission. I tried to give him a transfer and ended up getting marked with my fourth lesser. If Ambrose's looks could kill, the stars would have taken me home right there on the canyon."

Many years before, Kano had been in a similar concentrative state except his lasted the better part of two years with no stars to name. One day, it had occurred to Hadrian that if he transferred some of his energy towards Kano, it might give him a boost of sorts.

Kano sat there honed in, stubby legs crossed, peering into the welkin of his lesser target, sweat beading down his neck. Hadrian sat a few feet away as the idea morphed into action. He reached out towards Kano's back and began calling on the power of his stars.

Slowly and methodically, a small cloud of energy

transferred from Hadrian's outstretched hand towards Kano. Kano never saw it coming and Hadrian only told him about it days later when Kano's burned shoulders had to be healed by the Tribesmen.

Hadrian shifted in his barstool, stealing a glance towards Ambrose. "The stars have a way of humbling even their most beloved children. Looks like he's recovered quickly enough despite the growing pains. I trust you didn't teach him to transfer?"

"Of course not. I'm fairly certain our friend Ambrose would sacrifice his kneecaps to name a major, then use his chin to drag himself around less he blemish the mark. Best we keep transferring to ourselves for a while."

"Indeed," Hadrian responded, satisfied. "Now back to our business here. I'm afraid you're right about the Prothica. Their activity has caught all our attention and they have the majors to cause quite a stir. If they persuade Boyce to join them, we'll be in serious trouble. We must be ready if they strike. What word do you have from Nicolai?"

"He felt Lucian's death as well and shares my concern for Liz. There have never been this many vacant major stars available. The Prothica may be making a move to gain the majority of the Mozzaroth." Kano was cut off by Ambrose's shoulder tapping. The protégé stared wide-eyed at the entrance of the tavern as three very out-of-place gentlemen entered. They wore ash-grey hooded tunics, intricately embroidered with stars down the front, the Zodiac wheel on the back.

"Borin," Kano muttered, clinching his fists—worthless as the gesture was against a starborn. He took note of Borin's two minions, namers of minor stars, perhaps. The music stopped. Everyone in the tavern looked at the three newcomers as if they'd just barged into their outhouse.

"No need to stop the music on our account. We're just passing through," Borin said, a cloud of trouble about him like a brute looking for a bar fight.

The big guy sitting between Charles and the hunchback spoke up. "Those are fancy-looking clothes you girls got there. A copper for each of ya if you're willing," he mused, nodding to a room upstairs.

Borin peered round the tavern, ignoring the drunkard until he spotted the Zodans' table. He glided their way, his minions trailing on each side like a pair of trained hounds.

The drunkard didn't take to kindly to being ignored. He reached for Borin as they passed the hunchback, too slow to stop his friends' advances.

Borin was authentically surprised to find his arm in the big man's paws. His eyes came aglow and the big man's went wide. Above the bar, swords and shields hung decoratively on display. One of the swords flew from the wall, driving through the big man's temple and pinning his head to the table.

Charles flung himself forward like dead men do, stopping on the business end of a blade. Borin's accomplice eased Charles to the floor nice and gentle like. The tavern began to clear, cooks and whores alike, each clogged between the swinging doors.

Borin paid them no mind, focused only on Kano's party. "Well, well, well. Four Zodans in one place, and two of the twelve besides. Please don't get up, we won't be long. Allow me to introduce my associates Giles and Stephon." The pair looked ahead, all business.

"Nice to see you again, Hadrian." Borin smiled. "And you, Kano." He continued ignoring the Zodan protégés altogether. "Our business is simple but not personal. You and the half-man possess two major stars and the Prothica wish to relieve you of them. To dumb it down for your witless protégés, we're here to kill you." Borin finished.

Hadrian struck first, calling on lighting before making it up from his chair. A thundering bolt tore through the roof of the tavern, striking Giles and Stephon. Each of them was sent sprawling across the tavern, taking benches and tables with them as they went.

Hadrian cursed his aim for missing Borin and called on another bolt of lightning just a moment too late. Borin flipped four metal stars into the air. Kano stood closest to the Prothica major and was the first to see the killing instruments take flight. Behind them, Borin's eyes lit up, the metal objects twinkled in midair, separated, and flew towards the Zodans.

Kano ducked but not quick enough. Sharp, jagged

metal tore through his cheek and severed his right ear as it passed his face. Ambrose turned just enough to take a star in the shoulder, the impact knocking him to the floor. Torrez sat at the table paralyzed in shock. A star hit him in the neck and blood squirted through his fingers, draining the color from him as he slumped to the floor desperately trying to stop the bleeding. Kano looked back and saw Hadrian clutching a star that protruded from his chest.

Kano reared back as blue and white matter took shape in his hand, then flung it towards Borin with all his might. It staggered him back, but a second shot sent the Prothica major reeling through a wall out into the street.

Stephon didn't appear to have lived through Hadrian's lightning blast, but Giles did. The minor Prothica appeared out of the corner of Kano's eye, running towards him dagger in hand. Another blast of starfire sent Giles reeling once again through the tavern. Kano turned around to find Ambrose looking at his own hands in disbelief.

Borin staggered into the tavern through the broken double doors with another handful of stars.

"Run!" Kano yelled to Ambrose. He squared on Borin to give him time.

***

Agnen sat in his cell, leaning against an iron gate,

massive paws swallowing an old creped copy of *The Divine Comedy*. He avoided making friends with the others; most of them didn't last very long in the fighting pits regardless. He used to play chess with a Kotian named Vito who was as good a companion as one could find in the pits. That was until the two were matched and Agnen had to cut him down. It was no easy task, mind you. Vito fought as if the two were natural born enemies. Now Agnen had only a scar on his chin and the book he'd left behind to remember his old cellmate.

There were about fifty slave fighters imprisoned within the stonewalled Gorronian fighting camp, most commonly referred to in the north as Sarci Barnil, which roughly translated from Gorronian to Veronian as the Sacrificial Chamber. It rested slightly underground the fighting pit, which seated thousands of spectators.

Above ground, the pit was connected to Sacri Barnil by a narrow walled alleyway. Many a slave fighter would take the long soul-wrenching gut check of a walk from the Sacri Barnil to the pits but only the luckiest or most skilled would return. Agnen couldn't tell how many men he had killed in that pit of sand. One, two, sometimes three at a time. During his treacherous two-year stay he'd counted thirty stomach-knotting treks to the pit. A feat unsurpassed, earning him a red name: the Reaper.

Archers manned the walls with crossbows, honing their skills on men who would rather take their chances running than trial by sword. An outsider might curse the runner a coward after pulling the bolt from the slaves back. The fighters, on the other hand, were thankful of one less opponent. Anyone with a weapon can kill you. Death is simply a cut, a fall, even a spoonful away.

Agnen heard clanking armor coming down the corridor. A guard, most like. The fighters were prohibited from wearing armor unless they were in the pit.

The clanking stopped nearby. "Reaper. You have a visitor."

A visitor? Even with an arrow buried in his chest from the first day battling the Veronians in the Winsoot, it took a dozen men to subdue Agnen after the Gorronian Army returned home defeated. They bound him in rope, trapped him inside an iron cage, and carted him through village after village until he was thrown into Sarci Barnil. Since that time there were no visitors for anyone and memories of home and family were just painful afterthoughts.

The guard stepped aside, revealing a man Agnen guessed to be in his fifties. He had grey hair and wore a long red and black accented surcoat. Most noticeably were the visitor's grey eyes. They swam over each of the fighters as if he were in search of a good stud horse.

The Reaper found himself sizing up the man as he would an opponent. A practice he'd grown accustomed to and was now second nature.

"Thank you, Dolan," the visitor said to the guard.

"You've been most kind but the matter in which I have to discuss with General Agnen is of a private nature. Would you be so kind as to excuse us?"

Dolan looked at the visitor, then to the Reaper and the rest of the hungry-eyed fighters. "I cannot be responsible for your safety......"

The visitor smiled as if the guard had just told a joke. "I'll be fine, I assure you. That will be all, Master Dolan. You are dismissed."

"As you please, sir," the guard said, clanking his way back up the corridor.

The visitor strode past Agnen's open cell into the middle common area of Sarci Barnil. He retrieved an unoccupied wooden stool, pausing just a moment to take in his surroundings, not the least bit concerned at the many hard stares he attracted.

"My name is Abaddon. I have enough coin to open most doors and an army to splinter through those that won't. Take a look around you, Agnen. Your life in Gorro is over. You're a disgraced general turned slave, and despite your fighting skill you will surely die in the sand like the rest. I'm surprised you've managed to live this long, which is precisely why I'm here. Pledge me your sword and I'll buy your freedom and give you a chance at vengeance."

Freedom? A word he had once taken for granted as most people do. Truth was, there isn't much a slave fighter wouldn't do to escape Sarci Barnil, and pledging a sword seemed easy enough. Abaddon also spoke near-perfect Gorronian, which interested Agnen a great deal. The vast majority of Veronians thought the northerners a savage people and wouldn't dare lower themselves to speak their tongue.

Agnen set his book down. "And what will pledging my sword cost? Nothing such as freedom is free."

"A lot has happened since you were cast down here. True, the world has moved on without General Agnen, the Reaper of Sarci Barnil, but I intend to put you on the cutting edge of a new world. Veronia is on the verge of civil war and I'm giving you a chance to overthrow their kingdom."

Agnen sat in silence. Other fighters strained to listen, unbelieving of what they were hearing. Most of the lot would cut their manhood off with a rusty spoon to be offered their freedom.

Abaddon placed his hands on his knees and leaned in close to whisper, "I'm told that Leo Rosewood was near death amidst your own camp in the Frosbite, and it was your decision to let him live." Abaddon fixed Agnen with a questioning stare, no doubt wondering why he would let the commander of the enemy army simply limp away. Had he just killed Leo then, things would have been much different.

The memory put Agnen in a mood, and Abaddon poked the bear.

"That kind of blunder must rest at the forefront of your many mistakes, I don't doubt. For the Bloody Rose beat your army not once but twice and here you sit waiting for death to wrap you."

His prodding had the desired effect as Agnen rose to his feet, fists clenched, knuckles white. Other slaves left their seats as well to get a better look.

Abaddon lazily raised a palm and continued. "That leaves you and me with a common interest. Your cost of freedom is servitude in my Red Army as Commanding General. You answer directly to me until Veronia is conquered. You get freed of bondage, and an army to exact your revenge."

Agnen hung on Abaddon's every word, despite the sleight about Rosewood. Nonetheless, it had been ages since he'd heard any good news so his head swam searching for loopholes in the offer. He abandoned the search in lieu of improving his current situation.

Continue fighting in the pits a slave, or command an army of free men? "Get me out of here and I'll make Veronia bleed!"

***

Abaddon returned the next day, this time unaccompanied by guards. Dolan and Company must have grown tired of the scorn and left Abaddon to fend for himself.

"I've offered them a king's ransom for your freedom and they still refuse," Abaddon said calmly, easing onto a wooden stool. "It's your death they want, not my coin. There must be another way."

Thoughts about the offer and the fighting pit's refusal had plagued Agnen throughout a sleepless night. "They want a show."

"They want to make history, as most men do," Abaddon countered.

It wasn't just Abaddon's coin offer he had thought of all night, but the price he'd have to pay just to get out of the pits. *If it's making history they want, I'll give them a story to tell.* "Twenty men!" he muttered, pummeling fist to palm. "The fighting pits of my country are sacred ground. Many a freed man train their whole lives voluntarily competing for fame, fortune, and glory.

"Giltor Atillin was the best of those men. He once challenged the most praised slave fighter to a match. The fight was a disaster. Giltor killed the slave too quickly and many began to curse him for rigging the fight. Whether it was true or not, who could say, but Giltor had to save face, so he challenged the next best slave fighter, then the next, until he had killed all of them one at a time. Fifteen in all."

Agnen's blood ran cold as he sized up the other slave fighters from his cell. A glare like he was giving were the same as fighting words but the other slaves thought it healthier to just look away. "If it's a show they want, tell them I challenge twenty!"

The proposal seemed to please Abaddon. "I'll make sure you're provided with the weapons and armor of choice. You know, your Veronian isn't half bad," he said, turning to leave.

Agnen hadn't realized they had transitioned from local tongue to southern Veronian. Something about Abaddon made him uneasy but for now he would have to address the more pressing issue. *I'll be damned before dying as their entertainment. Twenty men, Veronia, Leo Rosewood, and then Gorro.* It was a large to-do list but one worth dying for.

A few weeks later, Agnen made his last trip between Sarci Barnil and the fighting pit. He would cut through twenty men and earn his freedom or die trying, and he hadn't given much thought on dying.

Despite reservations in trusting Abaddon, he had never seen nor had the pleasure of dawning such spectacular armor. Five smiths were commissioned, hammering day and night to make a sword, shield, and armor to Agnen's exact specifications.

The end result was a jet-black obsidian shield and armor with red accents. The dragon glass helm had two solid gold horns. His sword was made of Drago steel, fitted on an obsidian two-handed grip. The price for the Drago steel alone was worth more coin than Agnen had ever looted.

"You're my champion now, and you'll look like it," Abaddon had told him.

Agnen made his way through the stone tunnel, past the last gate and into the fighting pit where thousands of spectators voiced their lust for blood. Whether it was his arrival or impending death, he couldn't tell. The noise was deafening but somehow he made out the clash of iron on stone as the gate shut and locked behind him. A chilling sound that awakened all his senses like a hungry bear coming out of hibernation.

His introduction was brief; they'd come to see his death but wouldn't miss the opportunity to stain his name one last time. Something about his twice-failed military campaign and some emphasis on his pit-fighting skill as the Reaper, which drew mixed reviews.

They looked no more significant than ants on a mound from where Agnen stood in the pit. He spotted Abaddon's red surcoat easily enough, as well as the large, dark-skinned Kotian next to him. *A bodyguard, perhaps?* The two sat in tranquil silence, their attention fixed on their champion. So earnest were their stares that Agnen felt exposed despite his heavy armor.

Another roar of the crowd and the first of twenty entered the pit opposite him wearing a polished breastplate, wielding two short swords. Erion was introduced as a northern pit fighting champion with twelve victories. Losses were never mentioned because Gorronian pit fighters never outlived them like the Romas sometimes did.

For fuck's sake, I hope they're not all champions. He glanced towards Abaddon to see if he betrayed any knowledge of his opponents. Abaddon shook his head as if he could read Agnen's mind.

No indication to start the fight was given, so Erion took it upon himself to fly forward, delivering a backhanded left followed by an overhand right sword slash, which Agnen deflected with his shield. The clash on his shield snapped him out of his prefight daze and sent him on the attack.

The first pieces of advice his old cellmate Vitor had ever given him were to, "Never take your eyes off an opponent. You got one task in a pit fight—outlast your opponent, or water the sand."

Ever the showman, Erion crossed his blades back and forth before his next attack. The Reaper intercepted his attacker with a shield thrust that caught Erion off guard and sent him reeling onto his arse. Agnen never fancied style points. He followed Erion to the ground with an overhand swing that tore through helm and head.

He followed with a backhanded slash which severed head from neck, keeping in mind Vitor's other nugget of wisdom: "Kill them twice or thrice, leave nothing to chance or you'll bleed for it."

After his fifth victory, his nerves had subsided and his heart no longer pounded to get out of his chest. The ninth fighter, a stout-looking Veronian named Gregor, landed a slash to the back of Agnen's leg, causing it to buckle.

Gregor was now behind him, sword raised high for the finishing blow. Agnen timed it just right and rolled out of the way, landing a gauntleted right hook to Gregor's manhood.

He dropped to the ground, hands assessing the

damage. "You broke me balls, you son of a whore!" Gregor said, writhing in pain.

The crowd booed Agnen's low blow as if he gave a shit. The Reaper climbed atop Gregor and caved his face in with the Veronian's own helm. Agnen had learned a long time ago that pride and honor only get in the way. Ignorant shit like that will get you killed elsewhere just as fast.

After his tenth victory, the bodies were given ceremonial honors and individually carted out of the arena, providing him with a much needed rest. He slumped back against the stone wall, sucking air and dousing himself with water.

"You look tired. A tired fighter is more often than not a dead one. How's the armor holding up?"

Agnen looked up at Abaddon staring down at him. His armor had already paid for itself and he was only halfway done. It had absorbed and deflected more blows than he could block. The downside was that its weight was starting to bear down on him, causing his arms and legs to tingle from the strain.

"I expect your armor will survive the day. I'll try not to bleed on it." Agnen took a closer look at Abaddon's companion. He wore a grey surcoat, stars parallel to the buttons running down the length of the front. "Who's the Kotian?"

"This is Lyle, an associate of mine. The three of us will have plenty of time to get acquainted provided you live through the day."

Lyle looked down at Agnen as if he'd found the source of a foul smell.

Agnen had the notion to make Lyle a bonus kill for the crowd about the same time his eleventh opponent entered the pit. He stalked back to the center, cursing the Kotian as he went.

He tore through the next five opponents, wondering what life would be like after the pit. Slash, stab, four left. Sweat-soaked hair matted his face, and breathing became more labor than instinct. He shed his helm and some of the tension in his neck subsided.

They must have run out of volunteer champions because Micah, the seventeenth challenger, was a spear-wielding brown-skinned slave from Heron and a fellow pit slave. Agnen remembered sparring with him a few times using blunted instruments.

Micah, like most other slave fighters, liked to display his combat prowess during sparring matches as a means of climbing up the invisible ladder of hierarchy. Agnen, on the other hand, would usually only spar at fifty percent, being very careful as to what strengths and weaknesses he chose to expose. But when you're nearly seven feet tall and notoriously famous for all the wrong reasons, it's hard to be discreet about anything.

Agnen tried to close the gap after the first spear thrust but Micah was too fast. Three more spear thrusts in quick succession and the Reaper found himself backpedaling. Micah let out a war cry and charged forward. Foreign as it was for Agnen to be doing the backing, balance was natural and he stayed upright despite flailing his arms around.

Regaining any form of fighting stance came seconds too late, and in the pit you don't have seconds to spare. Micah's next spear thrust penetrated chainmail just below Agnen's dragon-scaled armor and lodged in his stomach. Being stabbed is a hell of a deal. Foreign objects such as spearheads aren't natural to have in one's stomach. It makes the other organs a little squirmish. Before the pain kicked in, Agnen felt his intestines warm the cold steel which scraped between two broken ribs.

All those Veronians, all those champions, and a fucking slave kills me? The thought pestered him more than the wound until all he saw was red.

For some reason Micah let go of the spear and stepped back in awe. Maybe he was surprised he'd actually hit pay dirt and the Reaper was still standing. A belly full of iron should put a man down.

Agnen tried to pull the spear out, and sudden pain threatened to drop him to the sand. About the same time he realized that pulling the head out now would leave a gaping bloody hole by which he had no means to plug. He wrapped both hands around the wooden spear and snapped it in half. The pain blotched his vision and watered his eyes but he was still in the fight.

Micah's bowels betrayed him as the Reaper staggered forward with the broken spear in hand. He drove it through Micah's midsection, lifting him three feet off the ground, and tossed him—spear and all—as far as he could throw the man.

Agnen picked up his shield and stood over Micah, watching him flop around the pit like a fish out of water. Some people just don't have it in them to die with dignity. Death comes to us all and yet people fear it. He took his shield and smashed Micah's face in, once, twice, thrice.

There was another pause before his final match as the dead combatants who had been dragged to the side were now carried out of the pit. Agnen took his rest on a knee in the middle of the pit, opting to focus on the task at hand rather than engage in meaningless chatter as if it would fight beside him. There was nothing left to be said anyways. He'd win or lose, live or die.

The crowd roared as Samson, a local pit-fighting champion, entered the pit. Introductions were given but Agnen paid them no mind. Apparently Samson cared less and little for them as well. He paused just long enough, adjusting his polished shield so the sun reflected into Agnen's eyes. As soon as it had the desired effect, Samson struck with a fury of slashes before the two men were properly introduced.

Agnen half ran, half fell, raising his shield to avoid the attack. He blinked furiously in attempt to readjust his sun-blotted vision while Samson lined up for another go. The second attack sent Agnen reeling. His legs burned something fierce and finally buckled under the strain.

Samson wasted no time or effort for show, instead delivering a hammering blow that Agnen absorbed with his shield. He rolled from the second blow and tried to rise to his feet, but his legs weren't quite ready and he found himself on one knee.

He dropped his sword to the sand. It became too heavy to wield. Behind the shelter of shield, he reached into his belt and drew a dagger. Samson came barreling at him as he tried to make little behind the shield. Samson's blow jarred his shield into his head, nearly knocking him out.

Agnen shook off the misery of pain like he'd grown so accustomed to. Beneath his shield he saw Samson rearing back for another blow and realized he wasn't going to stay conscious for many more of those.

The Reaper tucked and rolled forward, driving his dagger through Samson's leather boot as he went. The blade buried through the arch of Samson's foot and out the sole of his boot. He dropped his sword and hobbled off, cursing through clenched teeth.

Agnen picked up the borrowed sword, seeking an end to the madness with a sword slash of his own. The blow took off Samson's raised arm just below the elbow. The next one caved in his helm.

Agnen sank onto both knees, while the crowd shouted praise and cursed his birth in nearly the same breath. He wanted to run. To where he didn't know, didn't much care, just wanted to put as much distance between himself and Gorro as he could. If only he weren't so tired. There was also the matter of a certain spear in his stomach to deal with. The thought of it reminded him it was supposed to hurt but the shock of it must have dulled the pain.

Men grunted, pulling the heavy iron chains as the challengers' gate creaked opened once more. Dolan and his goons stepped forward to collect the dead and give Samson his honors.

"If you're expecting a freedom sword, you can go fuck yourself," Dolan said. "You are anything but a free man. I'm ordered to advise that if you step foot in Gorro again, you'll be skinned alive and hung to dry. Now get out of here before I cut your arms off and turn you into a pleasure slave."

Agnen's blood ran cold. There was a time not long ago when no man dared threaten him. He'd killed a few men just for their snotty remarks or hard looks. You let someone challenge you in Gorro and get away with it, you'll be cursed a yellow sword for life.

Dolan knew what such an open insult would do and his goons snickered in the background. Abaddon and his Kotian accomplice appeared on the other side of the gate. Behind them, Agnen's freedom.

***

Kano sat at the water's edge of Crystal Lake, boots removed and feet submerged. His cheek and ear stung with the nagging pains of healing flesh. He dipped his head in to dull the pain and dreaded the thought of leaving the water.

"Good morrow, friend. I hope you didn't call me out here for swimming lessons."

Kano exhaled his frustration. He had the ability to teleport and yet it was Nicolai who always snuck up on him. Kano turned his head towards the Zodan leader turned Priest.

Nicolai was something of an anomaly. His snow-white hair sat atop a square-jawed, youthful face. Kano wasn't exactly sure how old Nicolai was, but he was rumored to have been among the first twelve.

"Borin!" Nicolai answered his own question as he often did, looking at what remained of Kano's ear.

The mention of the name brought a vile taste to the back of Kano's throat. "He and two minors attacked us in Nebula. Hadrian and Torrez were killed. Ambrose and I made it out alive, but not without injury. Borin said they came to take our stars."

Nicolai stroked the stubble of his chin while he processed the news. "I felt his loss, as I did Lucian's before him. And Borin?" Nicolai asked.

"The thug's still alive," Kano spat, tugging a boot over his foot, "and stronger than I've ever seen. We were able to dispatch the two minors but it was all I could do to keep the Sagittarius spawn off us. Still uses the same bloody stars, though," he added, rubbing his wounded face.

"How bad is Ambrose?"

"He got hit in the shoulder. Could use the Tribesmen's attention but he'll live in any case. He shot a bit of starfire that saved both our lives."

"Interesting," Nicolai responded before attending his stubble once more. Most minor Children of the Stars can't shoot starfire until they name their second minor. Even then, many of them can't draw enough energy. If the two minor minions Boris had had with him were able to call starfire, Kano and Ambrose might not have lived.

"Notify the Tribesmen," Nicholi ordered. "Round up every protégé at our disposal and put them to work naming majors and minors alike. This blatant assault can mean only one thing. If it's a war they want, it's a war they'll get."

CHAPTER

5

The king's new dungeon lay beneath the Capitol's keep, the most secure structure within the castle walls. It was dark, damp and rank, housing nearly a hundred of Veronia's worst criminals. The design itself was very simplistic and perfectly square. Leo couldn't tell exactly how long or wide it was because in a dungeon with only four outside walls and no privacy, stepping on someone's real estate is a capital offense. You bump into the wrong person in there and you might end up on the wrong end of a crudely-made shiv.

It was the first time Leo had ever seen someone

stabbed with human remains. Overpopulation wasn't as big a problem as one might think. What goal fever didn't kill, the other prisoners did. Life sentences were laughable. From what Leo could tell, blue hairs had no place in Lawrence's dungeon and simply didn't last long.

Leo finished a set of pushups and rested his scarred back in the corner. A prime piece of real estate for a square dungeon.

After he'd been flogged, it took several weeks for his back to heal. General Soberal was well informed of the dangers in King Lawrence's version of the Pontefract. He had demanded that Leo be isolated and admitted to the infirmary at least until his wounds had healed, given his service to the empire.

King Lawrence granted part of the general's request, throwing Leo in the oubliette instead. The vertical shaft was designed so the prisoner was unable to sit or lie down. His meals were lowered down the shaft, his feet were covered in piss and shit that mashed between his toes. His back burned, itched, and ached beneath scarred skin he thought would never mend.

The pain and misery had driven him mad. So mad that after a month he began to refuse his meals. He'd rather embrace death than another sleepless night in this claustrophobic stone shaft. Leo pled with the general to have him transferred to the dungeon, healed or not. They both knew he would be a target down there but Leo would rather die fighting than rot away knee-deep in his own shit.

Cast into the dungeon, it took mere hours before one of the prisoners worked up the nerve to test the injured former captain. The Capitol Watch made sure everyone in the dungeon knew who the weak and wounded newcomer was when they threw him in and slammed the iron gate.

Weary as he was, Leo had managed to snap the bastard's neck, giving pause to the rest of the prisoners who thought about making a name for themselves with Leo's blood. A week later he'd regained enough strength to claim one of the four corners as his own.

The occupant had been a snaggletooth, tangle-haired, wiry man named Chaz who'd earned his stint in the dungeon by refusing to pay the king's taxes. When they tried to seize his animal trapping equipment, he killed a few coin collectors and ended up here. The king couldn't kill everyone or he wouldn't have any occupants at all in his pretty little dungeon.

Chaz had leaned into the corner, watching Leo make his way towards him. Chaz drew his shiv but sat where he was. Leo stood over him, weaponless but deadly as they come. His reputation was hard-earned and battle-tested, and they all knew it.

"I used to be a nice guy," Leo had said, knuckles clenched for a fight. "Never took anything that didn't belong to me. Always told the truth, even listened to my brother preach the word. Used to watch executions and wonder why good men made such ill-advised decisions."

Leo couldn't see the prisoners behind him, but they all watched him. Wasn't much else for entertainment in the dungeon, and it didn't get better than a corner spot challenge.

"Now I realize it takes something as small as the principle of things to push a man to killing." Leo had knelt at Chaz's feet, their eyes locked, each waiting for the other to make the first move. "You've never wronged me—Chaz, isn't it? I hate to do this but I'm going to have your corner one way or the other. I've had all I can take bumping elbows with the scum on the long wall."

Chaz twisted the shiv in his hands, silently weighing his odds. Leo's challenge had been subtle enough as to not insult Chaz's pride, but lethal enough to get the point across.

"I was wondering when you'd come challenging," Chaz said, standing. "I know a few things about principle too, and I sure as hell ain't going back to sleeping on top of bastards on the long wall. Martin!" he yelled to the occupant of another corner. "Time for a change of scenery. You're in my spot."

"Well fuck my mother," Martin said, gathering his things. "You hear that Quinton? Seems you're in my spot."

"Yeah, yeah, I'm moving already you dingle berries." Yusolf made way for Quinton in the last corner. "Get the feck out of my way," he barked, kicking a few people out of the way as he spread out along the length of the wall.

"Good luck trying to quill all the squabbles in this hellhole, bossman," Chaz had said, smiling. "I didn't realize I'd killed the dungeon boss when I took his corner either. A piece of advice"—he sheathed his shiv in his dirtied waistline—"always convene with the other cornermen before making a final decision or the prisoners will turn your bones into shivs." Chaz patted his bone-made shiv once more and walked away to claim his new corner.

Well shit. I should have known there were strings attached to these corner spots. Looking at the rest of the prisoners piled nearly on top of each other, he wondered why he hadn't challenged for a corner earlier. Leo had almost smiled, leaning back into his corner for the first time. It wasn't much, but at least he didn't have to look over his shoulder anymore. It had been far too long since he could say that.

They were served two meals each day, what Leo guessed was morning and night. If you wanted to call throwing half as many loaves of bread as there were people into an open space a meal. It was an unwritten rule that you scuffle for your grain, leaving what weapons you might have holstered. A rule that wasn't always followed. A starving man lives only to eat his fill.

Candlelight peered through the iron gate, illuminating the staircase that led from the outer entrance to the iron dungeon door. Footsteps patted down the stairs, signaling their next meal—or prisoner.

Leo walked amongst the crowd of prisoners across the room where they formed a half circle around the iron door. The Capitol Watch would not risk injury feeding prisoners; instead they would toss bread through the square holes in the gate.

A laugh rang out before the bread. "Get it while it's cold and stale, you whores' sons," George the goaler said, heaving loaves through the door.

Prisoners sprang into action, climbing and fighting over one another for a meal. Leo had noticed ole Georgy threw in about fifty loaves each time, so he routinely waited for the last few loaves before jumping into the mix. The first loaves were usually won by the hungriest men who'd scratch and bite your fucking face off to get any substance they could into their bellies. Screams rang out as men beat and trampled one another for a loaf.

"Har har har," George laughed, throwing them in one at a time, careful not to miss any of the action.

Forty-one, forty-two, forty-three. Leo sprang into action, eyes on his prize. Many of them cowered before him as he slung men out of his way, mindful not to turn his back completely, of course. He made it straight to the door and took a loaf almost straight from George's hand, catching it before it hit the ground.

Leo wrapped both hands and arms around his meal and walked alongside the wall back to his corner. He sat down, taking a swig of lukewarm water. Water was much more plentiful. As much as George loved a good show, he gave them their fill of water through a rusted shaft that ran from the iron cells above to a washbasin turned water well on the dungeon floor.

Beside him, he heard the growling only a hungry stomach could make. Leo ripped the loaf in half and tossed one end to his right.

The other cornermen were growing on him but they usually kept to themselves, unless they had decisions to make over thievery, fighting, and what have you. Boyce was the closest thing Leo had to a cellmate. "Thank you, friend," he muttered.

Leo nodded, not that Boyce could see it in the dark. He knew better than to befriend anyone in a hellhole such as this but for some damn reason he didn't have the heart to listen to the man slowly starve.

"Veronia will miss your loyal blade if it doesn't already," Boyce said between chews. It was more than Leo had heard the old man say in one sentence since he had arrived.

Somehow the mention of loyalty turned his stomach sour. "Veronia can go to the pit for all I care. There was a time I'd color the dirt red for it, but that time has passed."

"And yet given the chance, you'd do the same, if not for country then for God or family. Whatever reason you could find to wet your sword, I'd imagine."

You ungrateful bastard, Leo thought, watching

Boyce eat his bread between insults. "You presume too much of me, old man. Don't speak as if you know my doings." Silence. *Damn this old man.* "The sword is the only thing I've ever been good at. Don't mistake me for an honorable man, though. Truth is I'd fight for much less than God, family, and country. But enough of this shit. What did you do to end up here, anyways?"

Dungeon code prevented most men from prodding into other men's personal affairs. Perhaps no subject was more sensitive than asking a man what crimes he'd committed, but Leo had to know. There was another silence, longer than before. The shameful, awkward kind Leo recognized all too well. He swallowed the last of his bread. Wheat so hard he had to dunk it in water to get it down.

He took to the cobbles for another set of pushups; there wasn't much else to do. "Wrap your arms tight around your secrets for now, but I'll hear the truth before you share any more of my bread."

"Have you ever wished upon a star and got something so wonderful it tore your life apart?"

Doesn't take wishing upon the stars to tear your world apart. Leo was in no mood for riddles but for some reason he'd taken a liking to Boyce. He may not fight for his bread, but Boyce had iron in his voice. "I've wished for many things; never on stars, though."

Boyce's voice was calm and level as if they were fishing Crystal Lake on a cool summer's day. "Have you ever heard of the Mozzaroth?"

"Can't say I have," Leo replied, although he'd caught wind of something or another from his sister years ago. Some folklore about sorcery and such. He hadn't the time to waste on childish games if he were to be the best swordsman Veronia had ever seen.

"Care to hear of them?" Boyce asked.

Why is it old men always have a story to tell? "I suppose I've got time for a story."

"Very well," Boyce said, scooting closer. "Long ago, the ancient Chaldeans sought to unlock the secrets of Earth hidden within the stars. What they discovered is what we now call the twelve signs of the Zodiac. More than that, they learned how to use the twelve signs and its major and minor stars to control the universe.

"The first Chaldeans to harness the power of the Zodiac's twelve major stars were called the Mozzaroth, which are more commonly referred to as the Keepers of the Zodiac. They discovered power beyond belief. The ability to control wind, water, healing, shape-shifting, lightning, immortality, and more. While only twelve could name the major stars, lesser stars could be named as well.

"With such power available, a man named Abaddon sought control of the earth and stars by forming a group of his own called the Prothica. He recruited others from the twelve and sought control of the Zodiac by attempting to kill off those who would not join him.

"The others were forced into a group of their own called the Zodans who have fought to prevent the Prothica from controlling the Zodiac and unleashing hell on Earth."

Rubbish. "An interesting tale, but what does that have to do with your imprisonment?" Leo asked.

"If you do not believe what I've just told you, you would never understand any crimes of mine."

"Try me."

"I had a beautiful wife and son. Lilly and I had been inseparable during our childhood. We wed shortly after graduating from the university. She and I shared a knack for alchemy and were given the opportunity to pay our dues by selling various projects we made.

"After graduating, we moved from Mirta to Nebula. We had Gregor shortly after and I opened my own business selling alchemy lamps. It wasn't long before we noticed Gregor was different. He would pace back and forth, lost amidst his own world, covering his ears in public to block out excessive noise. He was emotionally unstable and could not be reasoned with.

"We traveled all over Veronia in search of an apothecary who could treat him. We had to sell our business to cover the debt and in the end, not even the physicians at the university could diagnose him. They all wrote him off as afflicted. A blanket diagnosis for the unknown.

"With nothing else to do, I turned to God and the stars for answers. I spent night after night wishing for answers and one night something strange and unexpected happened. An uncontrollable power coursed through me as if a star had reached out and touched me.

"Thinking it was a gift from God, a remedy for Gregor's affliction, I sought to cure him myself." Boyce's voice began to shake and he cleared his throat to reset. "One night, as Lilly struggled to hold onto Gregor, I placed my hands on his head to calm him. I'll never forget the wild look in his eyes before the starfire killed them both."

It took several moments to realize that Boyce was done speaking. Leo was still curious as to how Boyce had ended up killing his family and why he wasn't stoned or hanged for it. But you don't poke an injured animal nor inquire upon a broken heart.

Leo went a different route. "And what of this gifted power you possessed? This starfire, you say. What was it?"

Suddenly from the darkness two strange lights appeared. They shifted atop Boyce's palms in a blue and white cloud of mist. Behind them, Boyce sat cross-legged, looking nothing like the old man Leo had pictured. He had greying hair, finger-combed away from tear-filled eyes that flickered with light.

"Sorcerer," Leo muttered defensively.

Although Boyce had his back to the other prisoners, they weren't oblivious to the glow that lit up the darkness. Many shrunk away from the light as if it were deathly contagious. Others sat in amazement, none more so than Leo.

As quickly as it had appeared, it vanished. Darkness submerged the dungeon, leaving only blotchy pigments of light fading from Leo's eyes.

***

Jaminez sat at his desk, scribbling out a letter to his son beneath the flickering candlelight. Although it was well into the night, he'd not yet had time to shed his armor. Too many things to do and so little time.

He paused and set down his quill, flexing his fingers and exhaling the strain of command. Beside his parchment lay Leo's sword and hatchet. Jaminez unsheathed the sword, running his fingers down the length of the blade. Despite Leo's efforts in sharpening and smoothing out the blade after each battle, more than a few nicks remained. Each notch a memory.

Jaminez became lost in thought, looking at his second son's blade. Heart full of concern for what they'd been through and what lay ahead. It wasn't until he saw a tear run off the edge of the blade that he realized he'd shed it. He sheathed the sword and clapped his hands in prayer.

"Dear Lord, please look over Veronia in its most dire time of need. Give our soldiers the heart to do what's right and the strength to carry your cross. Bless the priesthood for their continued devotion and look after my family, for I am getting too old and fear my time is almost up."

Outside Jaminez's wooden door, two cloaked figures approached, each of them grasping the head of a diamond-eyed snake. One of them handed a coin purse to Sergeant Stone, the assigned guardsman to the general's chamber door.

Stone reached out and took hold of the bag with shaky hands. Sweat beaded down his face as what little conscious he had left was washed away by greed. One at a time the snakes were released beneath the door, slithering into Jaminez's chamber. The cloaked figures disappeared as quickly as they'd come, leaving Stone alone once again in the hallway.

After the Lord's Prayer, Jaminez reached for his quill to finish the letter.

Captain Juan Soberal,

Leo is finally out of the oubliette and has spent the last few weeks in the dungeon. How his back healed without infection can only be a gift from God. Perhaps he's too stubborn for life's ailments to bog him down. I've tried reaching out to him but King Lawrence has forbidden me to have any contact with Leo in the dungeon.

The Red Army grows stronger every day as our soldiers lured by coin desert us to join their ranks. I feel it's only a matter of time before King Lawrence orders us to disband them. As each day passes, the Reds grow stronger and bolder. It will be no easy task.

The officers and I can reason with the king no

longer. He and the closed council heed none of our advice but we continue our duty undeterred. Give my regards to Bishop Jewel, the High Priest and the rest of his council. They may be Veronia's only hope to survive this brewing civil war that threatens to tear Veronia apart at the seams. Your mother sends her love and we look forward to being together again. Until then be strong and of good courage, my son.

General Jaminez Soberal

Commanding General of the Veronian Army

"Come to bed, Jaminez," Lauralis called. "Whatever it is you're writing can wait 'til morning. You've lost more than enough sleep as of late."

"Just finishing up. Stone!"

Sergeant Stone heard his name from outside the doorway. He paced back and forth in the hallway, wondering if the general had discovered his betrayal or detected the snakes.

"Stone!" Jaminez called again, louder than before.

The sergeant was a ball of nerves opening the door, not sure if he was more afraid of the poisonous snakes slithering about or the general who stood beside his desk with two weapons in plain view.

"I have a letter that needs to be sent to my son in Mirta. Find Sergeant Holloway, tell him to take five of his men and hand deliver it himself."

Jaminez extended his arm to hand off the letter. Stone hesitantly moved forward to take it, but not before Jaminez noticed the sweat dripping off the sergeant's nose.

"You feeling all right, Stone?" Jaminez asked. Stone's eyes were too occupied with avoiding the serpents' path to meet the general's curious stare.

Stone swallowed a lump in his throat. "Must have been something I ate, sir. Been on the latrine all day."

"Get the letter to Sergeant Holloway, then summon Lieutenant Von Drake to relieve you for the night. I can't afford a security breach while you're paying for your sins on the latrine."

"Yes sir. Right away sir," Stone said, bolting towards the door.

"Oh, and Stone, one more thing."

Jaminez moved back to the desk and reached for the sword and hatchet. Stone nearly ran, thinking the general was onto him. Underneath the desk, one of the snakes coiled to strike.

"See that Sergeant Holloway gets these weapons to Juan as well."

"Yes, sir," Stone said, taking the weapons and closing the door behind him.

The general sank into bed next to his wife. She buried her head on his chest, and the two were sound asleep before one of the snakes slithered onto the bed.

* * *

Juan walked through Mirta's busy streets towards the church to meet Bishop Jewel. General Soberal had seen fit to station Juan as far away from the Capitol as possible after his return from Gwonda. Juan busied himself assuming command of Veronia's most elite cavalry unit, the Widow Makers, who were stationed at the port city.

With the Red Banks' coin-bought army in clear defiance of the king, it would be only a matter of time before the two armies collided. Jaminez was none too confident that Veronia would withstand their assault, which was another reason he ordered his best soldiers as far away from Bresdan as possible.

Captains Natalie Collins and Bruce Donnell were ordered back to Indigo. Bruce won a Guardian Sword just months after Gwonda and requested to command a unit of his own. King Lawrence approved the request and the Swords of Bane were born. With the Reds controlling Chaucer, Indigo was right in the middle of the two armies. In the event of a Red attack, Bruce's unit would most likely see first blood so he trained his men twice a day, making damn sure they'd be ready.

Juan didn't take very kindly to being ordered away. After Bruce won his sword, Juan entered the following year and tore through a notable list of Veronian and Red Army swordsmen. He was rewarded for his efforts with a two-handed Guardian Sword. Juan requested a pardon for Leo, which the king denied. Wanting nothing else, Jaminez finally convinced Juan to request command of the Widow Makers since he was stationed in Mirta anyways.

Despite the feeling of being held captive in Mirta, Juan knew it could be a lot worse. Leo was a prime example of that so he made the best of his time in the port city. It was General Soberal's idea to petition for the re-installment of the Guardians. Two centuries before King Lawrence's reign, the Guardians were a small army charged with the protection of the church and directed solely by the High Priest and his council. They had grown so powerful that King Isaac was rumored to have feared them and eventually ordered the Guardians disbanded.

Of course, King Lawrence would hear nothing of the Guardians' reinstallation. He had enough headache dealing with the Red Army. Despite Lawrence's disapproval, Juan and Bishop Jewel tirelessly petitioned the reinstatement to the rest of the Priest's Council who had yet to buy into the idea.

Juan hastily climbed the stone steps, reaching for the front door of the church to escape the sun's relentless heat. A raspy yet familiar voice called from behind, "Captain Soberal!"

Juan turned and found Wade wearing his usual sun-salted tunic, spitting a mouthful of chew before ascending the steps. It was awful thoughtful of him to resist the urge to stain the white-stoned entrance.

"Lieutenant Holloway." Juan shook his head at Wade's sergeant breastplate. "It's always a pleasure to see you, old friend. Still avoiding the promotion I see."

Wade was the Veronian Army's best recruiter. He

spent much of his time a nomad, traveling Veronia on horseback. The rest of his time, he carried important messages to and from the highest ranking members of the army. Lately, Wade carried only black news.

"No offense, but I ain't the officer type," Wade replied, spitting another mouthful of oil. His right palm and fingers were swallowed by Juan's banana hands as the two greeted one another.

Wade brandished his sealed scroll. "Good to see you again though, sir. I have a letter from your father."

Juan wasted no time breaking the seal and was refreshed to read of no major catastrophes. Leo's release from the oubliette was a double-edged sword, though. Jaminez had a habit of downplaying his troubles in his letters so Juan relied heavily on Ole Faithful Wade Holloway to tell him the truth of things.

Juan rolled the letter up and secured it in his belt. "How are things in the Capitol?" Juan asked, knowing Wade would cover the proper ground.

"Not so damn good. Not good at all. I spoke with a friend o' mine just south of Antick on the way here. He says the Reds are on the move and headed towards the Capitol. Not sure what their headcount is but—"

"They're marching on the Capitol?" Juan wasn't sure why he seemed so shocked. The Red Bank had been defying Lawrence for far too long and it was only a matter of time.

"I ain't seen em marching with my own eyes but I believe they are. I double timed the rest of the way here just in case. The general also wanted you to have these. Didn't speak with him directly, but they look like Captain Rosewood's to me. Don't know anyone else who carries the pair," Wade said, presenting the sword and hatchet to Juan.

Juan paled at the sight of Leo's weapons. His father cared for them like they were his own offspring. To give them up meant he knew the Reds were coming and didn't want them to fall into the wrong hands.

Juan's temper flared but he restrained himself. "Get to Indigo double time. Tell Bruce and Natalie to round up as many men as they can and meet me at the Capitol. With any luck, they've already started that way."

Wade acknowledged the order with a nod and was off in a flash. Part of Juan was glad Wade didn't take the promotion. Sergeants competent and trustworthy as Wade were hard to come by.

"Cederic!" Juan called to his lieutenant.

"Already on it, sir. I've sent Jaxon to ready the men."

CHAPTER

6

The Reaper sat atop his stallion, listening to one of his lieutenants babble something about castle walls and Capitol Watch. Behind them, his army of twenty thousand men stood in formation, eagerly awaiting the order to start the war. His soldiers wore light plate armor with red belted tunics and visor helms. Agnen had no reason to downgrade from his obsidian armor despite uniformity. In the north, beards were the closest thing to uniformity they had.

The Veronians sent out a handful of soldiers who stopped halfway between the Capitol and the Red Army to parley. *I'll never understand why these purple plates want to talk so much before a fight.* Nobles fled the Capitol for days as news traveled of the Red Invasion. Abaddon's orders were to bring the Veronian king's head back on a spike. Agnen wondered if the king hadn't fled already with his noble court.

"You want me cut down their parlay or have the archers blot them out?" Captain Visney asked.

Damian Visney, the Reaper's second, was a vile bastard even for Agnen's standards. Abaddon freed him from a Gorronian prisoner camp while trying to locate the Reaper. They called him Nightmare on account of the screaming and yelling he did when he slept. Damian never slept without daggers in both hands and the dreams kept his eyes peeled most nights.

He was one of a few unlucky former Veronian soldiers who got captured behind enemy lines at the Frostbite. Damian had been tortured by the Gorronians for intelligence he didn't possess and was forgotten about after the war, apparently thought dead. Most of the Veronian captives were killed off, except Damian. He was the example of what an uncooperative prisoner was treated like and put on display for any of the newly arriving prisoners.

Agnen stole a glance at his one-eyed captain and recognized the handiwork of the Gorronian Inquisition. "Tell them we're here for the king's head. Either bring him to us or we'll carve him out."

Damian rode off with four men of his own. Agnen

didn't care much for the killing, raping, and pillaging that comes with sacking a city, but sometimes it makes the next one easier to yield so he let Damian have his fun.

Agnen watched his earless captain address the Veronian convoy. He couldn't tell what was said from the distance but it didn't take long before the Veronians were red of face. Damian galloped back to Agnen's side.

"Well?" the Reaper asked though he knew the answer already.

Damian flashed a broken smile. The Gorronian Inquisition's handiwork no doubt, chipping away every other tooth piece by piece. "It seems they're rather fond of Lawrence's head and wish him to keep it."

Agnen hefted his golden-horned helm onto his head. "Burn anything that catches flame. Bring their king to me."

***

In the center of the dungeon, a removable manhole led to the outside world. It was used mainly to empty buckets of piss and shit, which were tied to ropes and hefted out of the dungeon by less offensive prisoners housed in the iron cells above.

On rare occasions, a rope would be lowered, Goaler George would call a name and that prisoner would be lifted to freedom. More frequently it was used to extract the dead.

Most of the prisoners in the dungeon passed their time in solemn silence, reflecting on the lives they'd once had. Living only to dull the hunger pangs that wrenched their aching stomachs. New prisoners learned the hard way that it was better to suffer in silence, less you get your teeth kicked in for disturbing someone else's peaceful misery.

The iron door offered the only source of ventilation when the manhole was closed. On hot days such as this, the stone flooring offered a little comfort from the hot, muggy prison. Leo laid stomach-to-stone, letting the flooring suck heat from his body.

"Do you hear that?" Boyce asked.

Leo detached his face from the ground but heard nothing aside from the rustling of other prisoners. "Hear what?"

At the outermost parts of the Capitol, the Red Army began sacking the castle. Boyce craned to hear panicked Capitol folk running about full of terror long before Leo could process what was happening above. "The Capitol is under siege. Sounds like trebuchets on the walls," he said plainly.

Leo, along with the rest of the prisoners in earshot of Boyce, were all on their feet.

"What is it?" Chaz asked, trampling over a few sleeping prisoners to Leo's corner.

"Shh," Leo hissed.

They listened intently, eyes fixed on the covered

manhole as the sounds of an attack became clearer. Yusolf, the displaced cornerman, rallied a group of prisoners and began assaulting the gate. They pressed and pulled on it with all their worth as shouts and screams began to flood the streets above.

Outside, the first of the battering rams made its way to the front gate. Capitol Watch and Veronian soldiers scrambled in a futile effort to man the walls. Catapults loosed huge boulders at the wall and fiery arrows rained down on unsuspecting citizens.

The dozen or more Reds it took to man the first battering ram were finally shot down by archers atop the wall. Two dozen more arrived to take their place. The gatehouse began to splinter and crack. Further down, catapults heaved man-sized boulders. They pounded a gap through the stone wall which filled quickly with Reds who spilled into the Capitol's streets like bees on honey.

The manhole atop the dungeon was suddenly ripped away, and a familiar fat face peered down at them. "We're under attack!" George said as if they were all blind, deaf, and dumb. To everyone's surprise he began to lower a rope. "Don't say ole Georgy didn't give you a fighting chance."

George lingered just long enough to see Martin and Quinton scrambling over one another in a mad dash to climb the rope.

"I'm a senior cornerman, and first to climb!" Martin yelled, kicking at Quinton just below him.

Quinton pulled at Martin's heels. "You climb like old people fuck. Get out of my way!"

Leo wasn't sure if George actually gave a shit about them or just wanted to get in one last game before they were all slaughtered.

Martin was only an arm's length away from reaching the surface when he and Quinton's weight snapped the rope, sending them sprawling back to the ground.

"Har, har, har. Your mothers shoulda swallowed you dummies," George said, taking his leave.

Leo ran to the iron gate and joined several others trying to pry the damn thing open. He grabbed two fistfuls of iron and tugged, but to no avail. He put his shoulder to the task and after battering himself bloody against the damn thing he fell back onto his arse and watched the others give it their worst.

"Damn gate's buried in the feckin' wall," Leo panted.

Boyce knelt beside him. "What would you do if you were able to get out, anyways? The Reds would find you even if by some stroke of luck you fled the Capitol."

Boyce was right for the most part. New prisoners reported that the Veronian Army was all but depleted. The Kiman Empire threatened to conquer his family's homeland. The same land he'd taken an oath to protect. The same oath his father had sworn, and his father before him. The thought of a Red king sitting upon the

Veronian throne made Leo's blood boil.

He remembered the oath of vengeance he'd made to himself hanging by the wrists on that whipping pole. The one of settling scores. An eye for an eye, a tooth for a tooth, blood for blood. "I'm going to kill Lawrence and destroy this traitorous Red Army. I'll wade through their blood and drown those who stand in my way."

The conviction in which Leo spoke made the hairs on the back of his neck stand, as if speaking the words aloud bound him to the task. He flexed his fists, ready for another go at the gate.

"So this is the Bloody Rose I've heard so much about," Boyce said.

Something burned above them, and a dark cloud of smoke filtered into the manhole. Light peered through as well, revealing Leo's stricken form. Scars wrapped his body like vicious words in a bloody book. Leo didn't like the way Boyce and Chaz stood gaping.

His first reaction was to pull his buckskin blouse over his head. The second prompted Leo to punch the bastards in the jaws to stop their staring.

As if reading Leo's mind, Boyce's eyes flashed, a light so bright it quenched the notion Leo had of taking a swing like water dowsing a flame.

Leo took a step back. "What are you?"

Stars began to shine forth from Boyce's hands. "If you would have listened you'd already know. I'm the Water Bearer, Namer of Sadalsuud."

Other prisoners shrunk back like roaches exposed

to the light. Leo stood his ground. Something charged through his body, tingling his extremities, leaving a metallic taste in his mouth.

Boyce raised his right hand and grasped a ball of light that danced on his hand. He rotated his palm towards the iron door, then light flew from his palm and shattered the iron gate as if it were stone passing through glass.

He turned to Leo. "Outside this dungeon, men and starborn grapple for empires, land, power, and gold. Each of us has a role to play, a job to do. You know what yours is. Get to it!"

***

Kano hadn't seen this many charred rocks at Zeus' Canyon since he'd stumbled across Hadrian all those years ago. Starfire was clean burning and much quieter than lightning so the Zodans were able to train without drawing much attention to themselves.

They broke up into two groups. Kano instructed the naming of stars and Chief Ansuk instructed calling of starfire. Amongst a crowd of people, Kano's dwarf stature would be lost. In a crowd of Zodans he was given a wide berth.

Likewise, the Vratta Chief's bone armor, deadly-looking hatchet, and savage appearance commanded fear and respect in any setting. Ansuk spent the majority of his time in Gwonda with his son Trechon who doubled as a protégé that named two minors. Despite his uneasy appearance and thick native tongue, Ansuk was a great teacher with a mountain of patience.

Kano rubbed what used to be the lobe of his right ear. Ansuk had healed both he and Ambrose upon his arrival, leaving only the missing lobe and a faint scar on the cheek as a reminder of the day he couldn't save Hadrian.

Ansuk could only work with what was given. "I can heal what's left, but only God can restore what's been taken away," the chief had said.

Out of the ten aspiring protégés they were able to round up, mostly from Nebula under the tutelage of Hadrian, Kano and Liz, only three of them had named minor stars. Of those, only Ambrose and Trechon were able to call upon starfire.

Ambrose lit up the canyon, slinging starfire with improving accuracy as Ansuk loomed over the protégé, pointing out different targets at various distances. The furthest were just out of reach, his starfire evaporating before impact.

Veronia was not the only kingdom on the verge of falling. Brielle de Luca was a displaced Itlan beauty. Children of the Stars have the ability to sense the presence of one another within a certain range. The more minors you have not only strengthens your abilities but also your senses, which allowed Kano to find Brielle and her family on one of his travels.

She sat away from the others on the edge of the

canyon, feet dangling off the cliff. Thick dark locks cascaded down her shoulders, having shed her hood to concentrate. She attempted to name her second minor while the others drained themselves trying to name the three vacant majors.

"What star draws your attention tonight?" Kano asked, sitting next to Brielle. He'd been watching over her as best he could since her mentor Liz disappeared. Luckily, Hadrian had charged her with watching over the others before the meeting that night at the tavern or she too might be dead. The sky above was clear and the stars shone bright as they dare. A good night for any namer, as far as Kano could tell.

Brielle rubbed her eyes, revealing the minor star burned into her left hand. "Vindermiatrix," she answered.

"Ah, the right hand of the Virgo Goddess. It would suit you well."

She brushed hair from her face and Kano caught wind of her jasmine-scented locks. Although he had lived centuries longer than Brielle, they were of the same age. He wondered how she had named her minor without having been taught to name. For now, that secret was hers alone.

The only other person he had known to do that ended up killing his family in a tragic accident. Nobody had seen or heard from Boyce since, although Kano thought he'd sensed him from time to time.

Her frustrated brown eyes found his. "I'm not sure

what good it will do against the Prothica. I haven't named a major and can't call starfire. I'd be of more use with a sword, or dagger perhaps. Maybe I can throw one of those and get lucky."

The weeks of intense training was starting to take its toll on Brielle and the others. Not to mention the worrying over Liz's disappearance that weighed heavily on them all. Many of them were clearly frustrated and wearing down both mentally and physically with little progress to show for their efforts. Kano wished Nicolai was there. The Zodan leader had a calming presence about him that put everyone at ease.

"C'mon now, don't be so hard on yourself." Kano smiled. "At least your Veronian is improving. It's a wonder you named that minor in the wrong tongue."

A brief smile touched her lips and laughter filled her eyes. It was cut off when the star of Zebeneschamali shone brighter than the rest, sucking all the nearest light from the sky.

Kano was on his feet in an instant. He turned in search of the Zodan naming the star, but was disappointed to find everyone gazing upon the Libra. Yet none of them were being marked.

"Damnation," Kano spat, realizing the Prothica had named another. He had half a mind to light up the canyon with his own starfire, but a childish meltdown like that would do them no good.

"Was that what I think it was?" Brielle asked.

Kano looked at Brielle as if she were the source of

the problem. She stepped back defensively as his eyes flickered aglow.

"I'm sorry if I said something wrong," she added.

A leathered hand clutched Kano's shoulder, sucking all the fight out of him. "Easy Kano," the Vratta chief rumbled in his ear. The closest thing to a whisper Ansuk had in him. "A word with you?" he asked.

Kano realized all eyes had diverted from the stars and onto him. "Have a rest, the lot of you. You can't name the stars without energy, so eat your fill. It's time some of you joined the twelve."

When they were out of earshot, Kano put a voice to his agitation. "Those bastards have some nerve. Of all the stars, they named Hadrian's first just to spite us."

Ansuk shrugged. "What's done is done. We must stay the course. Can't afford the Prothica to get stronger."

Kano's thoughts swam towards Boyce, who had never officially picked a side. If he decided to join the Prothica they would be doomed. He was tired of playing by the rules. "What if I told you there was a way to level the playing field?"

"What's this you speak of?" the chief asked thoughtfully.

The weight of a secret is oppressive. Kano was glad to escape it. "I promised an old friend of ours that I'd keep his secret. Given the circumstances, we have no choice. Soon there will be no majors to name.

There's a way I can transfer energy that increases naming ability. It doesn't come without risk, though."

"I don't like the sound of this... transfer energy you say?"

"Do you remember the burn you healed on my back years ago?"

Kano saw the chief fishing through a vast ocean of memories. It didn't take long to reel it in.

Ansuk snapped his fingers. "Hadrian said he touched you with a bit of friendly fire. A rogue bolt that hit you in the back, if memory serves. I had my suspicions then as I do now, but you healed all the same. Suspicions are sometimes better left a harmless thought rather than a poisonous question."

"Well the truth of it was that Hadrian transferred energy into me which increased my naming ability. I've tested it since then with Ambrose but haven't yet perfected the transfer process. I ended up naming a minor star, hurting only Ambros's pride. More importantly, he was unscathed."

Ansuk pondered a minute before loading his next question. "So this transferring of yours is dangerous, uncontrollable, and could risk the lives of the few protégés we have left. And you think this a good idea?"

"If you have a better idea, I'd like to hear it," Kano challenged. "I can't think of another one. And besides"—he reached up to clasp the Tribesman's shoulder—"if things go bad, who better to have at our disposal than Chief Ansuk and his renowned healing ability?"

Ansuk was less impressed with the idea but had nothing better to offer. "Volunteers only. I'll heal all I can, any deaths and the blood will be on your hands, not mine," the chief said, finger pressed into Kano's chest for added emphasis.

CHAPTER

7

Leo passed through what was left of the iron gate, up the stone steps of the narrow corridor and to a second gate, which was left ajar. He pushed through the gate and stood ground level in the cell room.

"Free us!"

"Take us with you!"

"Don't leave us here to die, brothers!" came the voices locked in the cells.

Leo moved to a heavy wooden door that looked to be the only exit. Outside, light peered in from beneath. He began pushing. "It's barred from the outside." If he had his hatchet, he'd be able to carve his way out. In this case a starfire-wielding Mozzaroth would have to do.

The room began to fill with prisoners from the dungeon. There was a healthy two-arm distance encompassing Boyce as he made his way to the door.

***

The Red Army slashed and stabbed anyone who dared stop them and many who didn't besides. Agnen had only two people he wished to see dead that eve. The king, because that was his mission, and Leo. But not particularly in that order.

Baldric, a former Veronian soldier turned Red, kept a quick pace as he led Agnen around yet another corner. "Just around here. There"—he pointed. "The outer passage. It leads to the cell room; the dungeon is beneath it. I'm not sure which one houses Rosewood."

Agnen pushed past the soldier, his eyes on the prize. The door was barred by a single wooden board held in place by two simple catches on each side. It rattled. Someone was pushing from the other side.

Baldric's confidence waned. "General, Commander, sir, there will be dozens of men inside. Perhaps we should wait for more men."

Bugger that, I've waited long enough. As he grabbed hold of the board, light burst through the door before any sound was heard. He was flung through the air, only a stone wall to stop his flight but it provided no comfort. Agnen's back and head thudded into the wall and he slumped to the ground, unconscious.

***

Leo was the first out the door expecting to be challenged. He saw only one soldier, wearing shiny plate armor and helm beneath a red, leather belted tunic. The soldier's eyes were wide. Leo wasn't sure if he was more surprised to see the door burst open or the dozens of prisoners who rushed through it. The Red took off, clinking down the street as fast as he could.

Darkness blackened the sky; smoke filled his lungs and watered his eyes. He fought to adjust his vision to the bright flames, setting out to look for the first weapon of opportunity he could find. There's no honor in a nighttime attack, but at day's end only victories and defeats are remembered, not the time of day.

"We must part for now, friend," Boyce said matter-of-fact.

Leo knew the voice to be Boyce's but it wasn't the voice that startled him most. It was the fact that he trusted it to watch his back as the rest of the prisoners filled the streets behind. Two iron rings lay against a nearby wall. He picked them up, gripping one in each hand, and made an arch over his white knuckled grip. They'd have to do for now. It beat punching steel plate and chainmail with bare knuckles anyways.

"Where will you go?" Leo asked. He hadn't known Boyce very long but they shared a bond nonetheless. It was strange to think he'd ever considered the sorcerer old or weak the way Boyce stood amidst the chaos without a care in the world. As if it was all beneath him. Perhaps it was.

Apparently, Boyce wasn't one for goodbyes, because he was halfway out of sight before responding. "To prepare!" he shouted before disappearing around a corner, cloak flapping in the wind.

"What are you waiting for?" Chaz said, running past. "Bunch of us are headed to Heron to lay low for a while."

Leo clinked his iron fists together. "Don't wait on me."

"Suit yourself." Chaz ran to catch up with the others.

From what Leo could tell, the keep was overrun. He could only hope Jaminez had made it out in time. A handful of Reds turned the corner, swords drawn.

They moved forward to circle round him. "What do we have here?" one of them said.

He wouldn't last very long with two metal rings against five armored men. But getting away wasn't the only goal that crossed his mind. He needed an upgrade in weaponry. He set his sights on what appeared to be the weakest of the five and made his move.

Leo sprang forward and drove an iron fist into the un-helmed Red. He had the falling soldier's sword in hand before the others thought to join in. A second Red tried a sword slash but Leo was too close. He ate the pommel of Leo's newly earned sword and dropped to the ground, clutching a broken mouth.

The three remaining Reds began their slashing and stabbing, careful not to hit each other. Leo managed to parry most of their fury but it had been far too long since he'd held a sword and it showed.

He managed to cut a third down, which cost him a slash to his left side. The cut oozed crimson, triggering the remaining two Reds into a lust of their own, like sharks sensing blood in the water. The wound also pissed Leo off a great deal, thrusting him into a rage reminiscent of old. Sometimes it takes a bit of pain to get your mind right for the fight.

Some swordsmen teach that it's better to fight with a clear head, else your emotions weigh you down, making you clumsy and predictable. Leo welcomed the rage like water in the desert. An intoxicating side effect that grew stronger and more enticing with each kill.

Say what you will about a soldier's temperament around common folk. How they're too rough around the edges or too high-strung. How war changes them, leaving them jaded and apathetic. It's those wounded souls who are left standing, raising the colors after the battle so those same common folk can sit gossiping, casting stones.

"You're leaking," the Red soldier said, licking a bit of Leo's blood from the tip of his blade.

Leo lunged forward with a slash that sent the blood licker off balance. He kicked another Red soldier to the ground, armor meeting stone, accelerating him into the wall with a clank and a crash.

The blood licker took his place. "You should have killed me first," he said, running at Leo behind his shield.

Leo had seen this move before. The brace before impact left the Red soldier blind as he crouched behind the safety of his shield. Leo stepped aside and watched the soldier stumble forward.

Not wanting to give the mad bastard a second chance, Leo drove his sword into the Red's lower back, just below the plate metal. He felt the sword pierce through flesh and bone, coming to a stop when it hit the man's chest plate on the other side.

"You're dying," Leo said, picking up the blood licker's shield.

Screams of men, women, and children cut through the air. The Capitol's main entrance lay on the north side of the castle walls. He figured it would be flooded with Reds by now and piles of the dead who had tried to escape. *There has to be another way out.*

Leo ran towards the south wall, turning one last corner before it came into view. He paused a moment to catch his breath, looking up at the twenty-foot wall that stood in the way of his freedom. Perhaps he'd have better luck trying to tunnel beneath it.

Suddenly a teeth-clicking jolt from behind sent him

stumbling forward. Leo turned to find a young woman staring up at him through frightened blue eyes. At least they appeared blue—in the dark of night who could tell?

She shrank away to the nearest wall, uncertain if Leo was friend or foe. His own attire didn't provide much reassurance, standing shirtless and bleeding behind a Red Army shield and sword. His expression fierce, like a wolf among sheep.

His hesitation gave her courage to speak. "They're chasing me," she said as if Leo couldn't put it together himself. Stating the obvious is much easier than pleading for help.

Two Reds came into view, one of which strained to keep his pants up during the pursuit. The second earless man bore the rank of Captain. He glanced over the girl, focusing on Leo's sword and shield, no doubt playing the odds in his head and wondering how Leo had obtained the Red weapons.

Saggy Breeches spoke first. "There's that little cunt. I'll make an honest slut out of her, I will. She'll father my bastard if she ain't carrying one already." The soldier unfastened his pants and looked up, wide eyes staring at Leo as if seeing him for the first time.

"You better move along if you want to live. Drop those weapons before you go," Captain Earless said, gripping his sword ready for a fight.

The girl was on her feet, moving to put Leo between her and the Reds. Thoughts of running clearly on her mind, her eyes darted around for the nearest exit, yet she clung to the cobbled street as if trapped in quicksand.

It wasn't Leo's business to intervene with the spoils of war. These Red bastards had even given him a chance to move along without a fight. But the Bloody Rose didn't like the lustful look in the first Red's eyes and felt compelled to intervene.

Leo squared on them. "The cunt you speak of is with me and we'll be leaving now. As for these weapons, they're mine. If you want them you'll have to shed red for them same as I did."

Apparently that hurt the rapist's feelers. He ran recklessly towards Leo, pants sagging round his knees, obviously more accustomed to striking down women and children than fighting men. A mistake he'd not recover from. Leo deflected the incoming sword with his shield, nearly cutting through both the rapist's legs with a slash of his own. He finished him with a sword thrust that pierced chest plate and cavity, and stepped over the dead, waiting on Earless to attack.

The Red Army captain was tall and broad of shoulder and omitted a dark and dangerous presence around a broken, knowing smile. "Your name and legend precede you, offering no favors of concealment, Leo. You can run for now but you can't hide. It's a small world closing in all the time."

Words are used to fill voids of uncertainty on the battlefield. Oftentimes the more a soldier sings his business, the less effective he is steel on steel. At least that's what Jaminez had always told him.

"You better move along if you want to live," Leo mocked. "Drop those weapons before you go."

The Red captain dropped nothing but moved along all the same, burning holes of hatred into Leo as he left. Making sure the Red was well and gone, Leo turned to the girl.

"What's your name?" he asked.

She began thawing from her frozen stance. "Mandy Strickland," she replied, eyes still darting for an exit but with less urgency this time.

"Drew's daughter?" he asked, mind already sifting through memories of seeing the two hugging outside the gate when he and Drew had returned home from the Frostbite. Another memory surged to the front, his last of Drew, one Leo hated himself for. She nodded in reply.

Small world.

"Listen. I'd go any direction than with me if I were you. I'm a magnet for pain and misery. With me your safety will be in constant jeopardy, death always nipping at your heels. You come with me and you'll have to squeeze steel to survive. You can start by picking up that sword, or you can run and hide with the others. The choice is yours."

"You're Leo Rosewood, aren't you?" she asked, calculating. It was his turn to nod in reply. "My father followed you and it got him killed."

Now his legs were frozen. To be fair, her slight wasn't too far off the mark. *Is this how it's to be? Killed by the daughter of a better man than me? If it's so, let it be.*

"But I'm not so naive to blame you for his death. War makes widows of wives and bastards of children. I'm coming with you," she said, walking to Saggy Breaches' corpse.

She stood over the rapist who had tried and failed to have his way with her—the same man who had killed her mother when she tried to intervene. Her mother's death gave her the chance to run but now she wanted to fight. The rapist didn't look so terrifying now, lying lifeless on his back, a pool of blood spreading around him. She picked up his sword.

"There's a rear gate, but we have to hurry."

***

In the darkness, two liberated prisoners hovered over Agnen's unconscious body, looting what they could.

"I'll trade you this blade for that helm."

"Go feck yourself, Marcus. These horns are solid gold. Help me with his breastplate, would you? The whole set will fetch more coin."

"I ain't going to stand here and watch you undress the man, Phil. We got to get moving before the Reds get us too. Last chance now. I've seen your kinfolk, ain't a one of them ever had a sword this fine," Marcus said, blade in hand, stretching it out grip first.

Phillip tugged on Agnen's breastplate. "I prefer coin, thank you. Swords are just so un-gentleman like."

The Reaper's eyes opened and his hand shot up, wrapping round Phillip's neck.

"Marcus! Sword....sword!" Phillip choked out, frantically trying to peel Agnen's grip from his neck.

"See now. I told ya you'd be wanting this here sword." Marcus chuckled.

Phillip's neck snapped; his body went limp. Marcus's eyes went wide as men's do when shit gets real.

Agnen threw the corpse aside and rose, helm in hand, to block Marcus's stolen sword slash. He parried the sword with his helm, then thrust the golden horns into Marcus' gaunt face. The would-be thief slumped to the ground next to his partner in crime.

The Reaper placed his bloody horns atop his head and retrieved his sword. Gorronians made a living of looting the dead. Most of the weaponry in his old army was pried from the cold dead hands of fallen foes. But a wounded man ain't a dead man. Any bugger with a sword can poke holes in you, so best make sure they're dead before you go pilfering.

Amateurs.

Agnen made his way down to the empty dungeon, cursing everything he knew on the way out. He stopped at the shattered wooden door, trying to remember what happened. Only the blinding light came to mind. He'd never seen a light so bright.

"There he is!" Baldric said, unbelieving as he led Captain Visney towards Agnen. "I thought you were dead, sir. There were prisoners everywhere. Hundreds of them burst through the door and took you with them," he continued guiltily.

"Was Rosewood among them?" Agnen asked, the name turning his mouth sour.

Baldric took a sudden interest in his boots. "I can't say for sure. There were too many of them to tell."

You can't say because you ran like a coward. Can't say I wouldn't have left his ass there either, though.

Visney rolled his boot over Phillip's face to make sure he was dead. "Not all is lost. King Lawrence awaits you in the courtyard. He struggled a bit when we killed the queen, but he lives."

"And his whelps?" Agnen asked.

"Prince Marion would not be taken and was cut down. The princess was not so lucky. She had a line of.....suitors, shall we say, when last I saw her."

And you were no doubt one of the first.

They made their way to the courtyard where a crowd of Red soldiers had gathered round the king who was bound by his hands and feet, clinging to life. Lawrence lay on his side, his face sticky wet with blood. Tears of mercy ran down his face, not for him but for his daughter who was ravished over and over again as he lay bound, forced to watch.

Princess Gabrielle's voice was hoarse now, crying

at each thrust, as man after man had their turn. She was naked as her name day, bent over the stone fountain and mounted from behind, her head dipping into the water.

The Reds cleared a path as the Reaper approached the princess. Only the soldier having his fun was left, unaware of the general's arrival behind him.

"You're done!" Agnen bellowed. "Find another."

"Wait your turn, damnit. Think I'll fuck Lawrence next."

Agnen drew his sword and drove it into the soldier's back, then threw his cursing body into the fountain. Princess Gabrielle slid to the ground, unable to bear her own weight. A cloud of shame smothered her. Agnen knew only death would ease the mental anguish that threatened to consume her soul. She appeared whole but Agnen knew she was broken inside. Not all wounds are visible—many bite deeper than the surface, scarring the mind, heart, and soul.

She said nothing as her father pleaded one last time to spare her life. Agnen's sword delivered her from a life worth living no more.

"Stretch him out!" Agnen yelled to his men.

Lawrence was secured to the chopping block that was rolled down into the courtyard. He had pled for his daughter's life just moments ago, but the king made no pleas for his own as Agnen drew back for the killing blow.

"Answer me one thing, mighty Agnen," Lawrence said, Damian pressing his royal head against the chopping block. They'd already tied his hands behind his back.

"Silence, fool," Damian spat, mashing Lawrence's face into the block.

"Did you find the scepter?" Lawrence asked, undeterred. Damian slapped him across the face but Lawrence held Agnen's gaze.

Scepter? What scepter?

Lawrence began to laugh, spit and snot running down his chin. "He didn't tell you, did he? You've no idea why Veronia attacked Gorro, do you? You fools are nothing but pawns on his board."

Damian wasted no time striking Lawrence for the slight as soon as it came out of his royal mouth.

"Enough," Agnen said, backing Damian away. "Fine, I'll take the bait. Your head will be mine regardless. What scepter?"

"Things would have been so different if Vrago hadn't got himself killed." Lawrence's laughter died as soon as he mentioned Vrago's name. "How fucking hard is it to trek through the mountains with a whole fucking army at your disposal to find a cave on the highest peak? What does he do though? Falls in a damn creek taking a piss and freezes to death." Lawrence began his crazed laughing again.

The name Vrago didn't ring a bell either. "You Veronians speak in riddles even on the chopping block," Agnen said, testing the distance with his sword.

Damian grew bored of the chatter. "Vrago

commanded the Veronian Army at the Frostbite. Rumor has it he froze to death after falling in a creek during the campaign and Rosewood succeeded him in command."

"It doesn't matter, you fools." Lawrence with his laughing again. "When the Reds are done parading your sorry asses around, you'll be headless too."

Damian drew a dagger and stabbed Lawrence in the side before Agnen could wave him away. Lawrence winced as air began sucking through the wound.

Must have hit a lung.

It took the Reaper two strikes to sever the Veronian king's head. Had he any fire left in him it would have only taken the one. Gabrielle's head took more from his conscious than his strength but Agnen felt bogged down nonetheless. The second swing cut through Lawrence's spine, finishing the task. He drove his sword through the base of the severed royal head and lifted it high in the air as his men began to cheer.

The Purple King was dead, the Capitol had fallen. Veronia was theirs.

***

Kano strode past the Zodans to the tallest hill within eyesight. "I need three volunteers," he said.

Ambrose was first to follow. Behind him, Ansuk nudged Trechon forward while the rest of the minors sat weighing their options.

"What for?" one of them asked.

"Where are they going?" asked another.

Brielle hesitated long enough to see Ambrose look back at her, motioning her to follow. She shook off her doubts and hurried to catch them. "This isn't the part where you offer us up as a sacrifice to Baraqiel the Watcher, is it?"

Kano shook his head. "Only the Prothica would contemplate something so foolish. I've got a mind to see you three join the twelve tonight."

"I don't like the look in his eyes," Brielle whispered to Ambrose.

"I've seen that look only once before."

"What happened then?" she asked.

"Borin resized his ear," Ambrose replied, looking a little worried himself.

The hill on which Kano set their course turned out to be steeper than expected but it offered the highest vantage point in the area and removed the distraction of Ansuk's starfire course below.

They had to walk alongside the canyon, around the backside of what turned out to be a jagged cliff rather than a hill. Darkness swallowed the canyon's depths below, but the view overlooking the Heron Desert was magnificent.

Kano sat behind the three minors who seated themselves alongside the cliff facing the canyon. Ambrose was on the left, Brielle in the middle, and tight-lipped Trechon on the right.

Brielle raised the hood of her cloak. "If he kicks

me in the back, I'm taking you with me."

"It's a date," Ambrose said, having already dawned his cloak like a shield of armor.

Kano would only allow them to name stars beneath their cloaks. If he told Ambrose once, he'd told him a thousand times. "You must minimize all distractions, revealing only your eyes and hands. The eyes are the windows to the soul, and your hands will bear the mark, should you be lucky enough to name the star."

He waited until they were all cloaked before he continued. "Naming stars is something like courting a lady. You have to start slow and easy but in the long run you'll have to bare everything you were, everything you are, everything you inspire to be. It's a game of matchmaking, a dance with the stars.

"Ambrose, you'll attempt Aries' brightest star Hamal, which offers the ability of invisibility. I can't bear the thought of you naming Aldebaran and reading my mind. Brielle, Aldebaran is yours if she'll have you. And Trechon, you will attempt Leo's brightest star Regulus with the ultimate warrior ability."

To their credit, the three minors knew at least where to find their assigned stars amongst the others, which eased Kano's mind ever so slightly. Ambrose and Trechon had been painstakingly taught all things astrology through Kano and Hadrian. Brielle somehow managed to keep pace having only worked with Liz a year or less.

Since the fight with Boris, Kano had neglected

sleep and skipped more than a few meals, traveling back and forth with supplies to train the others. Dark bags of sleep deprivation welled under his eyes and Ansuk warned of giving him his last freebee healing to restore his energy.

Kano's hands were aglow behind the three volunteers, focusing on Ambrose first. Slowly, he transferred energy from his hands towards his protégé. The mystic light formed a small cloud of energy that danced slowly from his fingertips towards Ambrose as he struggled to control its strength.

Kano began to sweat and shake from the effort. In what seemed like a never-ending torture, the effort only lasted a few agonizing minutes before the star of Hamal pushed Kano away and began to mark Ambrose.

Hamal sucked the light from the sky and Ambrose's eyes were first to change as they shone bright beneath his hood. A long, painful growl escaped from the depths of his stomach. His back arched, threatening to snap him in half. He was lifted into the air, his eyes never breaking contact with the star that began to mark his hand.

Brielle and Trechon scurried away, afraid the light energy would destroy them. A star appeared on Ambrose's right hand, light spilling forth to reveal the Aries sigil of the Ram at its center. The light vanished quick as it had come, leaving Ambrose slumped on the ground.

Brielle leaned over him, panicked hands touching

his face, Ambrose's skin warm to the touch. "Is he alive?"

Kano took a long pull from his water skin and wiped sweat from his brow. "He'll need his rest. The marking process sucks the mortality from a man, replacing it with the star's energy."

They heard footsteps padding up the backside of the cliff. Ansuk was first to appear, the rest of the Zodans close behind. He ran to Ambrose, who lay on his back. The healer lifted Ambrose's right hand to confirm his suspicions. "I can't believe it worked," the chief said.

"Can't believe what worked?" Brielle asked, with a few suspicions of her own.

Kano was too tired to think of a witty response and didn't want to give away his and Ansuk's secret just yet. "You and you," Kano said, pointing out two of the aspiring protégés. "Take Ambrose down to the wagons and keep an eye on him. He'll need rest."

The two Zodans hurried forward, grabbing hold of Ambrose by the feet and shoulders.

Ansuk placed his hand on Ambrose's forehead. "That may not be necessary." The chief's eyes and hands turned healing green and Kano felt heat sucked from the air as a shiver shot up his spine.

Ambrose opened his disheveled eyes and realized he was the center of attention. He looked down at the hand that bore his new mark and jumped to his feet in jubilation. "I'm one of the twelve! One of the twelve!"

He ran to Kano, teary-eyed, and lifted him off the ground. "We did it!"

A father's pride spread through Kano like the heat of a warm blanket. "Best calm yourself down and take it slow until you gain some control of your power. Your emotions can trigger your star's power if you're not careful." Kano pried away from Ambrose's grasp. "Ansuk, would you be so kind as to look after him for the night? Brielle, Trechon, and I were in the middle of something."

The Vratta chief placed a healing hand on Kano's shoulder. Kano inhaled a lungful of power, exhaling any pain and weakness that remained, leaving his limbs tingling. "Damnit man. Warn me before you go doing that." Kano shook the life back into his limbs.

"You'll need all the strength you can get. Just be careful not to burn out. You do that and not even I can bring you back."

CHAPTER

8

Leo glanced back at the burning Capitol as they ran. "We need to get to Mirta if we have any hopes in making a stand against this Red Army. What pissed a bank off so much, they hire an army to overthrow a kingdom?" He'd heard of the bank buying a mercenary army when he was in Gwonda but never expected it to be so formidable.

"I'm told King Lawrence couldn't pay his debts and spat in the bank's face when they came to collect," Mandy replied. Her hands rested on her knees as she tried to catch her breath. Leo stood in front of her, hands on his head and trying to do the same. She couldn't help but stare at the scars that covered his back.

The Red Army had begun setting up camp on the southeast side of the burning Capitol. Perfect position to cut off their route to Mirta. *Or perhaps Mirta is next on the list.*

"It will take us twice as long to go around Crystal Lake on the west, leaving us little if no time to make a stand. Surely a resistance is gathered somewhere, we'll just have to find them." Leo was all too aware of Mandy's eyes on his back. *I'll have to borrow a shirt from the next Red I kill.*

"Last I recall, Mirta wasn't a fortified city," she said, watching the flames consume what was left of the Capitol. Somewhere in the midst of the inferno, her mother's corpse burned.

Well shit, I forgot all about that. Been out of the mix far too long, a stranger in my own country. Lawrence's Capitol was foreign to him, a place best forgotten, but for Mandy it had been all she had. His father's words of wisdom came to mind, but he didn't share them. *It's better to have a sharp mind and a dull sword than to be a fool who charges into defeat with a razor's edge, as if dying once isn't good enough.*

Instead he settled on the present. "Right you are. Sweetwater Creek is not too far from here. We can follow it up to Tamore."

They were not alone as they rounded the outskirts of the Capitol from the west. Those who had been able

157

to escape the Reds' assault darted past, unsure of where they were going but full of flight all the same. In the dark of night it was easy to conceal one's self, not that the Reds showed much interest in giving chase. For now they seemed content taking the Capitol. That was until a small contingency of what could only be Veronian cavalry appeared, riding hard.

Even in darkness, Leo recognized the Widow Makers. They were perhaps the most feared horsemen in all the world, and Veronia's oldest active unit. Each horseman wore blackened plate armor with gold etching, their sigil etched into each chest plate depicting Lady Sorrow, a morning widow cradling her slain husband's sword in both arms. Even their destriers looked menacing covered in chain and plate mail as if they had broken forth from the gates of hell.

"They'll be cut down before they reach the gate," Mandy said as the horsemen neared a wall of Red soldiers who scrambled to form a line.

Faster and faster the horsemen came, closing the gap in seconds, trampling earth and men alike. Not many soldiers look bigger than the beasts they ride into battle, but Juan Soberal was one of them, and it was he who led the charge.

"The Widow Makers," Leo said before the clash of steel rang out. "That's Juan down there."

His freedom awaited him to the north, but something kindred pulled him towards his mounted brother. Maybe it was his outnumbered countrymen making an honorable last stand or just the thrill of the fight, before he knew it, Leo was running towards them.

"You're going to get yourself killed!" Mandy shouted.

"A fine night to meet my maker. Find us a horse, this will only take a minute," he shouted back, rushing towards the Red Army flank.

The horsemen ran through the Reds like arrows slicing the sky, until their mounts began falling to spears as more and more Red soldiers took to the fight. Leo ran into the Red camp, picking up a leather jerkin and helm from an unoccupied bedroll to match his red sword and shield.

He heard Juan before he saw him. Juan's mighty war cry unmistakable after having fought beside him what seemed a lifetime. The sound of it lit a fire in Leo's chest; he began slashing and stabbing his way through the flank.

It didn't take long before he had cut his way through and halted sword to sword with one of the horsemen. The Widow Maker began slashing. Leo would have to get rid of all the red.

Leo clasped hold of the horseman's boot and pulled him from the mount. The rider went down hard with not a trace of the grace they'd charged in with. Leo stood over him, sword on neck. "Get up and meet us at Sweetwater. No time to explain—just move, damnit."

Not far away, Juan dismounted, looking for real estate to swing his bastard sword. Leo cut down two more Reds from behind and deflected an overhand swing from Juan that put him eye to eye inside Juan's guard.

Juan wrapped both arms round Leo and began squeezing like big bastards do. Those who were still mounted began to circle their dismounted leader, providing what little shield they could.

"Friendly," Leo gasped, unable to find any more words as Juan's massive arms clenched tighter. *Well fuck you too then.* Only a nose-breaking head-butt loosened Juan's grip as he staggered back, holding his face.

"It's me, Leo, you fool. Stop trying to kill me. We don't have time for this. Heard you screaming like a damsel in distress. Is that a Guardian Sword?" Leo asked. He'd never seen a two-handed Guardian Sword. It must have taken a lot of convincing for the Drago Smiths to work twice as hard on one sword. A Red charged Leo from the right and received a belly full of steel. "Withdraw your men, the Capitol has fallen. We need to get to Sweetwater and regroup."

A cavalry unit too proud to fall back is usually just an infantry unit in the end. An effective charge consists of one that strikes fast and fierce.

Juan shook his head, men fighting all around him. "Right. Widows, fall back! Fall back!" he bellowed.

The cavalry unit disentangled themselves and fell back as ordered. The Reds gave brief chase until running became more work than they had signed up for.

Leo came to a stop fighting for air, lungs like frozen pipes. "Where's the rest of the army? And when did you become a Widow Maker?"

"Got tired of wearing purple, it did nothing for my eyes. Got the sword winning the tournament and took command of the Widows. Bruce won a sword too. Captain's got his own unit in Indigo now. Dubbed them the Swords of Bane. Wade was sent to notify them at Indigo soon as I got word of the Reds' invasion.

"Far as the rest of the Veronian Army, there isn't much left. Most of the men were bought out by the Red Bank. Their stronghold is just south of Chaucer. I'm told it's an impregnable fort called the Vault and unless you're wearing red you're not welcome there."

Leo didn't like the sound of that. It appeared the Reds had anchored down for the long haul. The end of an empire, the birth of the next. "And Natalie?"

"She's with Bruce's outfit. Not much of a rider, I suppose." Guilt took him. "Listen Leo, I'm sorry I wasn't there for you."

"There for what, the flogging, the imprisonment? That was mine to bear, we both know that. Jaminez was right sending you away. What's done is done."

A mount approached in the darkness. There was no mistaking the sound of the beast's deep breathing; foliage trampled underfoot despite the rider's silence. Juan and Leo hugged the earth as the rider began to take shape in the darkness.

To Leo's surprise, it was three riders making the

161

sound of one. The first two riders Leo recognized as Widow Makers. *Surely more than two of them survived.* The third rider was Mandy.

Juan clasped hands with the first rider. "Glad you made it out, Cederic. You as well, Jaxon. What of the others?"

Cederic squinted through the dark at Leo. "We've not had time to take a proper count but I'm guessing we lost around two hundred men and more horses besides. Is that really Rosewood?" he asked.

"Have you lost your wits in battle, Cederic?" Juan scolded his second. "But to answer your question, yes. Captain Leo Rosewood, the man, they myth, the legend in the flesh. Leo, meet Lieutenant Cederic la Mare my First Horseman, and Sergeant Jaxon Griffon."

Leo gave each man a nod. He was terrible with names but there was no mistaking Jaxon's face, the same he'd crossed swords with just moments before. "I believe I've already had the pleasure of meeting the sergeant. Our introduction was brief."

"And who is the lady?" Juan asked. His chivalry never far away from a beautiful woman.

"That's Drew's daughter, Mandy," Leo replied. "We ran into each other in the Capitol. Damn maze back there, couldn't have made it without her."

Juan gave Mandy a sweeping bow. "Pleasure to meet your acquaintance, m'lady. Any kin of Drew is more than welcome in our outfit."

The three Widow Makers began strategizing

amongst themselves. Leo made his way over to Mandy. "I see you found a mount," he said, stroking the palfrey's head.

"Actually I found two, yours is over there." She gestured to where a palfrey like her own stood nibbling at the grass. They were less menacing in battle than the destriers the Widow Makers rode but more practical for the riding that lie ahead.

Leo mounted and the two trotted back to the Widow Makers. "You sure you want to stick with us?" he asked again.

She thoughtfully stroked her horse's mane. "I'm not sure of anything anymore. I've heard stories about the Swords of Bane. And I've seen the Widow Makers live up to their reputation. If war it is, this ain't bad company, I suppose."

"Suit yourself," Leo said. For some reason not entirely clear to him yet, he was glad she chose to stay.

Cederic and Jaxon led them north to meet up with the rest of their company. To Leo's surprise it wasn't just horsemen who'd gathered. Hundreds of men, women, and children stood nervously huddled together. As he approached, their heads turned, gawking towards him. Many pointed, others whispered his many names like he were a ghost who'd came back from the dead.

The Widow Makers sat in formation atop their mounts facing Leo, Juan, and Mandy as they approached. Lieutenant Cederic called for the soldiers to draw their swords and together they sat frozen in salute. The mass of people to the left all took a knee, heads bowed. Those who had weapons set them on the ground before them.

"What the hell is this?" Leo asked.

"You know what this is, Leo. Veronia is bleeding," Juan answered.

"Stop right there." Leo shook his head. "Don't put this on me."

"This isn't about you or me, it's about all of us," Juan said, stretching his arms out to the crowd. "Our countrymen are being forced into the streets by an army of usurpers. You and I have a duty that reaches beyond sigils and sides. I stood at your side while you wet your sword in Gorronian blood defending our country and another besides. If Veronia is to rise from the ashes, she'll need a leader with iron bones and steel will."

Juan rode to the front of his horsemen. "Leo Rosewood. The Widow Makers pledge their swords to your charge. These sons and daughters of Veronia have nothing left but their loyalty, and that they pledge to you." Juan finished his speech with a salute.

The only movement occurred to his left as Mandy rode out, dropping to a knee amongst the others and pledging her sword. Leo thought to ride away. *But to where, to what?* Veronia wasn't there for him when he was flogged and imprisoned, why should he answer her call now?

"Well hell," he muttered. "To Tamore it is then."

***

Kano peered through exhausted eyes, watching the Aldebaron star light up the sky as it began marking Brielle. He lay quivering on his back, searching and failing to find his own strength.

"You okay?" Trechon asked, leaning over him. "Thought you died."

"Get the chief," Kano muttered.

As if on cue, Ansuk and the others made it up the cliff face. Brielle slouched to her side, an accomplished grin on her face despite barely being able to move. Ambrose ran to her.

"You fool. You're going to kill yourself," Ansuk said, mopping sweat from his brow after lending Kano a healing hand.

"One more major," Kano replied, slowly recovering. He looked at Brielle as the protégés surrounded her. Ambrose shot him a knowing glance. Perhaps he was onto Kano's transferring secret by now. Other Zodans appeared to have the same suspicions. It's not every day that two join the twelve from the same group in the same night.

"You ready to do this?" Kano asked Trechon.

The Vratta Tribesman shed his robe, revealing a long, lean mass of muscle. Kano had nearly forgotten that Trechon and Ansuk had just returned from the mundane war. Although Trechon healed of any wounds he had sustained, Kano could see where a slashing blade had marked his chin and chest.

Upon closer inspection, Kano noticed burned flesh on Trechon's hands and arms, like he'd been dunked into a cooking pot. His heart sank as he came to the realization that the burns looked a lot like the ones he'd received from Hadrian's transfer all those years ago.

Trechon dropped his cloak to the earth. "I've seen the man whom the Leo star awaits. The one whom the moon shines upon, red in his sacrifice. Regulus will burn away all others who seek him."

Kano thought about the possibility of the stars selecting their namers. If that were the case, everything would change. He'd heard of Mozzaroth who had abused their power in the past. Many years ago, a Macedonian named Davor Nikolovski sought to become the most powerful of the twelve by naming a second major star.

One night, Davor killed one of his starborn brothers while he slept. He then disappeared to begin naming the star, and spent night after night in attempt to name the Aries star, to no avail. His Aquarius star would have nothing of it and in the end they found only Davor's charred body left behind. Such a treacherous act—the stars refused his soul.

"Looks like we have company," Ambrose said.

Only burning torches used to guide what Kano thought to be a wagon was seen in the distance. As the torches drew closer, several menacing golden-skinned figures appeared. Four guards came into view, surrounding a creaking wooden cart. Each of the guards wore brown pleated kilts and brass wrist guards with black and gold striped headdresses. Their chest plates were brass wings that stretched across their front, over their shoulders and again across their backs. They carried wooden shields bearing the scorpion sigil of Heron with sickle swords sheathed in golden scabbards.

An older man in threadbare garments dismounted from the wagon, revealing a covered figure that lay in the back.

"Do you feel that?" Kano asked, sensing another of the twelve among them.

"I feel something, not sure what it is though," Ambrose replied, eyes wide as if it were a Prothica trap.

Brielle was the first to scramble down the cliff towards the wagon. "Liz! It's Liz!"

Kano and the rest followed, some more hesitant than others at the sight of the Heron guards who stood motionless as the Zodans ran towards them. He reached for Brielle to slow her.

"Good evening, friends," Kano said, slipping into his native Heron tongue. "Is that one of our companions you have in the cart?"

"So it's true," the old man said, sizing up Kano like a king would his champion. "We've heard many stories of your Mozzaroth. Listened to you blast our canyons for many years. Not until now did I believe a Heron Native was among the twelve."

The old man appeared to know much more than

Kano felt comfortable in him knowing. He also noticed how the old man avoided his question.

"Ansuk!" came a weary voice from the back of the cart. Kano recognized it immediately as did the others. They threw caution to the wind and ran past the menacing guards.

Liz lay on her side in a white gown. Her back was exposed, revealing a large bandage between the shoulders. She was drenched in sweat. Dark lines webbed beyond her bandaged wound spreading through the pale skin of her neck and lower back. Kano didn't have to take the dressing off to know it had festered.

Ansuk must have come to the same conclusion. He ripped off the bandage and placed his hands directly on the wound, puss seeping through his fingers. Ambrose hurled on a cartwheel and politely excused himself.

She cursed the world and everyone in it until the healing began to relieve the pain. Ansuk's hands pulsed green light into the wound, which turned black to pink and slowly closed up.

"Oh my Jesus," she said, rolling onto her back and trying to catch her breath. "I don't see how you're not married, Ansuk. I really don't."

The chief shook off the tingling in his limbs that comes before burnout. "Good to have you back. I take it you weren't on an extended vacation."

"The twins attacked me at the port. Said the accords are done with and declared war. Thought Borin was drunk until he tried to kill me right there on the port with everyone watching. Didn't work out too well for them," Liz said, pulling a borrowed shirt over her head. She reached back and fingered the scar that Boris' star left behind. She found Brielle in the crowd for the first time. "You're marked!" she said, reaching for Brielle's hand.

"Isn't it wonderful? So is Ambrose! I'm glad your back," Brielle said, embracing Liz in a bear hug. She stepped back and eyed Liz's borrowed attire with disapproval. "I've got another blouse in my bag if you'd like."

Liz hopped down from the cart and stretched her legs. "I'm in your debt, Killian," she said, pulling the old Heron cart driver into a warm hug.

Killian smiled and took hold of Liz's hands. "That makes us even then. My son told me what happened, how you saved his life and many others during the attack. Don't be a stranger, my dear, and that goes for the lot of you. My people are more fond of the twelve than you might imagine," Killian said, climbing back into his wagon.

"And Kano, it would be a great honor to have you at my dinner table sometime. Stay as long as you like. I have many beautiful daughters," Killian said as he and his guards rode off.

***

"How are we going to take care of so many people?"

Leo asked, looking over his shoulder at the growing number of men and women joining them each day.

Their group was strung out nearly a mile long as they made the wooded trek alongside Sweetwater Creek towards Tamore, avoiding the King's Road as best they could. Juan split the Widows up into two groups, half of which rode ahead and the other bringing up the rear, providing whatever security they could in the event of a skirmish.

"Food, water, and shelter," Juan replied between bites of an apple. "Desperate people require only the basic necessities in life. Not just shelter from the storm but protection from our enemies, both foreign and domestic. You give them food in their bellies and a fighting chance and they'll follow you anywhere."

Juan was right. The people had no place to go at the moment. Leo and the Widow Makers were their best hope to avoid bending the knee to the Kiman Empire. But it wasn't so much the people that concerned him. Leo wondered how he would ever be able to assemble an army big enough to defeat the Reds. They didn't have the bankroll the Reds had so they'd just have to harden the swords he already possessed.

"Any idea what kind of shape Tamore's in?" Leo asked.

Juan tossed the apple core aside. It had barely hit the ground before one of the dogs made short work of it. "It was stripped nearly bare when Lawrence moved his court to Bresdan, but that was two years ago and I haven't been there since. Last I heard it was occupied by peasant farmers but not much remains of the former castle."

The mention of farming made Leo's stomach growl. "Perhaps a little restoration is in order. A farming village is a good start, though."

They made it to Britta Creek in two days which meant they were heading in the right direction at least. Much as Leo wanted to increase their pace, he knew they were moving as fast as they could. The people on foot were just as anxious to get off the road but nightfall would be upon them shortly and it was time to set up camp.

The Widows set up their camp away from the others in an effort to maintain training and discipline. Many of them were already heavily engaged in sword training before the rest of the camp had their cook pots boiling.

Down the line, a middle-aged lady sang her rendition of "Momma Bear," a song about a mother bear who fended off a couple of lions that happened across her two cubs. It was a valiant fight that left the two lions dead, and sadly the mother besides. But in the animal kingdom, sometimes all you need is a fighting chance, and Momma Bear had given at least that much to her cubs. In the end, the cubs survived and thrived together, never separating the rest of their lives.

Leo distanced himself from the group to avoid

awkward conversation and forced pleasantries. It had been too long since he'd carried his sword and hatchet and the reunion gave his allergies a fit. He shared a fire with Mandy, cleaning and sharpening his weapons despite having been well taken care of under Jaminez's watch.

Juan, ever the showman, took on three sparring partners in the distance. They used wooden short swords, Juan doing more striking than blocking and battering his opponents into the darkness beyond the fire's light. "Again!" Juan shouted, as three more Widows circled him.

Leo felt Mandy's curious eyes on him as he finished shaving off the bulk of his beard with the edge of his hatchet. The kind of look that preceded a question.

"That's an unusual-looking hatchet. Did you get it in Gwonda?" she asked.

"I did," he replied, placing the leather keeper around its head. "You should keep that blade of yours at least polished if not sharpened. Rust will weaken the blade."

Her sword rested in her lap, but she had made no effort to clean her mother's blood from its tip. A keepsake, Leo suspected, although he wasn't the type to hang onto the past.

"May I see your sword?" she asked. "I used to watch the tournaments every year but I've never seen a Guardian Sword up close."

Obviously Drew never taught her the mannerisms of weaponry. He reluctantly handed her the Guardian Sword. The wooden scabbard was inlaid with silver and obsidian, and the pommel was solid gold, as was the cross guard. A smiths hammer and sword over a budded cross was engraved into the rain guard. The Drago steel blade was magnificently reflective despite a few years of hard use.

"It's beautiful," she said, running her fingers down the length of the blade. "When we get to Tamore, the women will break off into roles of service. Put me in the kitchen and you'll starve. Turn me into a laundress and I'll drown myself in the water before scrubbing out their sweat stains." The visual nearly gagged her but she soldiered on intently. "Can you teach me how to fight like the others?"

His blood ran cold. He'd taught many how to use the sword, most of which now lay frozen in time at the Frostbite. "I'm no sword master. You should train with Juan and the Widows if you're serious about it."

"My father told me you were the best swordsman he'd ever seen. Why aren't you training with the Widows? A marvelous mastery of sword for the whole camp to see." There was no venom in her question, just honest curiosity.

In the distance, the Widows were hard at it. Two children took up sticks and began hacking away at one another, mimicking what they'd learned to the delight of the crowd as Juan refereed their match.

"Too much public sparring will only give your next opponent ideas on how to beat you." He motioned to the soldiers in the distance cutting away at each other. "Take Cederic over there. Swift and cunning, always playing defense, looking for an opportunity to counter with the kill-shot. He's just as strong on the attack but he's not fool enough to play all his cards in the training yard."

"Sounds reasonable, I guess. So how am I supposed to get any better with the sword if I have to worry about giving away my strengths and weaknesses?"

"I doubt you have many strengths to conceal at this point," Leo said gently. "But when you learn the basics, select your training partners carefully. In the game of steel it's not the one who strikes first, but the sword who strikes last that declares the winner. It doesn't have to be pretty; most fights are clumsy and ugly as hell. Just remember even a wounded survivor looks better than a rotting corpse."

"Sounds like my lessons are underway. When do we begin?" she asked, smiling.

Stubborn ass, just like your father. But I owe her that much. "Watch the Widows for now and learn what you can. We'll have time for training once we reach Tamore."

***

They met a hunting party of three who claimed to be from Tamore. Two of them were just boys, learning to hunt and gather from the looks of it. The boys were led by a man big as Juan who went by the name Edger. Edger had a braided ponytail and a thick forked beard that cut men with envy.

As Edger and company led the way back, Leo noticed a limp on the hunter turned guide. He looked too long and was caught.

Edger broke the silence. "We heard the Reds sacked Bresdan. Man named Gregor said they took turns ravaging the princess and carried Lawrence's head off on a spike. Heard they violated the Bed Chamber Queen as well. Ain't no way to win their hearts and minds if you ask me. Who am I introducing to Nestin as the leader of this outfit, anyways?"

"The Widow Makers have pledged our swords to Leo Rosewood," Juan said. "With any luck, the Swords of Bane will join us shortly."

"Rosewood?" Edger said, stealing another curious glance past Juan and Cederic towards Leo. "Heard he was killed in the dungeon."

Leo followed behind a short distance, letting Juan and Cederic do the talking. Juan was much more diplomatic and had the best chance of merging the group with the villagers in Tamore. But he'd be damned before he sat back a third wheel and listened to them babble about him. "You heard wrong. Who's Nestin?" Leo asked.

Edger squinted as if deeper concentration would allow him to recognize Leo. The hunter turned to Juan, finally putting the dangerous duo together. "I'll be damned. Last time I saw you, you were beaten as close to death as one can get without crossing over. Leo the Unbreakable they called you afterwards."

"Guess they'll have to come up with a new name now that I've returned from the dead. Who's Nestin?" Leo asked again, annoyed for repeating himself.

"Right. You know how we lowly peasants like to chatter. Nestin Vorhees is his name. Former Reeve of Indigo. He and his wife Abigail traveled to Tamore when the Capitol moved to Bresdan. Not sure exactly why, seems they were better off in Indigo. Nonetheless, he's the new mayor of Tamore now."

"Take me to him," Leo said.

Nothing was as it were the last time Leo visited Tamore. What used to be the site of Veronia's empire was now tilled into farmland far as the eye could see. Log cabins, cottages, and wood-planked buildings sprawled out alongside the Gorro River and villagers were hard at work like ants on a mission.

For some reason, he'd expected Tamore to have been abandoned and was pleasantly surprised. At the center of it all lay the cobbled town square bursting with people buying and selling goods. Hammers pounded in the distance; Leo wasn't sure it was metal or stone being worked. Probably both. Nearby a woman turned what looked to be a dear carcass over a soot-covered stone fire pit. The smell of cooked meat made his mouth water and stomach rumble.

Edger stopped and Leo nearly ran into the back of him. "This is Town Square. If you don't mind waiting here a spell, I'll go find Nestin. Angela!" he shouted to the woman roasting the deer. "We've got hungry guests here. Would you be so kind as to cut them a slab while I go find the Reeve?" Edger sent his two hunting companions off to find Nestin and took his leave.

The savory smell of cooked meat had his feet moving before Juan caught hold of him. "Easy, Leo. I know you're hungry, we all are. God knows you deserve a cooked meal, but we can't afford you gobbling down a deer carcass, hooves and all, to be our first impression."

Angela sliced off two slabs of meat, each speared through and served on a sharpened wooden stick. He didn't realize he'd snatched the stick from her hand until she let out a gasp that drew the eyes of more villagers. Seemed George the Goaler's food games left a lasting impression.

Juan face-palmed but recovered quickly. "My apologies—Lady Angela, is it? We've had a long and fruitless journey." He stepped between the two so Leo wouldn't mistake her for his next bite.

She giggled. "Quite all right... Captain Soberal, is it?" she asked, eyeing Juan's rank and sigil. "I've got a cousin in the Widow Makers. Sergeant Gaxon Griffon's his name. Is he about?"

"He should be meeting us here any day now," Juan replied. "Off on an errand in Indigo."

"And you are, my lord?" She turned to Leo with a second serving.

"Depends on who you ask," Leo said while chewing. "You can call me Leo. The pleasure's all mine, m'lady." He bit off another mouthful.

Her eyes widened at the name but she was saved from further small talk when Edger returned with company. Beside the hunter stood a man and woman Leo assumed to be the mayor and his wife.

Nestin appeared to be in his early fifties, despite a jaw carved from stone and an aura of nobility that clouded his simple attire. Only a few wrinkles that webbed from his eyes to his salt-and-pepper hair betrayed his true age.

"Two of Veronia's favorite sons. Tamore welcomes you back home. I'm Nestin Vorhees and this is my lovely wife Abigail. How can we be of service?"

Abigail's age was more clearly on display despite a natural beauty. Rusty red hair streamed down her sun-weathered face. Both hands and knees were dirtied as if she'd just crawled out of a garden. She locked eyes with Leo, holding the curious stare just long enough to prove she could, breaking it only to welcome Juan with a warm smile.

Leo tongued meat from his teeth. *Did she just eye-fuck me? A warning, perhaps?*

"We are much obliged," Juan said. "We rode to the

Capitol's aid, but unfortunately arrived too late. The royal family has been slain and Bresdan lies in ruins. The Reds cut off our passage to Mirta so we've led as many people as would follow here seeking whatever refuge Tamore can provide."

"We heard about the Red Army's attack," Nestin said. "They hold all of Veronia's wealth and most of its swords. It was only a matter of time before they usurped the king. I'm told they offer sanctuary to all those who bend the knee to their Kiman Empire. How many people are in your company?"

"Five hundred soldiers and nearly as many villagers from the Capitol. They've got nothing but what they carried here," Juan replied.

Nestin and Abigail engaged in a brief whispered conversation. It occurred to Leo for the first time that they might not be accepted as warmly as he'd expected. His thoughts turned to killing his way out of the village. A mental exercise he'd grown accustomed to, though he couldn't remember when it had started.

Judging by the looks of the villagers, they had few soldiers capable of standing against the Widow Makers, but that was no way to gain allies. The mayor and his wife were no doubt discussing the same thing as Abigail shot Leo another stern glance.

Nestin nodded, as dutiful husbands do. Abigail stepped aside and the mayor spoke. "What are your army's intentions?"

"To protect those who follow and restore order to

Veronia," Juan answered as if he had anticipated the question.

This time Edger was waved into Nestin and Abigail's huddle. Tension began to build in the square, and Leo overheard his name too many times to still his tongue.

"If you don't want us here, we'll leave and take our stand elsewhere. But make no mistake. When the Reds come marching into your village with sword and flame you'll bend the knee or burn like the rest. We've made our decision and choose to fight, not for a slain king but for Veronia." This time it was Leo doing the eye-fucking. "Whispered words are often lost in translation. Speak plainly with us or not at all."

To say it got quiet gave the silence no justice. Only the crackling of Angela's fire could be heard as villagers held their breath. Tamore could stand neutral no longer, but Nestin would not rush his decision. To cast lots with Leo's army was as bold a statement as one could make against the Kiman Empire. A victory that would echo throughout eternity or an epic failure best forgotten than repeated. The toughest decisions are those with other lives at stake.

To Leo's surprise it was Abigail who stepped forward. More surprising than that, Leo found himself on his heels when she spoke. "We'll not be ruled by the coin of bankers"—she stood hands on hips staring at Leo so there was no mistaking her meaning—"or the sword of a bloodthirsty tyrant. As long as you remember that, Tamore embraces you and your men."

He couldn't remember the last time he was challenged in such a brazen manner. But something quelled the desire to bloody his sword as Abigail's fierce blue eyes held his. An inkling of fear could not be found in her. Leo gave only a nod in return, appreciation tasting bitter in the back of his throat and dying on his tongue.

Nestin took hold of his wife and ushered her gently away. "Edger, see that our allies are fed. They'll have to build their own shelters. Gentlemen, it would be an honor to have you at my dinner table tonight. There's much to discuss."

***

Leo wiped a salty pool of sweat from his brow as it began trickling down his face. It was all he could do to keep up with Juan's relentless pace as their wooden swords cracked and popped from impact, Juan announcing each movement for Mandy's benefit. Truth was, Leo needed the practice but he didn't like the idea of so many seeing him sweat. The whole village stopped and stared when the Bloody Rose gripped the pine.

"They're here," Cederic said, not bothering to dismount. His beast circled round, skin stretched tight over massive muscles, winded yet anxious to run again. "Our scouts spotted them about five miles to the east,

Jaxon at their front."

"Our horses!" Leo yelled at the stable boys who scurried off to retrieve the mounts.

Leo's muscles ached, his chest heaved, but he grew stronger and faster each day. Covered in sweat during swordplay was the only time his back didn't feel like shattered glass bedded within his muscles. As he cooled off waiting for his mount, pain flared slow and steady like the tide crashing ashore.

"You were throwing your backhand better than your forehand strike," Mandy said, handing Leo his sword and hatchet. "A little rusty feigning dungeon weakness, perhaps?"

He strapped the sword behind his back, hatchet to his belt. "What makes you think the dungeon weakened me?" The dungeon had no doubt taken a toll on his physical strength, but it was the mental anguish that bit deepest. But a prison's pain teaches life lessons that books and scholars cannot.

Captain Bruce Donnell's Swords of Bane were the only company of Veronian soldiers who had not been enticed by the Red Bank's coin. Even the Widow Makers had a few men trade their black for red. What started out as a few dozen Frostbite veterans requesting transfer to his command quickly grew to nearly a thousand of the toughest sons o' bitches Veronia had ever assembled.

They paid homage to Veronia with a purple 'V' dyed into the chest of their black belted tunics. Leather straps fastened their weapons and armor tight against their bodies. The Swords of Bane halted and Leo led a handful of riders out to meet them.

"Good to see you again, Jaxon," Cederic said, clasping the hand of his sergeant.

Leo felt inadequately armored standing between the Widow Makers and the Swords of Bane. "Good to see you again, brothers." He grasped hands and clapped the backs of Bruce and Wade. "And you, Natalie." He clasped Natalie's hand before sharing an equally awkward hug. She squeezed him tight, a little too tight, causing a ripple of pain to run down the length of his back.

"I was starting to wonder if you'd lost your way," Juan broke the silence.

Wade chuckled. "The roads aren't as inviting as they used to be. Dodged more Reds than trees out there."

"How has Indigo fared thus far?" Juan asked.

Bruce watered the earth with a mouthful of tobacco. "Not so good. The Reds came a'calling after they took the Capitol. Looks like they're being led by a giant from the Gorronian fighting pits. My swords blocked their passage to Indigo's gates but before it came to blows, they sent in their Light Priests who swayed the townsfolk to convert to the Book of Light and the Kiman Empire."

It must have been a bitter memory because Bruce spat again. "Damn Reds installed new government officials in Bresdan and Indigo. They got a priest carrying round a book full of garbage about stars and angels." He pounded fist to palm. "When they burned Indigo's Chapel to the ground, I ordered the men to kill every priest wearing white and every soldier in red. That's when Wade found us."

Juan shook his head. "My father was right, then. He sent me to Mirta to petition the Priest's Council to reinstall the Guardians. It didn't make much sense until now."

Natalie clasped Juan's shoulder. "Sorry to hear about your parents. Jaminez was like a father to us all."

"Aye," Bruce seconded. "So what's the plan?"

"The plan is simple," Leo said. "We're going to take back what's ours."

***

Leo knew Bruce and Natalie, having been born and raised Indigo, would be welcomed like long lost sons and daughters by Nestin and Abigail. With the addition of The Swords of Bane and hundreds more who had joined, Tamore was now a formidable resistance. None were more pleased than Nestin whose vision of rebuilding and governing Tamore was finally coming to fruition.

As the days passed, more and more structures were erected to house the growing number of people. Wade was given charge of a recruiting party and sent south to gather those willing to take up arms or seek refuge against the Reds.

Edger was given charge of constructing Tamore's defenses. He had men working on a wooden wall nearly ten feet high surrounding the innermost part of the village. Outside the walls, wooden barricades were sharpened to defend against cavalry charges and holes were being dug and concealed to slow an infantry attack.

"A visitor awaits, my lord," one of Bruce's sergeants said, standing at perfect attention.

Leo looked up from Wade's hand-drawn map, which stretched across the table of their command post. It was too damn similar to the Frostbite cave for Leo's liking. "Who is it?"

"He gave only the name of Jonas. Said he was here on business and would deal directly with Commander Rosewood or no one at all."

"Bring him in," Leo said, returning to the map littered with little red pieces. Fewer purple pieces on the map as each day passed, but he didn't need a map to tell him that.

"Um. The visitor requested you meet him outside, sir," the sergeant continued.

"Who the feck does this guy think he is?" Bruce said, shouldering his way past Juan and Natalie for the door. The messenger sergeant, well accustomed to his captain's, fury was already out of the doorway.

Leo reached for his armor resting on the chair's

back. "Juan, make sure he doesn't kill the man before we discover his business, will you?" *Wait a second. When did I become the rational one?*

Outside, Sergeant Jaxon Griffon and Lieutenant Cederic la Mare stood on either side of the visitor. The man wore a leather apron strapped over his shoulders which revealed his trade as a smith. His massive bare chest and leathered forearms commanded respect far away from any forge. On Jonas' right palm, Leo noticed a tattoo that looked strikingly familiar. A smith's hammer and sword crossed atop a budded cross.

"What's your business, traveler?" Bruce asked. A challenge more than a question.

Jonas stood cool as water in the forge and wouldn't be baited. "Business, as I've said before. Hopefully I'll not have to repeat myself to everyone in the village, which is why I asked for Leo to begin with."

The bastard has balls, I'll give him that. "You found him," Leo said. "What can I do for you, Drago Smith?"

"Ah, I thought the tattoo looked familiar," Bruce said, connecting Jonas' tattoo to the maker's mark on his Guardian sword.

"You could do many things for my order, but that's not what brings me here. My services were paid for by a mutual friend who wishes to remain nameless. You see, wars are hard to win without weapons but my order has a remedy for that. We've worked tirelessly at our employer's request to provide weapons for your army.

The fruit of our labor lies across the Britta in three covered wagons," Jonas said, waving a muscled hand towards the west. "Take them, they're yours."

While the Widow Makers and the Swords of Bane were well equipped, hundreds more of his men were left without. One thing Tamore lacked was a proper weapon-building forge. They'd already resorted to beating their plowshares into swords and their pruning hooks into spears.

But something made Leo question the smith's generosity. "And what was your price, Jonas?"

Jonas crossed his chiseled arms over his stomach. "The price is none of your concern. My employer has been more than generous in this transaction, leaving your army in no debt of my order."

Leo grew tired of being stonewalled and would hear no further in the company of so many ears. An invitation to the dinner table not only provided protection to the guests, but strong wine and good food has a tendency to loosen lips. "You look hungry, Jonas. Come. A hot meal is the least we can do for your generosity."

"That sounds great. You don't get this size turning down hot meals." Jonas laughed.

After the patrons were politely shuffled out of the tavern and invited to return shortly free of charge, Leo, Juan, and Jonas took their seats.

"What will it be, my lords?" Angela asked, giving Leo a warm smile. He'd made sure Angela had been built a proper tavern of her own. A much-needed addition to the rebounding village where food and entertainment could be found and business could be discussed.

Jonas eased onto the wooden stool, careful with his weight. "Meat, wheat, and water will suit me just fine."

"Make it three," Juan said.

Leo waited until Angela had stepped away; she knew her business and didn't dally about. "Now tell us of this employer."

The smith looked at Juan, then to Leo. Not dramatically like a storyteller before revealing the climax, but with the thoughtful calculation of trust. "He requested only to be made known to the two of you. It might cause a few ripples in the Church if Veronia knew that Bishop Jewel had spent a small fortune to fund your army. Your brother must have a lot of faith in your abilities."

CHAPTER

9

Mirta wasn't called the crown jewel of Veronia for nothing. Ships and trading barges filled the harbor day and night, sun or frost. Those docking at the ports were greeted with the finest wines, food, and spices from around the world. Goods manufactured all over Veronia, namely Chaucer, were sent to Mirta, where they were bought and sold, imported and exported, making Mirta perhaps the most diverse populace in the world.

The cobblestone streets made passage on horse and carts a pleasure, a luxury most Veronian cities couldn't afford. In the days before the Reds put the kingdom to the torch, thousands of traders, pleasure-seekers, and businessmen littered the streets. Order was maintained by Veronian soldiers. It was also home to Veronia's fleet, which docked on the northern port closest to the Gorro River spilling into the sea.

Stone walls can often feel constrictive and claustrophobic. Mirta needed room to stretch its legs; therefore no walls surrounded the city. The streets would overflow with patrons and there were few vacancies in the many whorehouses, taverns, and inns.

Charles Rinnick, the Fief Lord of Mirta, and his officials were constantly entertaining distinguished guests in the castle's keep, and the embassy was always full of allies from abroad. For all of Mirta's sins, it was also home of the High Priest and his five-bishop council, each of whom lived in and ministered out of Veronia's most treasured Guardian Chapel.

The fall of the Capitol was widely known and tension at the port swelled, forcing merchants and sailors to choose between red or purple. Others steered clear of the port, waiting for tensions to dissipate or run their course. The Reds were on the move, sacking villages all over the east and around Crystal Lake. Mirta's Fief Lord wasn't exactly a pillar of strength. He nervously paced the city at night, overcome by unanswered prayers. He'd sent his sons to Chaucer in hopes of avoiding a war, and hadn't heard anything from them in nearly a week.

Aside from Chaucer, the Kiman Empire established two more of their own Fiefs in Bresdan and Indigo, and word was Charles Rinnick of Mirta was next to get ousted. With the absence of the Widow Makers, Mirta's military force had dwindled down to only a few dozen Veronian loyalists and those among the fleet too stubborn to abandon their ships.

The perils of civil war looming overhead, the Church became Veronia's rock. Clergymen gathered and held services not only in the Chapel but also in the streets and courtyards in attempt to still the unrest.

It was on Port Hill that Bishop Jewel gave his sermon, just two hours after the sun started to rise in the cloudless sky. The port filled with families bartering stubborn ship captains for lower fares, trying to go anywhere they could to avoid the Reds.

Jewel had entered the faith at an early age, about the same time his brother chose the sword. Their father, John Rosewood, was a famous Veronian general who instilled within his children at an early age the values of hard work and dedicating themselves to finding their niche in life, whatever that may be, and never looking back.

Leo discovered his early and easy enough, gaining notoriety as a swordsman, winning not only the Defender Dagger but a Defender Sword to boot. Defender Swords were crafted only at the king's request, and forged by the world renowned Drago Smiths at Mount Drago.

The Defender Dagger and Swords were carried by those who earned them by besting their competition in the annual Veronian Open Tournament. The scabbards were made of wood, softened with leather, and tipped with obsidian and silver inlay. The blades were forged from Drago steel ingots, so rare they were coveted, protected, and only known to be mined at Mt. Drago.

Only there were the sword smiths able to dispel any and all impurities from the ingot, using heat from underground lava pools that flowed beneath their forges. The hand guards and pommel were made of solid gold, the pommel fashioned into a devastating point capable of piercing flesh and bone. The weapons were spared no expense in production, but make no mistake, they were designed for combat, not as mantle ornaments.

The tournaments were fought upon a grand stage comprised of two age groups. Eighteen competitors were selected to compete in each of the two divisions. Investors often sponsored competitors, seeking to capitalize on the king's request awarded to the Guardian Champion.

The Sword Division was made up of competitors comprised of grown men, most of whom were already hardened combat veterans or mercenaries. Each competitor was allotted his choice of two weapons. Armor was allowed at the cost of a weapon selection. The competitors fought hard, sometimes to the death. The Defender Sword, the most prestigious award a

Veronian swordsman could earn, often opened doors a birthright could not.

After earning the sword, it was custom for the winner to request something within the king's power to grant as a gift for winning the tournament. This was where sponsors circled like vultures on a fresh kill. Competitors also chose pieces of land, lordship titles, even gold for their reward. Whatever the reward, any Veronian could spot a Defender Sword and those who carried it were honored and welcomed among any setting.

The Dagger Division was made up of those not yet willing to claim adulthood. Wooden instruments made the competition less lethal. The winner received a Defender Dagger, forged of the same materials as the Defender Sword. However, the Dagger Champion wasn't allowed a King's Request, but the possessor was very esteemed regardless, and usually groomed for an officer's rank in the military.

After winning the dagger at the age of 16, Leo had enlisted in the army. He won his sword the following year as a lieutenant and was well on his way to following in his father's footsteps having already obtaining two achievements his father hadn't. But Leo didn't compete for the favor of kings. Truth was he loved to fight as warriors often do, and in Veronia the most elite warriors carried Defender Swords.

Jewel remembered watching Leo presented with his Defender Sword. It was the only time in his life he'd seen Leo show any raw emotion. Leo had stared at the sword, tears of honor welling up but dared not descend. When it was time for his request, Leo shocked everyone in attendance.

He didn't ask for silver or gold, lands or titles, but for the one thing his younger brother wanted more than anything. Leo requested Jewel be admitted into the Priesthood and one day serve on the Priest's Council. Becoming a priest was something Jewel had already been working on. Being a year younger than Leo, he'd been studying with priests in Tamore to obtain his Priesthood Medallion.

However, there were only a handful of priests on the Priest's Council and those slots were only available upon the death of a living member. Even then, the current council would have to vote in a new member, who would then need approval from the High Priest.

As luck would have it, High Priest Bishop Frances was in attendance of Leo's Guardian Sword presentation. He conferred with King Hendrich, Prince Lawrence's father, and many of the local priests who had been tutoring Jewel. The Capitol Priests spoke highly of Jewel and after a lengthy discussion Jewel was awarded his medallion.

During Jewel's appointment ceremony, Leo looked on from the back of the Chapel. It was customary for weapons to be left outside during services and award ceremonies; however, those who carried Defender Swords were allowed to carry even in the presence of the king. Leo swelled with pride watching his younger brother appointed to Priesthood, an appointment that Jewel was humbled and honored to receive. Their father, General Rosewood, watched from an honorary front-row seat.

The general wore ceremonial attire which consisted of a shot of purple and brightly-polished accents. Despite his many metals and awards, John Rosewood was a man who commanded respect in appearance alone. When he spoke, people listened, and he never said more than needed to get his point across. His two sons had distinguished themselves very early on, making him a proud father though he was tightlipped with praise. John Rosewood passed away shortly after Jewel's appointment, a stinging loss that Jewel felt for the first time.

Next to the general that day sat his daughter, Page. At 14, she was one of the most beautiful un-betrothed women in Veronia. She would have no problem marrying into a family of her choice given her beauty and family esteem, however, most suitors called from a distance, well out of Leo's reach and his father's glare.

Jewel was ordered to Mirta just days later to study under the Priest's Council tutelage. Just three years into his study, Bishop Gregor passed away white-haired and full of years. Jewel was unanimously voted aboard the council, not only because of the king's request, but because he was very much a warrior of God and well esteemed by the clergy and citizens of Veronia.

Back on port hill, Jewel began to close his service. "We live in troubled times, my brethren. Be mindful of false prophets who reach out through turmoil for weary hearts and minds, when destruction comes knocking at our doors. Now go and let the good Lord be with you!"

Jewel lingered, shaking hands with the mustered congregation, until at last he was approached by a flame-headed man wearing a leather jerkin and sword. Jewel was uncertain if the man were mercenary or soldier.

"Bishop, my name is Trion Baccus, a former soldier who served under your brother at the Frostbite." Trion took to humble knees before continuing. "I'm now nothing more than a shamed deserter of both the Veronian and Red Armies, who can bear the weight of my many sins no longer."

He'd heard many confessions, but this was a first. "A deserter of the Red Army, you say?"

Trion winced as if Jewel had twisted the knife. "Yes, Your Grace. I come bearing warning, not threats. The Red Army will offer no protection to the clergy. Their priests draw from a different scripture called the Book of Light, and seek to strengthen the bloodlines of the faith by resurrecting fallen angels and cleansing the world of nonbelievers. They've got starborn sorcery among them that no mortal man can stand against."

Interesting. I heard their priests were a bit radical but that seems rather extreme. Perhaps Michael will know more of this Book of Light.

"God will judge you, not I. Rise," he said, taking Trion by the hands and nearly lifting him off his feet. "You have the rest of your life to atone for your past; what better time to start than now? Your knowledge can be of great use to the Church, and all of Veronia for that matter. Follow me if you truly wish to make amends and become an instrument of faith."

***

Jewel led Trion through the crowded streets, up the stone steps of the Guardian Chapel, and through the heavy gold-plated doors, which were opened by two young clergymen that attended the entrance. In the old days, two Guardian soldiers stood watch, an honor among the elite. Now two young priests-to-be manned the entrance, with barely enough strength between them to open and close the swinging doors.

They padded over the marble floor and past finely-crafted wooden pews to the candlelit altar, which revealed a less impressive wooden door with silver ring handles that led into a side chamber. Candles lit the round table which centered the room accompanied by six chairs, each embroidered with budded crosses.

Bookshelves clung to walls, emitting a cozy aroma only old parchment can produce. The kind of smell that makes you feel more cognitive each breath you take. The ceiling was made of silver, polished to a bright shine that reflected candlelight below.

Jewel retrieved a chair from one of the six desks along the back wall and set it by the door. "Sit here and touch nothing. I'll be right back."

He found Bishop Malachi as he entered the church. Most likely returning from his own service held in the courtyard. Malachi was a few years older than Jewel despite being junior in seniority among the council. Nonetheless, the two junior-ranking bishops had become quick friends.

Jewel closed the distance. "A word with you, brother?"

"Sure." Malachi squinted curiously. Usually when someone has something to say, they say it. When someone asks for a word, the impending conversation is much more consequential. They sat down in a middle aisle pew where they could talk quietly yet out of earshot of those still worshipping. The Chapel was never entirely empty; the doors were open to all, day and night.

"I have a confession to make," Jewel said, eyes darting around the chapel to ensure he wasn't overheard.

Malachi massaged his temples with the thumb and middle finger of his left hand. "I'm scared to ask."

"I'm told the Widow Makers have pledged their swords to Leo. As did a few hundred other refugees towards Tamore. They've amassed a real army. A fighting chance. Even the Swords of Bane are rumored to have joined them. The Red Army has been too preoccupied with sacking cities to turn their eyes on Tamore but it will be a target soon enough."

"Yes, I've heard of the resistance in Tamore. Who hasn't? Must say I miss Juan around here, but what does this have to do with a confession?"

Jewel took a deep breath, the kind of breath you take to prepare yourself for reproach, and exhaled. He leaned in close to have his confession heard. "I borrowed some gold from the treasury to send supplies to Tamore. They'll need every bit of assistance they can get. When the Red Army comes for Mirta, we'll have to go somewhere after all."

Malachi's look was incredulous and for a brief moment his shock was louder than he could contain. "You took gold from the treasury without approval?"

Jewel ducked his head, wishing he could reach out and grab Malachi's words before they reached the ears of a passerby. "Hold your tongue lest you condemn me here and now," Jewel replied between clenched teeth, brows scrunched together in annoyance.

Malachi smoothed the wrinkles of his robe and slowly regained his composure. "Sorry for the outburst, but what you've done hasn't been fathomed since we enacted the Priest's Council. Actually it's one of the main reasons the council was formed to begin with. Exactly how much gold did you take, and what kind of supplies are you talking about?"

"I'll tell you, but control yourself. I can only imagine how animated you are holding confessional.

Probably why so many are turning to the Light Priests." Jewel muttered the last part but Malachi gave an apologetic nod all the same. "I employed our brothers at Mount Drago to supply Tamore with enough weapons and armor to equip Leo's army. Raiders have been pillaging what the Reds have not. We have to centralize what's left of Veronia in Tamore. If we don't stand together, we'll all fall."

He left out the part about giving the Drago Smiths what they desired most; something gold and silver couldn't always buy. Ten ingots of Drago Steel, each hammered down from the swords of dead Guardian soldiers many years ago to prevent grave-robbing.

"You risk not only your medallion but your life making such a decision behind the council's back. The High Priest will have no choice but to pull your chain, if Theodore doesn't pursue your head first."

Old as he was, High Priest Bishop Frances was well known for running a tight council, and refused to allow one of his bishops to taint the church's reputation. His council was made up of Bishops Isabelle, Michael, Theodore, Jewel, and Malachi who had been appointed in that order.

Theodore was the more domineering and bullheaded of the bunch. He led the Holy Inquisition charged with the disciplinary action of clergymen and crimes against the church. His team of inquisitors was rarely seen, but when they were, questions were answered and lives were mysteriously lost. Wasn't always easy work but Theodore did it well for the most part.

Michael was charged in training new priests and bishops alike. He spent the majority of his time reading at his desk or bartering with merchants at the docks for rare books. The sleeves of his robes extended past his hands; he avoided physical contact whenever possible on account of being deathly afraid of catching anything contagious after narrowly surviving the bloody flux as a younger man.

Isabelle was the senior bishop and perhaps the most beloved among her peers. Even though her 60th birthday loomed ahead, she was blessed with an ageless beauty and a servant's heart. She managed the High Priest's affairs and oftentimes stood in for him.

Malachi was a blessed public speaker. His charismatic sermons were famous throughout Veronia, resonating with the most stiff-necked nobles and humblest of peasants. He directed the Church's missionaries and assigned them specific areas or duties.

Jewel was no doubt the most recognizable, or popular if you will, of bishops. His Rosewood blood sometimes preceded him, although once you took the chain, your surname was left in the past. He was given charge of the church's treasury and worked with Bishop Michael to preserve historical artifacts.

Theodore doesn't scare me half as much as he should. "My choices are my own. I can do the Lord's work with or without this medallion. There's someone

I'd like you to meet. Perhaps he can be more persuasive."

"And who might that be?" Malachi asked at Jewel's heels.

They entered the council chamber, where Trion sat peering at the ceiling. Jewel made the introductions, pulling up two more chairs. "Trion Baccus, allow me to introduce you to Bishop Malachi." The two men shook hands, exchanged pleasantries, and took their seats.

"Trion isn't our average visitor, you see." Jewel leaned forward in his chair, casually resting elbows on knees. "He's not only served Veronia in the Frostbite, he's also aided the Red Army in overthrowing our kingdom." Malachi gasped in disbelief. "He's requesting pardon in return for full cooperation. Isn't that correct, Mr. Baccus?"

"I'm at your service, Your Grace. What would the church ask of me?"

"What to ask, indeed," Jewel said, leaning back to have a stare of his own at the ceiling. Given the totality of the circumstances, Veronia was sinking fast and Jewel didn't know where to start. "To the best of my knowledge, you're the first Red soldier to defect back to Veronia. You could provide essential first-hand intelligence, and right now we need all the help we can get. We've little time for the Holy Inquisition to test the aptitude of your servitude, however Bishop Theodore would disagree. Will you do as the church asks of you, Trion?"

Malachi interrupted as Trion began voicing his reply. "Before you answer that, it must be clear that any assistance you provide the Church is given of your own free will. Anything you confide in us will not be disclosed without your permission. I cannot deny that your intelligence may be of great use to Veronia, but you must know we are not goalers but your refuge."

Trion tapped the wooden arms of the chair, exchanging glances with Jewel and Malachi. *Doesn't appear you have many options to weigh.* Trion came to the same conclusion. "Mirta is next. The Reds will be here in three days."

* * *

Once Trion broke the seal of his Red Army past, Jewel and Malachi couldn't have interjected with a question if they'd tried. The clergy were well trained in hearing confessions. You don't stop a voluntary utterance. It's better to reel in the babbler than silence a quiet man.

"It all started after the Frostbite when King Lawrence decided to uproot the Capitol and move his court south to Bresdan. I was assigned gate detail as carpenters and stone masons poured through the gate, wagons full of stone, lumber, and marble. Their hammers pounded day and night. I've never seen a city built so quickly; Lawrence was hell-bent on its construction. Didn't take long before the townsfolk started grumbling about increased taxes and the king's excessive spending, but Lawrence wouldn't hear any of it and ordered anyone with a sour opinion to clasp the pine for a flogging."

Trion hesitated a moment and took a swallow that didn't satisfy the uncomfortable memory. The kind of hesitation that got Jewel suspecting Trion of handing out more than a few of those floggings himself, whether he'd enjoyed it or not.

"Sometime during the construction, the king's council realized they wouldn't have enough coin to pay their growing debt. Lawrence had already borrowed a king's ransom worth of gold from the Red Bank who was more than happy to let the king dig his own grave. The bank brought in two heavy chests totted along by Red soldiers. They were lifted with long wooden poles that ran through metal rings along the length of the chests. Took twelve men to carry them, both brimming with silver and gold.

"Didn't take long before those chests were just as empty as the king's treasury. Lawrence would have been laughed off his throne for completing only half a Capitol, so he turned to his coin-makers for a remedy. Their answer was to dilute their silver and gold currency with copper, passing them off as the same face-valued lunar as before.

"Seemed like a good remedy at the time with the bankers suffering the only side effects. Soon the diluted lunar drove down the prices of the bank's stockpiles of gold and silver, which caused banks to shut down overnight. Investors lost everything they had to the diluted lunar currency. Got messy fast when they started taking their own lives. Some even took their families out with them. First time I've ever heard of a shortage of hemlock.

"When Lawrence sent chests of diluted lunar to the Red Bank as payment for Veronia's loan, he unwittingly started a war. The bank began recruiting its own army and that's when I bought in. They approached me one day as I stood guard at the gate. Offered me twice as much coin to soldier in their army. I dropped my sword and shield right there at the gate and rode with them to the Vault.

"The lunar didn't just cripple bankers and businesses, though. Whole towns and villages were caught in the mess. Chaucer in particular was hit hard and the Red Bank stepped in to stop the bleeding. Wasn't long before Euric Van Damme, the Fief Lord of Chaucer, was wearing more and more crimson. When Euric ignored King Lawrence's royal summons, lines were drawn in the sand. The bankers crowned Xalvador Hayward as the king of their Kiman Empire. They unshackled Agnen the Reaper from the Gorronian fighting pits to lead their army. Isn't a man alive who wants to see Veronia fall more than that savage bastard." Trion reddened. "Um..... pardon my tongue."

The two bishops startled when the chamber door creaked open. "Gentlemen, I hope I'm not interrupting something," Bishop Isabelle said politely, though her demeanor required explanation as to why her brothers had allowed a man not of the cloth into the council chamber.

Malachi fidgeted in his seat and turned to Jewel. An unvoiced urgency for Jewel to give the explanation.

Betrayed, and we've only just begun. Well this is the bed I've made after all. "Bishop Isabelle. Allow me to introduce you to our new friend, Trion Baccus."

Trion took a knee as Isabelle glided forward to receive the customary kiss of the ring. "Well met, brother," she replied, lifting him to his feet.

Jewel clasped the ginger's shoulder. "Trion and I met on the docks this morning. He brings us warning of the Red Army marching on Mirta. Quite possibly as we speak. Malachi and I were just listening to a story that I'm sure the council would find very interesting."

Isabelle pulled up a chair and sat between her brothers to face Trion. "I do love a good story. Mind if I hear it, Mr. Baccus?"

Trion recited the story once again as Jewel studied his sister's silent reaction although she betrayed nothing. She sat straight, fingers interlocked, palms resting in her lap. She was always the most proper of ladies. "It seems a council meeting would be a great idea, Brother Jewel. How long do we have, Mr. Baccus?" she asked.

"They were attacking Antick when I left. Heard the Light Priests talking of putting the Guardian Chapel to the sword and I could stomach it no more. They'll arrive within a few days."

She stood, yet no hurry escaped her bearing. "I'll summon the council."

***

Outside Marie's cottage, the village of Antick smoldered as its people cried out for mercy and found none. Marie faded in and out of consciousness as the Red bastard thrust his prick in and out of her. The burning smell of skin on skin and torn lady parts filled the air. He'd already beaten the resistance out of her. Now Marie's vision blurred as her left eye began to swell shut, body numb, trapped under the weight of his lust. She focused on the chain links burnt into the side of his neck, marking him as a Gorronian slave although he looked Veronian enough.

Gorronians took great pride in marking their investments. Chain links for the lowest class of slaves, a miniature sword on the neck for its pit fighters, and metal collars around the necks of the pleasure slaves. She saw red teardrops tattooed beneath his dark angry eyes, the room spinning faster and faster inside her head.

When the attack began, her husband Christian had told her to get the kids to the hiding place, a small dugout beneath the kitchen floor, used mostly for winter food storage. The sounds of Red soldiers had gotten closer to their house so he picked up his sword and ran outside to buy them the precious time they'd needed to hide. Christian was met outside by five Reds, two of which he wounded before he was cut down. It's a shame how a man so full of life can have it all taken away in the blink of an eye, the slash of a sword.

"I'm scared, Mommy. Where did Daddy go?" Leah had asked as Marie lowered her into the dugout beneath the floorboards next to her brother Samuel.

"There's no time to explain. We have to hide, you can't make a sound or they'll hurt you," Marie told them. She had just enough time to get the two children inside the dugout before the front door was kicked in and her husband's murderers spilled into the kitchen.

The man in the middle was a ghastly sight. He stood one-eyed and earless above the rest. The eye appeared to have been plucked completely out, leaving behind an empty socket half-closed by a cauterized eyelid. "Burn the cottages," he barked at the Reds behind him. "I'll take care of this one."

The two Reds gave each other a knowing glance and darted outside. One of them turned back just before he reached the door. It looked as if the man were working up the courage to say something but his courage faltered. She'd be spared by no knight in shining armor today. The man gave an apologetic bow and chased after his companion, leaving Marie alone with the burned man.

She fought as hard as she could to spare herself the pain and shame. In the end the blow she gave him to the forehead with a wooden bowl only enraged him the more. Blood trickled down the gash on his forehead and onto her neck as he handled her. She could think only of her children's safety, praying they didn't cry out for her from beneath the floorboards.

Each thrust broke her more and more, a pile of shattered pieces left behind never to be reassembled. Her tormentor grabbed her by the neck and chocked her unconscious as he climaxed, spilling his seed onto her stomach and chest just to soil her one last time. "Fecken cunt," he spat, dabbing blood from his forehead and leaving her lifeless on the kitchen floor.

The rattling of the trapdoor woke her from below. Smoke filled her lungs and her children fought to push the door open. "Momma, wake up! The house is on fire!" they yelled, voices hoarse from effort. "We can't breathe, Momma, wake up!"

Marie woke with a pounding headache, her dress torn nearly in two. She covered herself as best she could and pulled the latch to let her children out. She rummaged her wardrobe, opting for a simple blouse and trousers. "No more dresses," she said, wiping his poisonous seed from her stomach. "C'mon kids." She grabbed her late husband's bedside dagger, and the three of them scrambled out the burning door.

***

Agnen sat atop his horse, watching his army flood the

streets of Antick. Tears of blood were freshly tattooed beneath his left eye to replace the salty kind he'd forgotten how to shed long ago. A lifetime of war, betrayal, and disappointment hardens a man inside and out.

The more he tried to flush the headless king's words from his mind, the more they bothered him. *What was the scepter he spoke of, and why was the whole Veronian Army looking for it?*

With the Capitol, Indigo, and a handful of smaller villages already behind them, his men knew their business well. They took the lives of those who stood in their way and gathered up those who didn't for the Light Priests. Agnen didn't have much of a preference in priests, but Abaddon insisted Berinon and his white brothers accompany him during the campaign to soften their image.

Agnen often wondered why anyone would bend the knee to the Red Regime when they marched on villages, leaving corpses strung out in their wake. He'd have to give Abaddon credit though, it was rather well orchestrated. The army would seize the cities and Berinon the Light Priest would speak and preach from his Book of Light before introducing new officials hand-selected by the Red King.

Xalvador was also the president of the Red Bank and a bearer of the Guardian Sword won years ago in his youth. An impressive résumé for perhaps the most powerful man in all of Veronia, but Agnen knew it was

Abaddon who pulled the strings.

"Something wrong, Commander?" Berinon asked, clutching the Book of Light beside Agnen's horse. Antick was theirs; it was time for the priest to be escorted in for the naming of new officials.

Agnen looked down at the priest, wondering what the consequences would be for killing the book-toting bag of bones right there. Something about Berinon made his skin crawl although he couldn't quite put his finger on it. Maybe it was the way the fat bastard always glistened with sweat like he was about to drip. He'd noticed the priest required his own tent and would often entertain young women at night. Those same ladies had a habit of being carted off and buried with the rest of the fallen before sunrise.

"Damian," Agnen called, looking about to find his captain. Damian approached on foot as always, wiping blood from a fresh cut on the forehead. 'Don't trust a beast to carry my arse around. Seen too many men crippled under the weight of the damn things,' the captain had said when Agnen offered him his choice of mounts.

"Let's go, priest, waiting on you," Damian said coldly. Agnen wasn't the only one in the Red camp who Berinon unnerved.

Damian led the handful of Light Priests through the streets of Antick. A sergeant rode ahead carrying their colors, a twelve-pointed white star on a red flag. The remaining citizens of Antick were herded into a single crowd surrounded by a wall of Red soldiers. Most of them mustered on their own volition upon the Red Army's arrival. Others were beaten and forced to the gathering although Agnen had noticed they had to burn and kill fewer and fewer each time.

Berinon climbed atop a podium to address the crowd. His clergymen stood at his back, each wearing identical white cassocks with gold piping, frock cuffs, and shoulder epilates embroidered with miniature stars and crosses. One of the clergymen stepped forward, introducing Berinon as the Reader and Bearer of the Book of Light.

"Blessed be you, brothers and sisters of Antick," Berinon said, wetting his lips. "The honorable Emperor, King Xalvador Hayward, would like to extend the utmost hospitality to those loyal subjects willing to turn away from the greed and darkness that plagued the Veronian Kingdom, towards the Book of Light and the Kiman Empire. Only death could expunge King Lawrence and his court of their many crimes but we offer peace and prosperity to you all.

"Fear not, my brethren, for out of Veronia's ashes the Kiman Empire will surge forth, bringing prosperity to a land the likes of which have never been equaled. But first a little restructuring is in order." Three men made their way towards the podium. Two appeared to be handlers, the third no doubt a noble, wearing a silken red surcoat embroidered with the Kiman Star. "It is with great pleasure that I introduce Gregor Martell, the new Fief Lord of Antick," Berinon said, adding a theatrical bow before stepping aside.

There was no applause for the new Fief Lord's introduction. Only mute silence and bewildered faces staring ahead at an uncertain future. An uncomfortable sense of fragility was common throughout the crowd, as if moving or talking might upset the unseen balance of power. It was reminiscent of the sickening feeling Agnen remembered so well walking through the tunnel from Sacri Barnil to the fighting pit. Oddly too similar, in fact, which is why he had chosen to sit atop his mount and watch from a distance.

"Thank you, Father," Gregor said, flattening his surcoat. He was all smiles as he addressed the crowd with a mouthful of perfectly white teeth. You can't necessarily judge a man by the upkeep of their teeth. There's nothing worse than a writhing toothache days away from the closest healer, so even soldiers and slaves see to their oral hygiene as best they can. It was Gregor's soft, moisturized handshake that drained any respect Agnen might have garnered for the new Fief Lord.

Even the soft ones are cunning enough to have you skinned. Maybe more so.

The crowd fell silent as Gregor addressed his new subjects for the first time. "It is an uneasy task to march into a city demanding allegiance be given to a new Lord and King, but unfortunately that is exactly the scenario we find ourselves in today. I wish no harm upon any of you. I seek the easiest transition possible as your lord; therefore I offer you all a choice. Either bend the knee to me and the Kiman Empire, or leave with great haste."

CHAPTER

10

Trion sat in a pew outside the council chamber at the nave of the chapel. Only bishops and senior clergy were allowed to attend the council meetings and he was neither. King Lawrence had attempted to sit in on a council meeting years ago and was awkwardly asked to leave by the High Priest. Lawrence was none too pleased, but smart enough to choose his battles. The church can be very persuasive in dealing with the people and even Lawrence, fool that he was, knew that early on.

"Thank you all for meeting on such short notice,"

Jewel said, addressing the High Priest and his council who sat in their assigned chairs at the council table. "Our issue today is one that can wait no longer. The Kiman Empire has declared war on Veronia. They've killed our king, sacked several of our cities, and now we've been warned that Mirta is next on the Red agenda."

Only the sound of bishops shifting uncomfortably in their seats could be heard over the sudden hush of Jewel's crowd.

"Now, I know better than to announce a problem without offering a solution so I propose this. We give the people of Mirta notice of the impending attack, empty our treasury, and move all who will follow to the Shield. The island is well equipped with natural defenses and our most sacred relics are secured there. We should also think about aligning ourselves with the Tamore resistance. We have a duty to protect the church and its people."

"We need no reminders of our duties, Brother Jewel," Bishop Theodore said. It was no surprise that he would be the first to voice a retort. "You speak of swords and soldiers as if you command an army. Might I remind you that we are not soldiers but disciples of God. Panicking the people will only complicate our situation. Perhaps we should seek a more diplomatic resolution."

Malachi pounced on the opportunity. "And do you wish to volunteer for such a task, Bishop Theodore? To ride into an army with no moral compass, to break bread with those who seek to defile our church, and propose diplomacy?"

Theodore stirred uncomfortably in his chair. Jewel caught the faintest hint of a smile creep across Bishop Michael's face.

"Twas merely a suggestion," Theodore fumed. "I'm open to hear any others. Perhaps you have a better one, brother?"

Michael usually said less and little at council meetings but when he spoke all eyes and ears were drawn to him and today was no different. "I'm told the commander of the Red Army is none other than disgraced former Gorronian General turned fighting slave, Agnen the Reaper. I daresay we'll find no diplomacy in a man like that. If it's a treaty we seek then we will have to call upon King Xalvador Hayward himself. The Shield may be a good place to buy some time."

The council looked upon Bishop Isabelle to share her opinion. She sat in comfortable silence, legs crossed, hands resting upon her right knee, patiently awaiting her turn to speak. "I recommend we do as Brother Jewel suggests and relocate to the Shield for a time. Notifying the people might cause a panic, but who are we to withhold such a warning as this from them?"

Old as he was, the High Priest commanded his council chamber and all his bishops knew it. His body may have been slowly failing but his mind was still sharp, the fire of youth still roaring in his eyes. "I'll hear your votes now. Our first matter is that of the Shield. Who would have us uproot the treasury and relocate those willing to follow to the island? All in favor, say I."

The council voted in order of seniority, junior members first. "Aye," said Malachi. "Aye," voted Jewel. "Nay," said Theodore, surprising no one. "Aye," voted Michael and then Isabelle.

The High Priest sat stoically, wiping dust from his chair. "Now to vote on notifying Mirta of the invasion. We've all heard Trion's testimony. Who is in favor of spreading a warning?"

Again all said "Aye" in quick succession, save Theodore who again voiced his objection.

The vote for sending a representative to attempt diplomacy was slightly more dramatic if not entertaining. Malachi voted in favor of it, which drew a questioning glance from Jewel who voted against it. "What harm can it do?" Malachi asked with a shrug. Only Michael stood with Jewel opposing the diplomatic approach as Theodore and Isabelle voted in favor.

The High Priest interlocked his milky-white, age-spotted hands atop his golden staff of office that rested in his lap. "You have approved the move to the Shield, a diplomatic parlay with the Red Army to discuss terms of treaty, and preparing Mirta for a possible invasion. Is there anything else that requires our immediate attention?"

The council exchanged glances but no items were added to the agenda. The High Priest continued. "Very well then. Brother Jewel, you will be responsible for the treasury's relocation. It might behoove you to employ at least one hundred swords to accompany the treasury to the Shield, although I'd be as discreet as possible about the contents of the cargo."

"As you wish, Father," Jewel responded.

"Brother Theodore," the High Priest continued. "It was your suggestion of diplomacy. Ten swords will accompany you on your diplomatic journey. Seek peace for Mirta, and find out what they want to prevent any further attacks on Veronia. Be mindful of their radical Light Priests who'll seek to snare you. You are authorized to make any necessary payment arrangements, within reason of course. Should you require anything else before the council is adjourned, brother?"

The longer the High Priest talked, the more Theodore's confidence in their decision waned, but he was too far committed to back out now. "No, Your Grace. If peace can be found then I will seek it."

"Very good. Brothers Michael and Malachi and Sister Isabelle, you will notify Mirta and gather the flock for the move to the Shield with Brother Jewel. See to it that you gather necessary food and shelter to accompany you on the journey."

"Will you be accompanying us to the Shield, Father?" Jewel asked.

The High Priest looked up at nothing in particular. Jewel noticed he did that from time to time as if searching for strength. "I will remain in the Guardian Chapel and tend the flock of Mirta awaiting Brother Theodore's return. Send a rider ahead to notify Brother Dondarion at the Shield of your departure and heed any counsel he offers. You'll find that he is a very wise and righteous man." The High Priest stood to adjourn the meeting, pausing to look each of his bishops in the eye. "Now go. Be strong and of good courage until we meet again."

If Trion's story held water, the Red Army was just a few days ride north in Antick. Each of the bishops had much to do and was quick to carry on about their business, but only two or three hours of daylight remained. Malachi and Isabelle accompanied Michael in his room to discuss their plans. Michael was a walking map; the visual aids he had sprawled out in his chamber were for Isabelle and Malachi's benefit, not his own. They had to determine the safest route possible to avoid raiders and potentially hostage villages.

Jewel made his way back to the docks, this time looking for a mercenary army rather than an audience. Veronian soldiers were few and far between, either joining the Reds or following the Widow Makers to Tamore. Many villages were left hiring mercenaries to maintain order and Mirta quickly became Veronia's largest sword market. Jewel had to exercise an abundance of caution, though. He didn't want them turning on him in the middle of nowhere and make off with the treasury.

"Brother Malachi told me I'd find you here." Trion finished the last of his meat on a stick and tossed the wooden spear to the ground. "Told me you were looking to employ a few swords. If you'll have me, I'm at your service."

"I couldn't find you after the council meeting. Thought your feet chilled and sought Antick's warmth."

"Had a few preparations of my own to make," Trion said, polishing a new set of plate armor. "How many swords are we looking for?" He rested his left hand on the pommel of a short sword.

Too bold to be a spy. Or is he? "A hundred will do." Jewel crossed his arms and took a hard look at Trion. "I'm told my brother can look into a man's eyes and foresee what kind of soldier he'll be in a fight. I know less than he in judging the capabilities of a swordsman, but for this task I need more trustworthiness than fighting prowess."

"I don't recall many soldiers willfully meeting your brother's gaze. Leo's always so intense. Whether eyeing his next target on the battlefield or spooning through a pot of stew, you could never quite tell if you were his next bite or not." Trion mimicked Jewel's stance. "I'm no dullard, Bishop. You don't enlist one hundred swords to protect a food wagon; you're moving the treasury. My sword is yours, all I ask for is fair dealing, Your Eminence."

Fair dealing, huh? Such a polite way of demanding the truth of things. Not an unreasonable request from a man pledging his sword. "Very well then. We're moving the treasury to the Shield. Now, we'd better start recruiting before it gets too dark. And amongst ourselves, Trion, just call me Jewel."

***

At daybreak Malachi, Michael, and Isabelle set out preparing the citizens for the Red Army's attack. Some ignored the warning, others panicked as expected, opting to flee the city immediately.

A tired peasant in the crowd took his frustration out on Malachi. "Veronia is broken and the Kiman Empire doesn't seem so bad if you ask me. I'm sick and tired of all the fighting, and sure as hell ain't got the energy to run nowhere. We're bending our knees!" the man said, leading his family away.

Theodore assembled his escort in front of the Guardian Chapel. The High Priest was there to see him off. "You put yourself at great risk negotiating with the Red Army. I cannot bear the thought of sending you to meet your demise for a cause you don't believe in. There's no shame in opting out of this task. Perhaps Brother Michael had it right in seeking the Red King's ear."

"I didn't sleep a wink last night," Theodore said as the last of his luggage was carried into the carriage.

"Too busy thinking about what I'm going to say, wondering if they'll hear me. But fear has left me. In its place is a calming peace I've never felt before." Theodore ran his hand down the horse's mane. "I'm not coming back, Father. The next time we meet, we'll both be in a better place. Tell my brothers and sister I love them." He knelt before the High Priest. "Goodbye, Father."

Frances let the age escape his breath and he lifted Theodore to his feet. "Your faith is strong, brother. We'll meet again sooner than you think." The High Priest kissed Theodore on the forehead, then watched the bishop duck into the carriage and ride away.

***

The treasury lay beneath the Guardian Chapel in an underground vault. Only two entrances allowed passage—the first, a man-sized door concealed in the chapel, the second and much larger of the two concealed in the mountains on the eastern side of Crystal Lake. It was the latter location where Jewel had Trion meet him with the wagons.

Jewel withdrew a long brass key from the depths of his robe, inserting it into a keyhole hidden within a crack in the rock. The stone door was placed on several perfectly rounded wooden logs that allowed the key-holder to simply slide the stone door to the side.

"This isn't a ploy to lead me to the belly of your

sacrificial chamber, is it?" Trion asked, lighting a torch and peering at the carvings that covered nearly every inch of the stone tunnel. One in particular caught Trion's attention, a smith's hammer and sword intersected over a budded cross.

Jewel ignored the jape, jumping from the cart to unlock the second door as Trion readied to roll it to the side. "It will take two carts, most likely. The first will carry the silver and gold. The second... miscellaneous artifacts I prepared last night in those three boxes there."

Try as he might, Trion couldn't resist the urge to run his fingers through the silver and gold chests. The precious metals have a strange way of enticing a man's soul, an intoxicated euphoria which Trion couldn't withstand. "I've never seen so much gold."

Jewel watched Trion bury his hands in the chest of gold. "Reach your hand into the chest of silver and count out thirty pieces," Jewel instructed. His voice echoed through the chamber, snapping Trion from his gold-lust.

Trion plunged his right hand into the chest and silver spilled from his grasp, clinking back into the chest. "Twenty nine and thirty," he'd determined. "Know my letters too, in case you were curious."

"Thirty pieces of silver. An amount held in just one hand, yet it was the price paid to betray Jesus by his own disciple. I can't think of any life worth so little." Jewel grabbed a handful of his own, dropping the coins piece by piece back into the chest.

The shiny metals seemed to have lost its luster and Trion emptied his hands of it. "No life is worth so little."

"The spirit is strong but the flesh is weak," Jewel quoted from the book of Matthew. "There's much to do, we better dally no longer."

***

Bruce led a party of men across the river to retrieve the wagons Jonas had left behind. Two Drago Smiths, Val, and Mortis, guarded the cargo on the opposite side of the Britta, each bearing the same ink as Jonas. He examined the contents of the wagons, picking up a sword for inspection. The blade was well struck, but only Drago steel swords like his Guardian bore the mark of Drago. The swords in the cart revealed the smith's individual mark.

He had always admired the craftsmanship of a good sword, something his father had instilled in him at an early age. As a young lad, Bruce was never one to get many presents. His family lived a frugal life in the eastern slums of Indigo. At the age of fourteen, his father, Victor, noticed his son spent the majority of his time marring other children with wooden limbs, emulating the sparring Veronian soldiers who trained at the river's edge.

Victor had sustained a crippling leg injury during

the Norse invasion of Kotah years before. Not the heroic kind leading a charge or being the last man standing. It was dumb luck that had crippled Victor, trampled underfoot by his own men at the front lines while he had been grappling with a Viking. His right leg shattered and never set correctly which led to his discharge shortly after.

The injury forced Victor to make a living using his hands so he turned to carpentry, making chairs, tables, odds and ends. Bruce grew up helping his father make ends meet in their small broken-planked workshop.

One day, Bruce's father presented him with a finely crafted wooden sword that he'd made while Bruce was out and about. "In this life you have to earn the sword you carry. That is unless you have a fortune to pay for one, in which case we do not. Master this one and one day you'll earn a steel blade of your own. When that day comes, keep your blade clean and sharp. It will be there for you when your friends are not, like a lover in the night. And name it, for it's an extension of who you are."

It was a lesson with more and more significance as Bruce grew older, earning his first sword, which he dubbed Rose after enlisting in the army. He didn't have the heart to shelf her after winning his Guardian Sword, opting to drop the shield and dual-wield instead.

He and Rose made it out of the Frostbite together and shared a bit of a bond but Bruce was a realist at heart. If the Drago Smith swords were of better quality, then it would only improve his chances of survival and Bruce was fond of breathing. He unsheathed Rose and compared her to the sword from the cart.

Nearby, Val observed Bruce's internal dilemma. "May I?" the smith asked, both hands extended to receive the swords.

Go fist yourself was on the tip of Bruce's tongue, but it died there. You don't ask a man if you may hold his weapon; you admire the damn thing from a distance. On the other hand, the smith had to have known his business to sport that tattoo so Bruce handed him the swords.

Val turned Rose over in his hand. "The Veronian Army makes a decent sword, but they don't have forges hot enough to temper out all the impurities that bed in steel. The base of the blade closest to the handle is the strongest part of the sword. As you move further towards the tip, it gradually weakens. The sweet spot of any sword is in the middle where it vibrates the least upon impact. It's there that you determine if you have a sword or a switch. Mortis, if you please."

Mortis, the other smith, moved forward, relieving Val of both swords. He clasped both hands around the grip of the sword from the cart, extending the blade out in front of him. Val drew his own sword, Drago steel no doubt. Bruce blinked and almost missed Val strike the sword Mortis held. The blades bounced off one another, the sound of steel on steel filling Bruce's hearing and for a time he was lost in the past.

Bodies were strung out in front of him, far as he could see; their stench choked him, his lungs more ice than organ. The savages sent their next wave up the hill, and for a brief moment, he could feel his aching limbs again, his heart pounding inside his chest. He locked eyes with the nearest barbarian who sprinted up the hill impossibly fast, leaving him to brace for impact.

From the corner of his eye, he saw Captain Rosewood fly down the hill to greet them. Bruce would have to select another target because Leo blocked the sword slash with a battered shield and thrust through the Gorronian's stomach, lifting the savage off the ground and tossing him aside, eyes wild, looking for more work. Juan came into view close on Leo's heels, wielding what had to be the biggest sword in all of Veronia and cutting men in two.

Bruce selected another target and ran to meet him. A bolt ran through the Gorronian's chest, rocking him backwards and to the earth. Bruce glanced back and saw Natalie reloading. With no shortage of people to kill, he chose another who'd worked his way behind Juan. Bruce shouldered into the back of the barbarian and cut him down as they fell, and a wave of purple comrades descended to join them.

Snap! Bruce was brought back to reality when Val struck the second sword: Rose. The Veronian sword snapped in half, tip twirling into the air. "Well, you've made the decision easy enough. Probably would have taken your word for it," Bruce said, taking hold of the cart sword. "Think I'll call you Nora." He strapped her across his back next to Lilith.

Bruce waited until his men had crossed the Britta with the wagons before burying Rose at the riverbank. "Thanks for being there for me," he whispered before returning with the others.

***

Bishop Theodore's carriage came upon the Red Army camp a day's ride south of Antick. He was greeted by a lookout demanding to know just what in the hell they were doing there. The lookout's tone softened ever so slightly when Theodore shook off his riding cloak, revealing his white robe and violet mozzetta issued exclusively to the High Priest's Council.

"Hello there, my name is Bishop Theodore. I come on behalf of the High Priest's Council requesting an audience with your leadership."

The lookout seemed genuinely amused. "My leaders aren't the kind who entertain. You should heed my warning and ride away. Once you enter the camp, you might not have the same opportunity."

"I'll take my chances if you'd be so kind as to notify them of my arrival."

The lookout shook his head. "It's your skin, Priest. Your escort stays behind. Follow me."

As Theodore was led through the Red camp, soldiers eyed him with the disdain of a foreign object, some menial relic of the past. One soldier cursed him aloud as the lookout left him waiting outside a large tent in the center of the camp. Nearby, the lookout argued with a handful of soldiers over who would notify the captain. One of them hesitantly entered the tent and moments later a tall soldier emerged with a chain burnt into the side of his neck.

"What do you want, Priest?" the captain asked.

"My name is Bishop Theodore. I come on behalf of the High Priest's Council, humbly seeking an audience with your army's leadership, or a representative of the Kiman Empire."

The captain's demeaning gaze swallowed Theodore a moment, before entering an even larger adjacent tent, leaving the bishop outside. Inside, the Reaper sat cross-legged next to a low-burning fire, sharpening the edge of his sword. As his eyes adjusted they found the sword burnt into the side of Agnen's neck. It was the first time Damian had seen Agnen without armor. He paled, unprepared for the visual.

Damian bore more than a few scars of his own, but the commander was littered with long and deep, nasty scars. The kind left behind after dozens of scrapes with death, battling men and their various weapons of war. A few of Agnen's scars even matched a few of Damian's. The captain's mind wandered to the heated dagger burns on the back of his legs—silent reminders to answer when questioned or wail when burned.

Fire and silence were the only two things Agnen

enjoyed anymore. Damian's interruption was annoying but Agnen had overheard the visitor's arrival through his buckskin tent. "Is it Jewel?" he grumbled.

Fear and weakness can bleed through the hardest of men, leaving a puddle you can't conceal. Whether it be a nervous tick, beads of sweat, or the breaking of a strong voice, more times than not, the Reaper could sense it. Damian, on the other hand, would rather jump in the fire than give Agnen the pleasure of his discomfort.

"Said his name was Bishop Theodore," Damian replied. His presence sucked the heat from the tent.

Agnen held his sword in front of the fire, inspecting the edge of the blade for blemishes. "It's time we go then. Kill the bishop and be quick about it. I'll not give Berinon the pleasure of a new plaything."

Damian took his cue and exited through the tent flaps, drawing his sword and cutting Theodore down before the priest could instinctively raise his hands in defense. The cut started at the shoulder and buried deep into the chest clear to the back. Damian lifted his boot, placed it on Theodore's chest, and kicked him off the length of the sword until it was free. "Prepare to march!"

***

Jewel and Trion loaded the carts themselves, small amounts of coin at a time. A third cart was loaded with food and they quickly realized they would need much more if they were to feed a mercenary army besides. Precious metals are the most fundamental storage of wealth and are recognized as currency throughout the world, but food is everyman's gold.

While hunting for mercenaries at the docks, Trion located a chiseled, ebony-skinned man named Clarence Atney who led a group of fifty mercs from Kotah. They called themselves the Cleombras, which Clarence translated to Veronian as the Chosen Ones. Clarence also claimed to be the only one in the group to speak Veronian, however, Jewel suspected most of them understood it well enough.

They employed fifty more, a handful or so at a time to make it a hundred. Now Jewel, Trion and their hired swords awaited the other bishops at Crystal Lake. Isabelle was first to arrive, accompanied by a mass of people. Michael arrived shortly after with nearly twice as many, each carrying as much food and supplies as they could. Didn't take long for the crowd to grow impatient, waiting on Malachi's arrival.

"What's taking him so long?" Jewel asked, fearing something amiss.

Michael confirmed their course with the Cleombras and casually rolled up his map. Beside him, a second mount carried bags of books he staunchly refused to leave behind lest they be forgotten. "Saw him heading towards the Chapel when I left. One last farewell to the High Priest, I suspect."

"I hope so," Isabelle added. "We need to be moving. The people are getting restless and we're running out of time." In preparation for the ride, she braided her brunette locks tightly beneath her headdress. A subtle mockery to the conservative extremists who dared to declare women harlots for uncovered hair.

Guess we can hardly blame them. Warn them of an attack, muster them together, and have them hurry up and wait for it to come. "I'll go get him," Jewel sighed. "If I'm not back by high noon, you should start moving. We'll catch up."

Trion nudged his mount forward. "Can't stomach sitting here any longer. I'm coming with you."

They rode hard for the Chapel, Jewel struggling to stay upright, kicking himself for not accepting Juan's riding lessons while Trion rode effortlessly ahead. From the commotion in the streets, the Reds had been spotted north of the city and the townsfolk were in full-fledged panic.

They pulled up in front of the Chapel, horses circling nervously around the frightened people. Jewel dismounted and handed Trion the reins. "Hold onto these, will you? Would sure hate to ride double with you on the way back. I'll go see what's taking him so long."

Inside the Chapel, Jewel found Malachi pulling the High Priest by the robe, pleading with him to go with them, but Frances was having none of it.

"My place is here, brother, you know this." Frances snatched his arm back. "Jewel, take your brother. There's no time for this."

Outside the Chapel the Red Army had arrived and began swarming the ships at the dock first. Trion struggled to maintain control of the two mounts as his began bucking.

Malachi's shoulders slumped. "I'm ready then. Couldn't live with myself if I hadn't tried one last time."

Frances extended his golden staff of office to Jewel. "Take this, Brother Jewel. I'll not suffer it falling into ungodly hands. Can't think of a better successor besides."

Jewel took the staff, heavy in his hands. "Thank you, Father." The words caught in his throat but he fought them out. Sparing a glance back would have made it harder and it was hard enough already.

Malachi and Jewel hurried out the Chapel doors and were abruptly met by two Reds running up the steps with naked steel. Trion let loose of his bucking mount and intercepted them halfway up the steps. "Ride, I'll catch up," he barked as the two Reds turned their attention towards him.

Jewel and Malachi raced to the horses. The beasts were half mad given the commotion. Jewel mounted and looked back to find the two Reds slain on the steps. Trion ran for the horses but found himself cut off by two more. They were everywhere now.

"Persistent little buggers, aren't we?" Trion mused

as they circled him.

He lunged forward, slashing at the soldier to his front and was knocked down with a shield from behind. Trion fought to get up but was kicked down. "Just don't have the time to properly burn you alive," one of the Reds said, raising his sword to cut Trion down.

Jewel drove his dagger into the back of the swordsman's neck. The Red fell, staining the steps crimson. A leg sweep took the other Red down, the dagger following him to the ground and piercing through chest-covered chainmail.

He quickly wiped blood from the dagger and stowed it within his robe while Trion tried to process what he'd just seen. "Don't look so surprised, I'm a Rosewood, after all."

Trion made it to his feet, brushing himself off. "Had to wait till they were done kicking me around, did you? I thought priests weren't supposed to carry weapons anyways."

Jewel tapped the weapon beneath his robe. "Guardian Dagger. A gift from my brother. He wouldn't let me refuse it, said even a shepherd had to protect his flock. Guess he was right, don't tell him I said that though. Let's get out of here."

They rode for the lake as fast as they could, Malachi riding double with a frowning Trion, and Jewel laughing all the way.

In the Chapel, the High Priest knelt in silent prayer. A Red approached from behind, sword in hand. He was stopped short by a white-robed clergyman with slicked-back hair, who took the sword from the soldier's hands.

"It didn't have to be this way, you know," the clergyman said, running his fingers down the length of the blade.

"Berinon," Frances declared without turning around. "Rumors of your blasphemy have stretched far and wide. Couldn't make it onto the Priest's Council so you turned away from God to worship the starborn?"

"Our faiths are not so different, yours and mine. You just fail to give credit where credit is due." Berinon ran the blade down Frances' back. "It was the Watchers who helped sustain us when God sought to smite us off the earth. They gave us knowledge, wisdom, and power beyond belief. The Nephilim and the Mozzaroth, yet you turn your back on them as if they didn't exist. For that you will be punished, my old friend. Today you will be judged."

The High Priest stood and faced Berinon. "You're an abomination. Not even the Twelve can be controlled and you speak of Watchers and giants as if they can? They were buried for a reason. Only God's army could dig them up. If it's my death you seek, take it now. I can stomach your impiety no longer."

"Not all were buried," Berinon whispered. His borrowed sword rose and fell and the High Priest was no more. It took the Reds several hours before they located the hidden door to the treasury only to find it empty.

CHAPTER

11

Abaddon watched his army return home through the cutout window of his command post atop the Vault. A single wooden bridge allowed entrance over a murky watered moat surrounding the fortress. The majority of soldiers lived outside its stone walls in small huts and cottages. Others commuted to and from Chaucer where King Xalvador was seated. The Red king expressed a keen interest in moving his throne to Mirta but Abaddon would hear none of it.

Chaucer was a merchant's battleground for industry. Factories, businesses, and banks littered the city with no shortage of visitors and traveling entertainment. It was there Abaddon had planted the seeds of the Kiman Empire so many years ago, silently operating one of the first banks in the Veronian Empire. A prestigious bank with roots deep as Veronia, it was the only bank the crown trusted to borrow or store its wealth. At least it was before the Red uprising.

Abaddon's char-skinned assistant, Lyle, awaited Agnen at the bridge. "Master Abaddon has requested your presence. Follow me."

He was led up a narrow staircase guarded by two massive soldiers sworn to secrecy for all they saw and heard. Not that it mattered much because as far as they knew Abaddon was a distant cousin of the Red king, assigned to the Vault as the empire's Master of Coin. "Lies fused with fragments of truth are more easily believed," Abaddon had told him on the carriage ride from Gorro.

Lyle opened the double doors and waited for Agnen to enter, careful enough to never turn his back. Agnen thought it odd he'd never seen the Kotian carry a weapon.

"Have a seat, Commander," Abaddon offered, easing into a chair of his own behind a mahogany desk, lacquered and polished to a bright shine. The twelve-pointed star had been carved into its center, strange-looking symbols within each of its points that Agnen couldn't decipher.

"I'll stand." *Can't fit in the damn things anyways.*

"Suit yourself." Abaddon poured himself a cup of red, not bothering to be refused twice. "I'm told Veronia's High Priest is no longer with us. And that the Guardian Chapel treasury was empty upon discovery?" he asked, all hospitality gone from his piercing voice.

"We no longer have the element of surprise we did before Bresdan. You wanted Mirta, now it's yours." *Did your spies tell you of the priest we killed outside Antick as well?*

If Agnen's bluntness crossed Abaddon, he hid it well. Gorronians are well known for their lack of tact anyways. "I'm also informed of a growing resistance in Tamore, led by none other than Leo Rosewood. How you let him slip from a dungeon is beyond me but only a minor inconvenience nonetheless. Was his brother Jewel found in Mirta?"

Agnen fumed at the gape, but knew better than to voice excuses. *I start spewing shit about getting struck by sorcery and I'll end up in the fighting pits again—or worse.* "No," he clipped in response.

"This vexes me, Commander," Abaddon said, taking a swig from his silver chalice. "I'd hoped to use the bishop as a bit of leverage against his brother. Bloodshed is a necessity when forging an empire, but spill too much and it's your head that will roll. A crimson balance best not forgotten."

The Reaper shuffled around his chair to get a better look at the twelve-pointed star on Abaddon's desk. Aside from a wine bottle, it was clear of debris.

"Something wrong, Commander? You seem at odds."

Fuck it, why not? "Why do these Veronians seem to think Gorro invaded them?" Agnen blurted, surprising even himself. There was a pause while Abaddon and Lyle exchanged glances. "Before I took his head, Lawrence mentioned a scepter as well."

Abaddon leaned forward on the desk, fingers outlining the Zodiac symbols inside the stars. "The Mozzaroth. More commonly known as Zodiac symbols," he answered the question Agnen didn't ask. "The warrior star of Regulus suits you, you know." A wicked smile crept across Abaddon's face.

Silence filled the room yet again. Abaddon shrugged and set his chalice down. "Fine. You want to know about the scepter, I'll tell you. Although I'm surprised you've never heard of it. The mountain men who protect it are Gorronian after all. Are you a religious man, Agnen?"

"I don't believe in anything I can't see for myself. If I were blind, maybe."

"Suit yourself," Abaddon said. "There once lived a man named Nebuchadnezzar who led God's mortal army. Angels delivered onto him a scepter that gave him dominion over all the animals of the earth, and with it he marched monsters onto the battlefield and no army could stand before him. After disobeying God's commands, Nebuchadnezzar's scepter was taken from him and his power vanished. Master Lyle and I have spent many years researching the validity of the scepter through scripture and have concluded that it does exist and that it's hidden in those mountains."

Agnen fumed. "You started a war to look for a magical scepter?"

"Careful, Commander." Abaddon's eyes flashed and narrowed.

"My apologies, sir," he muttered, throat suddenly dry, wishing he'd taken a seat and wine.

"A thing of the past," Abaddon continued. "Contrary to what you may believe, not all things are within my control. Yes, Lawrence was tasked with finding the scepter but perhaps my orders were too vague for his understanding. It was Lawrence who fabricated the lies and letters of a Gorronian invasion. Why? I don't know. Perhaps he wanted to flex his imperial muscle. He should have sent a few dozen men to the task but instead he sent an army led by an incompetent general who got himself killed pissing in the river."

"Vrago?" Agnen asked.

"Yes. Rosewood took command after that and things went from bad to worse. Tell me one thing, Commander," Abaddon said, "I know you took an arrow to the chest. Perhaps it clouded your judgment, which explains why you let Rosewood leave your camp that night. But after losing so many men in the mountains, why go to Gwonda next?"

The memory was a sour one. "As you said before,

not all things can be controlled. Generals don't come home defeated in Gorro. They win or die trying. We didn't expect resistance in Gwonda. Just wanted to pass through and get into Veronia."

"Hmph. I see," Abaddon said thoughtfully. "Well as they say, the show must go on. I've another assignment for you. One of the utmost importance."

Dread took him. Memories of the mountains chilled to the bone. "The scepter?"

"Not this time, Commander. Perhaps we'll revisit that quest another time. Prepare to leave but tell no one. We depart in the morning."

***

They'd been on the road for two days, most of the group on foot so the going was slow. Trion rode ahead as a lookout, trying to avoid bands of raiders who constantly fought for control of the few roads west of Crystal Lake. The Cleombras rode in front; the other mercenaries were divided bringing up the rear, right and left flanks.

Isabelle shielded her eyes from the sun to look ahead but restrained from asking how much longer their trek would be. "So what's the plan when we get to the Shield?"

"I suppose we'll secure the treasury and reach out to Tamore," Jewel responded. He hadn't really thought that far ahead but it seemed as logical a plan as any.

"They should have received the weapons by now."

"What weapons?" Michael asked.

Jewel's mind hadn't stopped racing in days. He'd forgotten to have only told Malachi about employing the Drago Smiths to supply Leo's army. "Tamore may be the only land in Veronia not yet molested by the Red Regime. The Swords of Bane and the Widow Makers have assembled there providing the only organized resistance, however they are in dire need of supplies. I employed the Drago Smiths to craft enough weapons to arm those willing to defend what's left of Veronia."

Even Isabelle was slightly taken aback. She stared at Jewel in wide-eyed disbelief. "Without the council's approval? I know your heart's in the right place, brother, but you must consult amongst our council the next time you decide to make such a decision. Need I remind you why there is a council in the first place?"

Michael's surprise faded but he'd yet to divert his judgmental gaze. "Isabelle is right, we should be consulted, but Brother Jewel's foresight was spot on. If Tamore is armed and Leo is building an army, then our brother just saved us valuable time. I've no doubt the people of Veronia will stand behind Leo's sword. At least until the threat is neutralized."

The Cleombre leader fell back until he was in the midst of their discussion. "Pardon the interruption but I thought you might want to know this. Word is some of your hired swords are chattering about the contents inside those wagons," Clarence said, gesturing to the cargo he'd never questioned.

Jewel wondered how the dark-skinned mercenary could ride beneath sun and armor without shedding a single bead of sweat.

Life on the road didn't agree with Brother Malachi. He was grumpier than Jewel had ever seen him. "Is this some type of ploy where you try leaching more coin from us, only to split it with them later?" Malachi asked.

The accusation appeared to strike a nerve with Clarence who addressed Malachi with a cold stare and a thick Kotian accent. "If the Cleombras wanted your coin, your band couldn't stop us from taking it. My Bucca pride ourselves on completing contracts over riches. They are what sustains my people."

Jewel had never seen black hands turn white. Clarence's leather reins wilted under his grasp. "Pardon my distressed brother," Jewel said. "We are grateful of your loyalty. How do you propose we deal with the issue?"

Clarence cursed in his native tongue, most likely directed towards Malachi, before returning to the common tongue. "We agreed to provide you safe passage to the Shield against Reds and raiders. These sullied sale swords of yours were not part of the deal and will require a separate contract, but is well within my Bucca's expertise."

Jewel wasn't quite sure what a Bucca was but got the gist of the offer. "If it's a second contract you require, consider it done." Clarence nodded, sealing the deal, then rode off to inform Mondo, his second.

"Didn't we just have this discussion?" Isabelle fumed after Clarence was out of earshot.

"Oops," Jewel replied.

She shook her head and sighed. "What can you tell us about these Kotian mercenaries, Brother Michael?"

"Brother Jewel could have done a lot worse in selecting a band of hired swords. However, I would caution against any more contractual agreements with Clarence's outfit. Kotah is a very poor country. After barely surviving the Norse invasion during the Viking Wars, they sought to create an army of their own. Because they are a free people and despise centralized government, that army turned out to be several loose, independently-operating bands of Kotian patriots instead.

"We call them mercenaries in Veronia, but in Kotah they call themselves Buccas, which roughly translates to Battle Brothers. Boys and girls alike start their swordplay at a very young age in Kotah. They've even adopted an annual tournament of their own called the Bemarda Lam Atombre, which means Rite of Passage, to which there is no age restriction.

"They bludgeon each other with wooden or blunted instruments without the luxury of armor. You see, to become a leader of a Bucca you start your own, or challenge the current leader to a duel. Those duels are fought in a sacrificial circle surrounded by shield holders. The object being that two men enter and only one leaves after the earthen circle is ceremoniously watered with the blood of the loser."

"Classy," Malachi muttered.

"Indeed," Michael continued. "The leaders of the different Buccas are cast into an annual tournament of their own, to establish the Bucca hierarchy. The hierarchy affords the top Bucca's first selection among the most fearsome young Bemarda Lam Atombre competitors. A draft order, if you will. Our friend Clarence and his Cleombras sit atop that hierarchy."

Malachi swallowed the lump in his throat. "Why would they risk intervening in a war that isn't theirs? I know being a mercenary right now is a profitable endeavor, but if they're caught assisting us, wouldn't that jeopardize their whole country?"

"Can't blame them for seizing an opportunity," Michael said, staring at the backs of the Cleombras riding ahead. Even their horses were dark as night. "But they aren't as greedy as it sounds. The Buccas are beloved in Kotah because they share a percentage of each purse with the Dalmienar, a group of Kotian elders who distribute the coin evenly among the people. As far as intervening in the war, I wouldn't expect them to travel any farther north than Crystal Lake."

"What's the significance of the contract count?" Jewel asked.

"Good question. Wish you would have asked before agreeing to the second." Michael smiled. "The

Buccas are bound by blood to complete any and all contracts they accept. Who wants to employ a band of unskilled, untrustworthy mercenaries after all? But such an esteemed mercenary group is costly, and the Kotian Buccas have a saying well known in the south. A disclaimer, if you will. *The first is worth the price of gold. The second double, a warning behold. The third may bind your body and soul.*"

***

They set up camp just north of King's Road, a morning's ride from Nebula. Giant trees lined the road, providing more than enough shelter to conceal any smoke that escaped their underground fire pits. Jewel and what remained of the council sat around a fire of their own, struggling to find sleep while Malachi lay on his back, head perched on a stack of Michael's leather-bound books, fighting for air.

"For heaven's sake!" Isabelle muttered, rolling Malachi onto his side. He stopped snoring just long enough to smack his lips a few times and went right back to sleep.

Snap. The sound of a broken stick underfoot is unmistakable to the most amateur of woodsman. The sound froze Isabelle where she stood brushing herself off, paralyzed at the sight of a dozen crouched mercenaries easing towards their fire, weapons in hand.

"Shhh," the ringleader said, left forefinger pressed

against his lips, right hand tapping the pommel of his sheathed sword. "We're taking the carriages and riding out. That is all. Now be a good little priestess and lie back down. No need for anyone to get hurt now is there?"

Jewel sprang to his feet in alarm. No one within earshot of Malachi was getting any sleep that night. "If it's gold you want, take it and be gone, the lot of you." *Seems Clarence was right after all. Was Malachi right about Clarence?*

Michael stood in front of Jewel and Isabelle, drawing the cloak over his head as if he'd done it a thousand times. The sullied swords, as Clarence had called them, began climbing atop the carts. "We weren't asking permission, Priest," the ringleader snarled. "Now where's that fancy-looking staff of yours?" he asked, unsheathing his sword.

"Such a greedy lot." No mistaking Clarence's thick Kotian accent. He appeared from the darkness, a black cloak drawn over his own face. Apparently the Cleombras were fans of all things black.

The mercenary's voice quivered as his eyes found more and more shadows in the darkness. "There's plenty of gold for all of us. No reason to wet our blades."

Clarence shed his cloak, cycle sword in each hand. "*Ondalmo neifrap bustiago le sette.*" The words were lost in translation but Jewel surmised the Cleombre leader wasn't inquiring about the weather. The rest of the Bucca appeared at his side, shedding their cloaks in unison.

The ringleader back-pedaled until the treasure cart stopped him. The cart triggering fight or flight, the latter of which was out of the question, so he took a wild sword swing towards Clarence. The Kotian crossed his blades, catching the incoming sword in midair, then delivered a stomach-emptying kick that knocked the mercenary off his feet.

He raised his empty hands to beg pardon. "Please, I......" The ringleader's plea was stopped short by Clarence's merciless sword. The rest of the Cleombras were already on the task of killing the others. Those that fled, which happened to be the majority, were rode down and dragged back.

Mondo shaved his head to hide the grey. Jewel put him in his late forties, and figured Clarence had dragged him along for wisdom and experience rather than muscle. But Jewel had been wrong about many things. Mondo ordered the slain would-be thief stripped naked. To deter any other attacks, he cut out each of their hearts and piled them nice and high in the center of King's Road.

To Jewel's surprise, little objection arose from the crowd. He suspected most of them were too shocked by the magnitude of the brutality to voice their discern. Others helped pile the corpses facedown behind the hearts.

After the deed was done, Clarence split his men up

around the camp and began briefing Jewel as if his men had done nothing more than fix a broken cartwheel. "My men will cover the flanks but we should move a bit faster tomorrow. I daresay this won't be the last time your treasury is sought after."

"Are you suggesting a change in course, good sir?" Isabelle asked. She was much more receptive to the man responsible for saving their lives. Her attention drawn to the piled corpses that Michael knelt beside in prayer.

"I'm no navigator. Just go where the contract takes us," Clarence said, turning the dead ringleader's head to face them with the heel of his boot. "But a chest of gold will turn a friend to foe."

Malachi stifled a yawn. "Perhaps Tamore would be more suitable for our growing company," he suggested.

Jewel wondered how anyone could have slept through an incident such as that. Malachi and Isabelle were equally surprised when he had woken to her cradling his head thinking he'd died during the commotion. "I'm not opposed to sending our company to Tamore, but the council has business we must tend to at the Shield. We should send riders to Leo immediately and find out what his plan is."

"If I remember correctly," Trion interrupted, "only the clergy are allowed entrance upon the Shield's holy ground. I suppose that leaves me as the messenger."

"We would greatly appreciate that," Jewel said. "But we must ask more of you than carrying a message.

Take the group with you as well. Makes no sense for them to travel all the way to the Shield when they can go to Tamore from here. We'll make better time without them."

"Fine by me," Trion said. "We'll leave at first light."

The bishops spent the rest of the night huddled round the fire drafting their message. As day broke, Trion roused the followers from a near-sleepless night and prepared them for the change of course as Michael's deft hands jotted down the last of their message with perfect precision. He passed it to the others who signed their approval.

Jewel bound the scroll and handed it to Trion with a hug rather than a handshake. "You've sure earned your keep around here, friend. When this is over I'll not forget."

"I wish I could forget a lot of things," Trion replied, taking the scroll. "I've decided to join the army in Tamore if Leo will have me. No use trotting back and forth to Veronia when the fight will sure enough reach Tamore."

"Free men do as they please. It takes a lot of courage to ride back into an army you've betrayed. But a man set on bettering his future shouldn't be constantly reminded of a dark past. Perhaps this gift, a token of my appreciation, will improve your chances of acceptance."

Jewel pressed a tightly-bound bundle of sackcloth against Trion's chest and walked away before it could be opened. Trion unraveled the cloth over and over in his hands, until finally Jewel's Guardian Dagger was visible.

***

They made it to the Bay of Bones a couple of days later. It was an easier journey without hundreds of men and women afoot. The Guardian Chapel had occupied Shield Island for hundreds of years, making it the oldest church in all of Veronia. It also hosted the Church's annual convocation where clergymen from all over the world assembled for elections and to discuss the most important matters of the Church.

The island itself was a near-perfect circle, which most people assumed was the reason the island was dubbed Shield Island. However, high-ranking bishops who attended the annual convocation were more privy to the actual reason. The bay was approximately two miles of choppy rock-bashing water that stretched from the mainland to the Shield.

It didn't take long for a small vessel of clergymen to make its way from the Shield to the mainland. Jewel and company would have been easy enough to spot across the bay in their white and violet attire, offset by the black as night color of their Kotian companions.

They were greeted by a young sharp-eyed priest who introduced himself as Brother Joshua. "Brother Dondarion has been expecting you. Please come aboard, my brothers will see to your luggage."

Malachi and Isabelle were the first to board, Michael close behind, head buried in the Book of Enoch like he was preparing for an exam.

Jewel handed Clarence a coin purse containing nearly triple their agreed-upon amount. "The Church owes you and your Cleombras a debt of gratitude, my friend."

Clarence took the purse without counting, tossing it to Mondo who would divvy it out evenly amongst the Bucca after paying their dues to the Dalmienar. "Truth be told, it wasn't chance alone you found us in Mirta. We've completed two contracts for your council and await a third. But know this."

Clarence's cool and collected demeanor, which Jewel had grown quite fond of, turned intense as he'd ever seen and Jewel felt himself very uncomfortable and quite aware of the close proximity in which Clarence delivered his warning.

"The first is worth the price of gold. The second is double a warning behold. The third may bind your body and soul."

A chill crept up Jewel's spine that escaped his body, leaving his skin with gooseflesh. *Just when I thought we were becoming friends.* "My soul belongs to the Lord. My temple is but a vessel to serve the faith. Your warning is heeded nonetheless. If ever a favor can be returned, don't hesitate to ask."

The two clasped hands then turned away. Jewel

climbed aboard with the others, watching the Cleombras ride south along the coastline towards their homeland.

***

"Get off your heels! Balance! You have to stay on the balls of your feet or you'll end up back-peddling," Bruce warned, hacking away at Mandy with a wooden sword. The Swords of Bane tirelessly trained the Tamore resistance from sunup to sundown, using sticks in place of swords. Once they displayed a working knowledge of simple stick fighting, they earned a shield and had to master it before they were allotted armor.

Only then were they able to spar with Bruce and his officers to enter the final phase of training, to earn a sword. A task that left many bruised and disappointed. But time was not on their side and Bruce's standards relaxed a bit, passing more of them through to the Widow Makers who taught them archery and simple battle formations. Edger posted lookouts a day's ride out in each direction to capture any spies snooping about. Wade was dispatched with a small contingency to recruit more swords, and slowly more and more trickled in.

Wade found Marie and her two children near the ruined Capitol. Under Natalie's tutelage she became one of the top shots with the bow. Each arrow she loosed dulled the edge of the blade that twisted within her heart—a nagging reminder of her husband's loss. Chain links were at the center of each target she zeroed in on. The thud of arrows on impact was the only thing that stopped the bile in the back of her throat when she remembered what had happened.

Leo spent what little free time he had on the practice field with Bruce. Mandy had earned her shield and armor quick enough but had failed her sword test for the second time. Each time Leo lurking in the background, leaving Mandy to suspect he was responsible for Bruce's increased exertion. Although his breathing was steady as a gentle wind, the effort left Bruce with sweat trickling below his hairline the third time she failed the test.

She was now a far cry from the frightened girl Leo had found not so long ago. On more than one occasion, he caught her staring at the blood on the Red sword that had taken her mother. It was a tangible reminder that kept her sharp as the blade.

Mandy lunged at Bruce with a thrust he deftly parried away. Regaining her balance, she littered his chest with a fury of slashes. He blocked the first two and sidestepped from the third, knocking her off-balance with a push to the shoulder. He tried landing a backhanded slash of his own but she tucked and rolled under it, springing to her feet several yards from his reach with a smile on her face.

"You're getting quicker," Bruce said, pressing on to close the gap, stick swinging in a blur before him.

Mandy focused intently, trying to gauge the timing. He sidestepped, clamping onto her stick hand as her thrust came forward. "But your eyes give away what your posture does not." He popped her atop the head with his blunted sword. Just enough force to leave a reminder of her fourth sword challenge failure.

She cursed everything from Bruce to the oak trees that grew their swords.

"He's right you know," Leo said. "You're swift and agile but predictable. Your vision's too narrow. There are more killers in this world than men with swords."

For a moment Leo thought she was about to chuck her shield at him but thought better of it. "This is horse shit, Leo. I'm no sword master, but I could bludgeon half the swordsmen with this stick alone and you know it."

"Prove it," Leo rasped, flexing a muscled hand on the sword he'd drawn faster than she noticed.

Pissed as she was, her anger died as soon as he brandished his blade. His eyes darkened and a cold wind blew between them. Her legs suddenly rooted into the earth like the massive oaks of Crystal Lake. The stick slipped from her hand onto the ground.

He sheathed his blade and drew in whisper-close. "Your father would want better for you than the life of the sword." *As do I.* "But I won't tell you how to live your life; that's nobody's concern but your own." Leo nodded to Bruce and walked away.

Bruce made a custom of burying the tip of the

sword to be won in the earth next to the fighting circle. A visual reminder of what each challenger was fighting for. Now the sword master pulled Mandy's from the earth and presented it to her. "Don't fall on it. Report to the Widow Makers tomorrow." He drove another sword into the earth beside the fighting circle. "Who's next?"

***

As night fell, Mandy sat around the cook fire with Natalie and Marie. Nearby soldiers reminisced of battles fought and scars they'd earned. Others belted out drunken songs of fair maidens and the Headless Copper King.

Five soldiers, each deep in their cups, sat beside a roaring fire of their own. One of them nursed a bandaged hand. "Need to talk Leo into getting us some entertainment out here. Ain't no injury a tribal whore can't mend."

"I'll second that," another said. "Hear they'll suck the skin off your prick. Bet Rosewood knows a thing or two about that. They had to have given him more'n a damn hatchet for saving their necks in Gwonda."

Mandy tensed at the mention of Gwonda. Funny how simple words can trigger memories of the past.

Natalie had heard enough of their obnoxious blabbering. In the blink of the eye, she crossed into their drunken fire circle, kicking the cup from the funny man's hand. "Oops, pardon my clumsiness. I couldn't help but overhear your dire need for a whore. If pain is your pleasure perhaps I can be of assistance." Her slap caught him square in the face, silencing the song from adjoining fires.

The funny man cupped his face, rubbing the shock from his temple. She lined up a backhand to even him out. "What's wrong, can't handle a little foreplay?" The second slap nearly knocked him over.

The twice-shamed soldier began to rise. Rage sobered him long enough to stand with hands balled into fists.

"Is there a problem?" The looming figure cast a menacing shadow that revealed Juan clad in full armor and devoid of his usual jovial presence.

"Keep your mutt on a leash and we'll not have problems," the shamed soldier snarled.

His bandaged friend stood to reel him in. "Pay him no mind. Just a bad batch of brew, methinks. We'll see to it that he sleeps it off."

"Very well, don't let us keep you," Juan said, doing a bit of reeling in himself, shuffling Natalie back to her fire.

Natalie shook him off. "And to what do we owe the pleasure of your company?"

"Nestin had a feeling the Netche Brew might light a few fires in the men. Guess we'll have to start watering down the Tribesmen's next peace offering." Juan's joints popped as he knelt down between Mandy and Marie.

"What happened in Gwonda?" Mandy asked, watching the drunken soldiers stagger off. "Everyone seems to know of my father's death but me. I can't stomach any more of your pitying looks."

Silence strung out as Juan and Natalie exchanged glances, each wanting the other to speak first. "It's not my story to tell," Natalie replied.

Mandy turned her glare to Juan. "Why does Leo look at me like it was his sword that killed my father?"

He let out a defeated sigh. "Okay, I'll tell you." He pointed a meaty finger at Mandy. "But you have to be damned sure not to speak of it in front of Leo. Being called a traitor or a coward has never settled well with him as you can imagine. There's a reason you see little of him around the camp at night. One of the guys' mouths gets too loose around Leo and he'll start killing by default."

Mandy nodded in reply. "Just give me the virgin truth. I can handle it."

"Fair enough," Juan said. "The Frostbite was unforgiving. The Gorronians pushed us to the brink of defeat but we held the high ground, a mountain pass we called the Grinder. Wave after wave of them charged up the hill at us. When we'd nearly had enough, Leo snuck into the Gorronian camp under the cover of darkness and made one hell of a name for himself. I don't know exactly what happened in the camp that night but before the sun came up, Leo returned bloody as the moon that lit the night. *Bucha Enut*, they called him. The Bloody

Rose.

"When we got back to the Capitol, he defied King Lawrence and led an army to Gwonda. The Tribesmen were already heavily engaged when we arrived. It didn't take long for Leo to break the line and run headlong into the middle of it."

Juan reached over and took a pull from one of the drunken soldiers' abandoned wine skins. The strength of it made him wince.

Mandy surmised the rest of the story on her own. "And my father followed after him and didn't make it out."

Juan took another pull to calm his nerves and steady his voice. He could almost feel the weight of the savage round his neck as the memory took him back to the forest. The flash of Leo's sword delivering the killing blow that saved his life. The sound of the armor-piercing thrust that took Drew's.

"Your father was slain saving our skin. Leo and I would have done the same for him if we'd been given the chance," he choked out before clearing his throat and taking another pull. A strong drink will do little to erase the past but it sure takes the edge off the pain. "Leo saved mine and Drew saved his. Now we're left paying a soldier's debt. The kind bought and paid for with a life. A debt I owe Leo, a debt he owes you."

***

Tamore's governing officials crowded around a rectangular table nestled inside Old Tans Tavern, which had been converted into the Town Hall. Nestin Vorhees sat at one end of it, his wife to his right, and beside her their Castellan, Edgar Loveless. Leo sat at the other end of the table, Juan to his right accompanied by Bruce and Natalie.

Nestin didn't appear the least bit troubled with the council having more soldiers than politicians. Politicians wouldn't protect them when the Reds came calling anyways. "I know our main focus is strengthening the army and the city's defenses but we're running out of living space. We're short of hands in the sawmills and the people are growing tired of cramming into overpopulated shelters. I request twenty-five of your least-skilled soldiers to be reassigned to the sawmill, at least until we can put roofs over everyone's heads."

Leo remembered the first time he'd seen Nestin draped in humble peasant clothing. After further observation he realized the mayor's garments were anything but humble. They were handspun fustian cotton which left Leo wondering how he could afford such a rare textile on the wrong side of Chaucer. *Is anyone truly as they appear?*

"Twenty-five?" Bruce said, unbelieving. "We've spent a lot of time training the few swords we have. Losing any at this point will be critical to the city's defense."

"We'll give you the next twenty Wade brings back," Leo replied. As a captain in the Veronian Army, he would go out of his way to avoid Officer's Meetings. Now he realized wars aren't all fought on the front lines but at crowded council tables as well.

"Very good," Nestin replied, waving away a cup of wine from the serving girl. "Edger, would you be so kind as to update us on the city's defenses?"

The question caught Edger in the middle of finishing his drink and reaching out for the cup Nestin had turned away to quench his thirst. He was clearly unaccustomed to the finery of such sweet Mirtian red. At least it was Tamore's version of the wine, either way, Edger didn't know the difference.

He downed the second cup and slammed it onto the table, causing Abigail to startle. Edger leaned back in his chair, stroking his wine-dyed beard. "When the Reds come we'll make them bleed for it. Every forward step a snare of pain and misery until they seek out death or settle for retreat."

The council fell silent, each member staring at Edger's red-toothed grin. "I'll have what he's having," Bruce called to the serving girl.

Lieutenant Cederic la Mare rapped at the door before entering. "Excuse me, but we have another visitor," the Widow Maker said, drawing the council's attention. "Goes by the name of Trion and carries a message from the High Priest's Council."

"Send him in," Leo said, already making his way to

the door when the redheaded visitor entered. *A mercenary, perhaps?* "What word do you have of the Priest's Council?"

Trion entered far as he dared, eyes to the ground like a man not wanting to be recognized. "I bring a letter from the remaining members of the Priest's Council."

Hearts sank, none more so than Leo's.

"Is Jewel harmed?" demanded Natalie. "Out with it, man!"

"Jewel is fine. My apologies, I should have led with that," he said. "Other members of the council are unaccounted for. Namely the High Priest and Bishop Theodore. Theodore was selected to treat with the Red Army to seek diplomacy and has not yet returned. When the Reds attacked Mirta, the High Priest is thought to have been captured or worse. Bishop Jewel carries the golden staff now and has led the rest of the council to the Shield to stow the treasury."

Leo extended an impatient hand. "Their message?"

Trion retrieved it from his tunic and handed it to Leo. Leo broke the seal and began reading. He scanned the contents, then sank into his chair. Juan took the letter and read it aloud.

Greetings to the Shields of Veronia,

By now you've met our trustworthy ally, Mr. Trion Baccus, who we owe much. He brings with him a host of displaced and burdened citizens of Veronia, whom we hope you will take in as your own. High Priest Frances is thought to have been captured or slain when Mirta was attacked and Bishop Jewel currently presides over the council until we can select Bishop France's successor at the Shield. We will send another request for assistance to our brothers at Mt. Drago to arm those willing to stand at your side as the Defenders of our faltering empire.

The Red Army has slain Veronia's royalty and it appears they are unwilling to negotiate a treaty of peace. The Kiman Empire must be eradicated so Veronia can stop the bleeding of our wounded kingdom. The Priest's Council hereby exercises its lawful authority, and hereby authorizes and commissions Leo Rosewood as the Shield of Veronia.

The High Priest's Council will be arriving in Tamore as soon as possible to make the official appointment and continue to serve as instruments of the faith in Veronia's time of need. Until we meet again, be strong and of good courage.

High Priest Jewel
Bishop Isabelle
Bishop Michael
Bishop Malachi

CHAPTER

12

Underground the thick vaulted stone walls of the Shield, what remained of the Priest's Council sat with Bishop Dondarion, discussing the appointment of a new High Priest. Dondarion was voted into the council as their first order of business despite reservations of having to depart the island. The pale-eyed, sea-weathered bishop had dedicated the majority of his life to the Shield, first as a deck-scrubbing teen clergymen aboard the Shield's many transport vessels and now as its High Bishop.

Veronia was already without a king and queen, and

the council had nearly as many vacancies as living members so they had to fill what gaps they could. The voting for High Priest was a formal affair. Each bishop was given a piece of parchment to cast their vote in writing. They were forbidden to vote for themselves and once each bishop wrote down their vote they had to reveal it openly. The bishop receiving the majority vote was given the opportunity to either accept or humbly decline the appointment.

After each bishop had cast their vote they turned their parchment facedown awaiting the others. Bishop Dondarion was the first to reveal his vote. "I, Bishop Dondarion, hereby select Bishop Jewel as High Priest and successor of the deceased High Priest Frances."

An elderly hunchback scribe sat in the corner like a fly on the wall, recording the election. Brother Joshua stood outside the door to ensure the council was not disturbed.

"I, Bishop Malachi, hereby select Bishop Jewel as High Priest and successor of the deceased High Priest Frances."

Two of five, Jewel thought to himself, trying to unwind a stomach full of knots. As a kid he'd dreamed of one day earning the golden staff that lay in the center of their table. Now he wondered why the office hadn't preferred a sword. The thought of swords made his mind wander to Leo, then to his sister in Gwonda. That was until he felt all eyes at the table resting on him.

He straightened and cleared the nerves from his

voice. "I, Bishop Jewel, hereby select Bishop Isabelle as High Priest and successor of the deceased High Priest Frances."

Like the others, Jewel struggled with the word 'deceased'. Such a permanent word, spoken without confirmation, yet Michael was steady as the rising tide. "I, Bishop Michael, hereby select Bishop Isabelle as High Priest and successor of the deceased High Priest Frances."

And like that, Jewel and Isabelle were tied with only her vote remaining. She couldn't vote herself into office but a vote for Dondarion, Malachi, or Michael would result in a tie vote, in which case the most senior member of the Priest's Council would be elected.

She took a moment to share a satisfied smile with Michael, as if the two couldn't have choreographed it any better. The golden staff rested motionless, yet Jewel felt as if the table tilted and it rolled further away from him.

"I, Bishop Isabelle, select Bishop Jewel as High Priest and successor of the deceased High Priest Frances."

Michael was the nearest and first to grab him by the shoulder. His perfect teeth as white as his hair. "Congratulations, Father. We had to make it somewhat interesting, didn't we?"

"Your staff of office, Father," Malachi said, extending the staff out towards Jewel with an overemphasized sweeping bow. "Unless you would like to pass the staff?"

"I wouldn't think of it." Jewel took hold of the cold gold that warmed in his grip.

Above ground, Jewel was sworn in quickly as he could get it over with. Brother Joshua was selected as the fifth bishop to the Priest's Council and was awarded his purple mozzetta by Dondarion.

Jewel wasted no time calling his first council meeting to order and they found themselves underground once again. Truth be told, it had been Michael's idea to appoint Leo as the Shield of the Kingdom. It's not every day the most deadly sword in all of Veronia is wielded by the High Priest's own flesh and blood. The appointment also reinstated the Guardian Church, making Leo the commander of both the Veronian and Guardian Armies. Without a king, Veronia was a theocracy once again.

Michael also revealed to the council a secret High Priest Frances took to his grave—a secret the clergy of the Shield lived and died to protect. Mysterious artifacts hidden on Shield Island had been tugging at Jewel's curiosity ever since Michael had revealed them while they wrote their letter to Tamore.

Jewel wasn't happy about being in the dark in regards to the Church's relics. He took the opportunity to set a firm foundation of truth with his new council. "Brother Dondarion, perhaps you could be so kind as to explain why the Priest's Council wasn't made fully aware of King Solomon's golden shields, which are secured here? It makes me wonder what other secrets have been withheld from the council."

If Dondarion was surprised, he did well concealing it. Joshua, on the other hand, looked pained, defensively drawing his closed fists into his lap.

"I withhold no secrets from the council," Dondarion spat with venom. "High Priest Frances was fully aware of the shields that my clergy have dedicated their lives to protect. If it's secrets you're after, perhaps you should ask our ageless brother Michael about a few of his." Dondarion's eyes widened at his own outburst. "Please excuse me, Brother Michael. That was unbecoming."

Michael's calm was absolute. His fingers traced inscriptions carved into the stone wall. "Secrets are merely undiscovered knowledge. This island is full of wonders, many of which are hidden in plain sight."

Jewel fixed his gaze on the walls as if seeing them for the first time. Intricate carvings of the Church's history scattered throughout. He knew most of their stories. Others he was unsure of but hadn't until now thought to inquire as the image Michael was outlining became more clear. The Arc of the Covenant was surrounded by menacing-looking soldiers, each carrying shields. Other carvings came into focus: giants, sea creatures, and astrology symbols.

Malachi's head craned upward, taking in the scene for the first time as well. "They're beautiful."

"What does it all mean?" Isabelle asked Dondarion,

opting to go right to the source rather than stare open-mouthed at the ceiling like her brethren.

"The clergymen who make up the monastery here at the Shield are a separate entity of the church. When the Holy Temple was sacked by the Egyptians, the church saw fit to designate a select few tasked with the preservation and security of the faith's most holy relics. But it extends much farther than the Shield. Long before Veronia, King Solomon had five hundred shields of beaten gold crafted. They were issued to the mightiest men of valor to guard and protect the forest of Lebanon. They were the first of the order.

"It's said that each of the golden shields was inscribed with holy runes, etched into the gold by the hand of God. These runes enabled the shield-bearer various protection and powers. Whether or not the shields held any divine power was highly debated, especially after the shield-bearers were killed off and the temple looted by the Egyptians. All of King Solomon's golden shields were thought to have been lost after the temple was looted and King Rehoboam replaced the shields with his own, crafted of a lesser metal.

"But legend told of a different story, one where those golden shield-bearers fought their way out of the Egyptian invasion and led the Arc of the Covenant to safety. It's recorded that the runes inscribed in each of the golden shields were aglow the night the Egyptians came, and that no man or army could stand against the mighty men who carried them. When they escorted the Arc of the Covenant to safety, each of the shield-bearers were mysteriously struck down. Some say the shield-bearers now serve in God's Angel Army."

Jewel was speechless. Michael was not. "Care to elaborate on the separate entity part?"

Any reluctance Dondarion may have had in protecting the secrets of his order crumbled under Michael's request, as if he was compelled to do what Michael asked.

"To aid in the effort of securing and protecting our church's past, the early church convened and established a fraternal order. Perhaps the first ever assembled made up of church officials, blacksmiths, woodworkers, stonemasons, and soldiers—all sworn to secrecy. The order was given no name, only a symbol. One you might recognize today worn openly by the Drago Blacksmiths."

Dondarion wore two chains about his neck. The first was his priest's medallion, worn in plain view. He fished the second from his robes. It revealed a smith's hammer crossed by sword over a budded cross. Brother Joshua reluctantly exposed his matching medallion.

Jewel shook his head. *I should have noticed their second chains before. And why does Dondarion seem so edgy around Michael?*

"The shields are more than a novelty," Dondarion continued. "They are God's gift to the righteous men responsible for binding the world's most monstrous of monsters. If they were to fall into the wrong hands, the havoc they could cause would be catastrophic."

The Bible speaks of several mysteriously divine entities, most of which have been bound or destroyed to prevent a premature Armageddon. The book of Job makes mention of a few; one in particular surged to the forefront of Jewel's mind, and his face turned pale. *The Hunter...* "The Giant of Orion."

"Yes. Nimrod, the Giant of Giants, bound in the constellations is but one of many," Dondarion said. "Leviathan the Fire Breather is so terrible that no man can stand before him. Unfortunately, the list goes on. The order believes the shields serve as the monsters' goalers. Like keys to a cell, if you will. We don't know how to summon the monsters or whether or not it can be done by man, but we suspect the shields to be our only defense against them."

"And what of the Arc? Is it here with the shields?" Malachi asked anxiously.

The arc has a past bloody as its mercy seat. It's recorded to have killed those bold enough to place their unworthy hands upon it simply for their irreverence. "I wish it were so, but no," Dondarion said. "The Arc will reveal itself again before the end of times, but not yet."

"Are you planning on arming Leo with the shields?" Isabelle asked, apparently reading Jewel's mind as he sat twisting the staff in his hands.

"That all depends," Jewel replied. "I wouldn't want my brother struck down by the hand of God. Leo, on the other hand, would welcome such an opportunity." He stared at the golden staff but it offered no advice on the matter. "How about we have a look at them first?"

***

Deep in the Gwonda Forest, the Tribal Leaders convened to discuss their diplomacy status with the Kiman Empire. Chief Dretchel was accompanied by Nico, his liquor-breathed son, and Tekrano, the three of whom represented the Antucha-whahs. Chief Bretuka and Marchuke represented the Netches and Chief Ansuke and his son Trechon for the Vrattas.

It was midday. The sun beamed down through the thick canopy of trees, which made for a humid afternoon. The three tribes didn't convene very often but when they did they met in the neutral territory of Chamood. The Netches controlled the southwest portion of the forest all the way to the Gorro River. The Antucha-whahs controlled the northern part of the forest from the Gorro River to the Dorian Sea. The Vrattas controlled the smallest southeastern portion of the forest, which also stretched to the sea.

Although the three tribes were often at odds with each other, years of fighting off Gorronian attacks had bound them as one despite their many differences.

The Antucha-whas were a tribe comprised of the most elite native warriors. Every tribe member was taught at an early age to master the kwatina. The weakest fighters were cast out of the tribe and forced to gather at Chamood where they would await acceptance into one of the other two tribes.

The Netches outnumbered the other tribes nearly two-to-one and found their niche in the trading market, which proved to be a lucrative endeavor. It was known far and wide that if you couldn't find what you were looking for at Mirta's trading port, you'd find it at the Netche Bridge or you were shit out of luck. The tribal market showed no prejudice selling and trading goods to Kotians, Veronians, Herons, and even Gorronians during peacetime.

The Vrattas were masters of alchemy, runes, and all things misunderstood as dark magic. They were the smallest of the tribes and most unaccepted outside of Gwonda. They traded their buckskin attire for tattoos, piercings, and bone armor. Many of their concoctions were highly prized and sought after and the Netches had no trouble trading them to paleskins far and wide.

Tekrano sat cross-legged, his kwatina casually resting atop his knees. Sweat beaded down his neck and chest as flame began to rise in the pit. His kwatina provided the steel, Marchuke the flint, and Trechon the wood to ignite the traditional peace fire that bonded their tribes together. Traditions aren't always convenient but their symbolism serves the greater good.

"I'm not saying we march on the Kiman Empire and crack our heads against their walls," Tekrano said, half-cooked from the heat. "Take a look around. We've got far too many enemies and not enough alliances."

"We've given the paleskins no cause to attack us," Marchuke replied. "We are a peaceful people and have little that would appeal to them."

Peaceful? I can't remember a year of my life that we haven't battled the barbarians or paleskins besides. Our land is what they want, you fool. Tekrano shook off his annoyance and continued. "That scent you can't quite decipher is bullshit, Chief," he said to Dretchel.

The sight of Tekrano always put Marchuke on edge. Marchuke fancied himself as the most powerful and wealthy Tribesman in all of Gwonda. A noble Tribesman if ever such a thing existed. But the Antucha-whahs who lived and died by instruments of war were less impressed.

"If they come, they come. We've been repelling the Gorronians for decades, why would it be any different with the paleskins?" Marchuke asked as if pressed for time. The meeting was a mere inconvenience among his business affairs.

"You would rather have enemies bordering our north and south?" Tekrano asked. "You speak of paleskins like they're all beneath us. As if a paleskin army didn't save your sweet-scented skin not two summers ago."

Tekrano's prodding had the desired effect as Marchuke sprang to defend his honor. None too quick, mind you, but with enough spry to show he'd made the effort before Nico separated the two.

"Enough!" Chief Dretchel bellowed, halting all that Nico could not. "Spit it out, Tekrano. What would you suggest?" the chief asked when they were seated once more at their appointed places round the fire.

Tekrano buried the blade of his hatchet in the earth. "You all know what needs doing. Leo's army chose Tamore to make their stand but we all know they're outnumbered. If we combine our forces we'll squash the Red Army and more importantly pay the blood debt we owe the paleskins."

"Reaching out to Tamore would be considered an act of aggression," Marchuke hissed. "The Reds would be in our forest as soon as they caught wind of us crossing the river. Not that they won't anyways if you keep shipping supplies to them in the night."

Chief Bretuka could hold his silence no longer. "We are grateful for what Leo did for us, but we are not so naïve to think he did it out of his heart's kindness. Had the Gorronians defeated us, they would have had a stronghold that much closer to their kingdom. Self-preservation is a mask that fits heroes, cowards, and countrymen alike."

Tekrano couldn't refute that. Nonetheless, he found himself wanting to cut a man and was growing tired of being talked out of war.

Dretchel saw the fury rising in Tekrano like a steaming kettle. "The Bloody Rose might very well have had some ulterior motives of his own, but a debt we owe him and our debts we pay."

Wars are good for trading and Marchuke would no doubt turn quite the profit. On the flipside, such a fabled war might propel a warrior such as Tekrano past him on the tribal hierarchy ladder and that was a risk the trader couldn't allow. "Perhaps we should wait until Leo requests our assistance before getting directly involved," Marchuke added.

"I don't recall sending a fecking distress raven when the Gorronians came slashing and stabbing us last, do you?" Tekrano spat.

It was not uncommon for the Vrattas to sit mute throughout the course of such meetings. Chief Ansuke seemed more occupied staring into the fire as if it held the answers they sought. Trechon was only slightly more interested outlining the two star tattoos on his left hand.

"Enough squalling or we'll be here all day. By then we'll all be extra crispy," Dretchel said, shifting uncomfortably around the fire. "What say you, Ansuke?"

The Vratta chief didn't bother to look away from the fire. "Many will die. Perhaps all of us. The Kiman Empire will not relent until they're struck down by sword and fire."

Tekrano thought he saw a flicker of light come alive in Ansuke's bottomless pits for eyes, but shook it off as a side effect of the heat. He tore his hatchet from the earth and stood as if already dismissed from the fire by his chief. "War it is then. I'll ready the men."

***

"I don't see any reinforcements. It appears that whatever group was led from Mirta is well on their way to Tamore by now," one of Agnen's lieutenants reported, overcome by the urge to state the obvious.

Behind them, his small contingency of soldiers hacked and cursed the timber into submission and rafts slowly began to emerge. He leaned against a sea-weathered palm tree and peered out over the choppy, green-watered Bay of Bones. The beachfront of Shield Island appeared deserted, but white- and purple-robed figures scurried about the lone-standing Chapel, readying themselves to fight or flee—Agnen could not tell.

Berinon slithered beside him, brimming with excitement. "We mustn't allow them to sail away, Commander."

The Reaper didn't take too kindly to being ordered about, especially by a fecking priest. Before he knew it, Agnen found himself clutching the handle of his sword.

"Easy now, Commander." Abaddon casually glided into view, accompanied by Lyle, whose eyes flashed aglow.

The Kotian, too? Just what in the hell is going on with their eyes? Agnen thought back to the light that hit him in the Capitol.

"He's right, you know," Abaddon said, resting a

hand on Berinon's shoulder. It was a heavy hand that cowered the Light Priest like a wolf scolded by the pack leader. "We mustn't allow them to flee, but Berinon sometimes forgets his place."

"Forgive me, my lord." Berinon stepped away from Abaddon's touch as politely as he could.

"His eyes," Agnen said, pointing his sword at Lyle. "They lit up like the sun. What kind of sorcerers are you?"

Abaddon reached out, lowering Agnen's sword with his hand. "Patience, Commander. All of your questions will be answered soon enough, but first you've an island to secure."

***

Inside the Chapel, priests and clergymen scrambled about, yelling of the Red Army's arrival. Jewel ran above ground to survey the scene, his council in tow. Across the bay, Red soldiers launched nearly a dozen rafts into the choppy waters, paddling with tree branches and shields for oars. They took their time crossing. Not much of a choice with the howling wind battling the choppy green waters. White caps tall as a man roared towards shore. One slip and they would discover just how difficult it is to swim in chainmail.

Blast. We've run out of time. "Brother Dondarion, how many boats do you have on the west side?" Jewel asked.

"Enough to get us out of here, but we'll have to be quick about it. The shields will take some time to load," Dondarion replied. As if reading his mind, Joshua bolted below ground.

"Sister Isabelle. See that Solomon's Shields make it to Leo. He'll distribute them as he sees fit after you appoint him as the Shield of Veronia." Jewel handed the staff to her. "Keep an eye on this for a while, will you? The rest of you better board the ships and get out of here."

Tears welled in Isabelle's tired eyes, but she dutifully took hold of the staff. "What will you do?" she asked.

"My guess is they're here for the shields or the council, if not both. Any leverage they can find to wield against Tamore. If I surrender to them, maybe they'll not chase the rest of you. Tell Leo to stay the course, or thousands of Veronians will have died for nothing. We must hold Tamore. Now go, the lot of you, and be quick about it!"

Malachi held onto Isabelle like a pillar of courage. He said nothing, only looked at Jewel and bowed his head as he pulled her away.

Jewel walked towards the bay to meet the Reds as they slowly made their way onto the beach. It didn't take a life's worth of combat experience to realize something was off about the Reds' approach. A quick count revealed only about twenty-five soldiers advancing to take the island.

Twenty-five men? If the clergy was armed with bows they could have killed most if not all of them as they struggled to cross the bay. *Where is the rest of their army?* His heart sank to the pearl sand. *God strengthen my brother. Sharpen his sword for the slaughter. Polish his blade to strike like lightning and let death not find him until it is Your will.*

The first raft beached, carrying a handful of soldiers who clutched the earth and cursed the water. That was until they saw Jewel approaching.

"We don't get many welcome parties," one of the Reds said mockingly. "We're here for Bishop Jewel, now be good little priests and point him out and we might just let y'all live."

Priests? Y'all? Jewel turned and found Michael at his back. The white-haired brother had ripped the sleeves from his robes, exposing tattoos on each of his ungloved hands. "Did you bump your head and lose the fear of the flux?" he asked, not expecting an answer. "Thought I told you to leave with the others? These guys will kill you, ya know?"

Michael aligned himself with Jewel, a devilish smile on his face. "Only sinners fear death. You didn't think you could just order me away like a stable boy, did you? Besides, I've been looking forward to reuniting with a few of these gentlemen."

"You boys hard o' hearing? Where's Jewel?" one of the Reds asked.

"You're looking at him. What can I do for you?"

The rest of the soldiers trickled onto the beach and began circling around the two priests. "We've got orders to take you back to the vault," the soldier said, reaching for a set of shackles on his raft.

"I figured as much, which is why I thought I'd meet you halfway. Let's get on with it." Jewel stretched out his wrists.

The Reds wasted no time hammering metal pins into heavy iron shackles around Jewel's wrists and ankles with practiced precision. "What are we going to do with the other one?" the shackler asked.

"We only had orders to take the one. What's your name, priest?"

"Bishop Michael at your service," he replied, welcoming a matching set of iron accessories.

The Red soldier shook his head and spat. Killing a priest is an unnatural thing even for this lot. "Best beat it before our patience runs thin, priest."

"They're giving you a chance to go. Take it!" Jewel said in the most commanding tone his shackles would allow. "You'll do us no good dead. Get out of here."

Jewel wasn't the only one surprised when Michael hefted a pair of shackles from a nearby raft and clasped them on his own wrists. "I appreciate your concern, brother, but Tamore will soon be a battlefield and I've never been much use with a sword."

A scrawny-looking Red with bug eyes and something to prove had grown tired of the charade. He reared back with a right hook that caught Michael square in the stomach and buckled his knees. "Care for another, priest?" he said, drawing a round of laughter from his comrades.

Michael caught his breath quicker than Jewel thought possible. The tattoos on his hands flickered alight, the iron shackles clasped around his wrists burned orange as if in the forge and then crumbled away before their eyes. The Reds shrank back. "It would be ill advised to try that again. Which of the twelve command you? I can sense them nearby."

The twelve? Those tattoos? What in Sheol is going on here?

"Sorcerer!" one of the Reds screamed, bearing his sword half-full of terror. The gap between the soldiers and priests began to widen. The crowd of Reds separated and a mountain of a man emerged wearing a golden-horned helm with Dragon glass armor.

"You Jewel?" he rumbled, with no patience for games.

"I'm Michael. That is Father Jewel." He pointed. "You must be General Agnen, Commander of the Kiman Army. I've heard many stories about you."

A moment of silence passed. Agnen looked genuinely surprised to be recognized. His eyes darted from Jewel to Michael before lingering on the white-haired priest's tattoos. "Leave us!" he bellowed to his men. "Secure the Chapel. Let no one escape and burn nothing just yet."

The Reds swarmed the Chapel, leaving three

figures behind the general. The first was a white-robed priest carrying what could only be the infamous Book of Light. The Light Priest's attention seemed fixated on the Chapel rather than the two prisoner priests. The second figure was a Kotian wearing a black star-patterned jerkin. His eyes cautious, never leaving Michael.

"Nicholi," the third man addressed Michael. He wore a crimson surcoat embroidered with the stars of the Kiman Empire. "Nice to see you're not hiding your stars amidst a faith that shuns the twelve for once. I was wondering when you would turn up."

"Nicholi?" Jewel questioned aloud. "You know these men, Michael?"

"I'll explain later, but yes. We're well acquainted. Have been for quite some time. Careful not to cast stones from your glass house, Abaddon. Or the Vault, as you call it. The twelve have always been firmly established within the church. That was until your Prothica broke the accords," Michael spat, conduct unbecoming of a priest but the crowd didn't seem to mind. "And now you bring the conjurer to this holy ground seeking the Shields of Solomon? To what end, Abaddon? Your blasphemy shames us all!"

A conniving laugh escaped Abaddon's knowing grin. "Oh, Nicholi. Smart as you are, sometimes you forget to see the forest through the trees. I'm sure the shields are aboard a ship by now and sailing for Tamore. Am I right?"

A pause as Michael's eyes diverted to the northwest and the ships that carried the shields. "Then what is it you want here?"

"It's time the Twelve are made known once again to the world. And what better way to do that than to bring forth a tidal wave of misery that only the Twelve can withstand?"

"You're mad. You'll kill us all. I can't let you do it." Michael's eyes and hands were aglow in an instant, flinging starfire at Abaddon who braced for the impact with outstretched hands.

Abaddon was driven back, his feet digging through the sand like a knife through butter. Jewel found himself on the ground next to Agnen's massive form. The general didn't seem the kind to take to the earth for cover, but a wise man knows when to fight and when to get out of the way.

The Kotian flung a bit of his own starfire which drove Michael back. Michael's hands were outright, shielding the steady streams of starfire coming from Abaddon and Lyle. Michael struck first and fast, just like Jewel figured Leo would have done, but he was being driven further and further back.

"You'll have to kill me," Michael gasped through clenched teeth. He dropped to a shaky knee but managed to keep his hands up, fending off their attack.

One last surge of strength and the Kotian tumbled over, writhing in pain as if he'd been splashed with scalding water.

Abaddon relented just long enough to let Michael sag to his knees. He took a knee next to Michael and whispered in his ear. It was meant only for Michael but Jewel could hear it loud enough.

"Long live Azazel!"

Michael collapsed onto the sand. Jewel tried running to him but found himself bound by the ankle in Agnen's iron grasp. Abaddon slid a golden ring from Michael's finger onto his own. The stars on his hands and eyes came alight. He fixed them on Jewel. "You'll do as I say or everyone you love will wish you had."

CHAPTER

13

It was the end of another long day in Tamore. Despite the moon's watch, Leo heard Edger barking orders at his work crew who scrambled to make final preparations to their wooden walls. Others were restless and heavily engaged in sullen conversations, speculating when the Reds would arrive.

As usual, Leo immersed himself in the solitude of a crackling fire next to the Gorro River. He found himself strangely at odds with the Priest's Council's letter naming him the Shield of Veronia. Had the church and his brother not been the authors, that letter would serve only to kindle his fire. *What good's an extra title when it can't bear a shield or swing a sword to cover my ass?*

The fire wasn't the only thing crackling that night. In the darkness, twigs snapped underfoot. Juan's steps couldn't have been louder not because his size hindered his stealth, but because he knew damn good and well you don't want to surprise a man with sharp weapons in the dark.

"Sheath your sword, it's just little old me," Natalie said from the tree line, carrying a familiar-looking tribal pot. She'd shed her armor for simple leather pants and a form-fitting violet jerkin that exposed her navel. Leather straps pulled tight around her breasts, fastening the material that covered them yet exposing just enough cleavage to make the mind wander.

Leo slid the letter inside his waistband and set his sword down, struggling to divert his eyes from her breasts as she came closer. A witty reply eluded him; instead he flexed his jaw to make sure his mouth wasn't gaping open.

"Care to share a tribal drink with a lady?" She chuckled, sitting next to him. She took a swig and passed it to Leo. From the smell of her breath, it wasn't her first pull, but Leo wasn't necessarily focused on her breath.

His suspicions were confirmed when he hefted the half-empty bottle to his nose for inspection. The strength of it curled his nose but he warmed up to the smell quick enough. "Fire Water is a better-suiting name." He cradled the bottle cautiously. "Haven't had any of this stuff in a while and for good reason."

The familiar smell of alcohol assaulted his senses. He found himself reminiscing of nights that seemed so very long ago. Nights spent in the Antucha-whah village with his friend Tekrano. Both battered and bruised but deep in their cups recovering from a long day of weapons play. Back then Tekrano was just as thirsty, learning the sword and shield as Leo was the kwatina and bow.

He took a swig. The liquid fire spilled into his mouth, spread and tingled throughout his entire body. He closed his eyes and tilted his head back, exhaling the heat only to open his eyes and realize he may have enjoyed that little moment a bit too much. It only amused Natalie that much more.

"Sorry. This Netche Brew and I go way back. You're up," he said, handing her the bottle.

"We all have our scars and secrets. You don't have to explain anything to me." She scooted closer and he felt her knee touching his. "What were you looking at?"

Her curious green eyes met his and he took another gulp to steady his nerves. "Nothing interesting. Just waiting on my clothes to dry." He gestured at his laundry draped over a log near the fire.

Natalie pulled the bottle from his grasp and took another impressive pull. "You're a terrible liar," she said, leaning back to look at the sky. "The Kotians say the stars shine brightest the night before a bloody morn.

Guess we don't need the stars to tell us when the Reds will be here, but they look awfully bright tonight," she said more seriously.

He lay beside her now, both of them gazing at the stars. Funny how many times he'd thought about a night like this, just the two of them under the stars by the fire, but he wouldn't dare make such a reckless move as asking her to share a drink. She found the courage easily enough but he suspected most of her courage was brought on by the brew. Either that or the battle preparations diminished her apprehensions.

Leo didn't care either way. He hadn't had this much fun in a long time. "When we were kids my father would read to us from the Book of Job. I was less infatuated than my brother but one story in particular caught my interest. The story of a Greek slayer. A man so devastating that only God's angel army could subdue the giant to stop the slaughter."

Leo threw caution to the wind, taking her by the hand to outline a cluster of stars. He stole another glance at her tits and wondered what his cock would feel like between them. "If you look closely you can see the giant trapped within Orion's Belt."

Natalie leaned into him as he outlined the giant. His heart raced as he drew in her rosemary-scented hair, more intoxicating than any alcohol could ever hope to be.

"The three stars here make up the giant's belt. And here his legs. There his arms," he said, pointing.

"I see it!" She turned to face him. They were so close he felt her breath on his lips.

Leo panicked and turned nervously away to sit up. She took the bottle and slid it between Leo's crossed legs. The backside of her hand raked across his rock hard prick, which he'd leaned over to conceal.

She winked at him, a provocative smile stretched across her face. "Your shot."

He downed the remainder of the bottle. It seemed as good an idea as any at the time. When he exhaled, the heat made his head tingle. Whether it was the liquid courage or the moment, he couldn't tell. But he mustered the confidence to place his hand on her inner thigh. He clamped down like it was his. His other hand cupped the back of her head, drawing her into him.

She hungrily welcomed the kiss, and for a moment nothing else in the world mattered. He slid his hand forward up her inner thigh until it rested on her lady parts and could go no further. He squeezed again and Natalie gasped, her back arched, exposing her neck. His lips moved to it, kissing gently at first and then harder until red marks began to form.

Snap, snap. The footsteps stole his attention. "Someone's coming, and fast."

"Let them watch," she replied, pulling him back towards her.

To Leo's surprise it was Wade who barreled into view clad in full armor, his voice distressed. "Leo, you must come quickly. We've a mess on our hands. A couple of the men tried to bed Mandy. Juan and Bruce are after their blood. The whole camp's in an uproar."

Quick as a flash, Leo was on his feet and striding off sword in hand, Wade and Natalie struggling to keep up. They made it to camp pushing through a crowd of shouting spectators. What they saw was an all-out brawl. In the center of it, Juan and Bruce were fighting off nearly a dozen men. Leo caught sight of Mandy being dragged away out of the corner of his eye. Her hands clasped her torn shirt and fear filled her eyes.

Something inside Leo bent when he saw the dozen on Juan and Bruce. At the sight of Mandy it snapped and he shouldered forward, knocking two of the men to the ground from behind. A few of the smarter ones took notice of his arrival and lost themselves in the crowd.

Juan was being held from behind while another man punched him in the front. Leo cut the puncher down and Juan fell. A blink later, Leo drove his sword into the neck of the man who'd been doing the holding. The three men surrounding Bruce shrank back with swords drawn.

"What's the meaning of this?" Leo yelled. The rage carried him forward, cutting another man down as the others tried to flee. Their escape was barred by a wall of Widow Makers. The Swords of Bane closed in from the other side, creating a shielded circle.

Juan and Bruce slowly got to their feet. Cederic stepped forward with two swords to arm Bruce and Juan. He met Leo's gaze and the lieutenant gave him a reassuring nod. The circle of justice was set. In it, sharpened steel was the judge and jury.

"You brood of vipers!" Leo spat. He paced around, beside himself. "How dare you raise your hands against your own brothers. And to our women besides! Death won't erase the stain of your lives fast enough!"

He didn't wait for the men to charge. It's easier to swing a sword than block one anyway. Three of the assailants moved forward, swords at the ready. Leo recognized them as Gregory, Claudius, and Merrill. From the crowd Natalie recognized them as the same trio she'd encountered the other night when Juan stepped in.

Juan and Bruce were not in the best condition yet they stood beside Leo nonetheless.

"What's wrong, Leo? Need Bruce and Juan to fight your battles?" Merrill said. "Ain't none o' your business who we fuck. I bet Mandy's got a sweet little cherry. Claudius and Gregory here can share Natalie. That cunt will probably beg for more."

"They're mine," Leo rasped, pushing Juan and Bruce a step back with either arm. He drove the point of his sword into the earth and walked past it.

The three circled Leo as all of Tamore watched. They moved round and round. Gregory positioned himself at Leo's back and was first to attack, lunging forward but Leo dodged the blow. He countered with a bone-crunching elbow that landed square against Gregory's left temple and dropped him to the ground.

Claudius and Merrill moved as one, slashing and stabbing. Leo ducked, dived, and rolled out of their assault. Again they came but Leo was a blur of motion.

"My turn." Leo burst forward towards Claudius who swung his sword in defense of the charge. The Bloody Rose deflected the sword with his forearm, not the least bit concerned about it biting into bone. He delivered a left hook that dazed Claudius long enough to throw a knife hand that landed directly on Claudius's Adam's apple. The man went down, gasping for air through a broken windpipe.

Merrill saw an opportunity and lunged forward to deliver a thrust, however Leo saw it coming, sidestepped, and parried the blow. Leo's right forearm was numb and blood began to trickle into his hand.

"You think you're invincible because you've survived a couple wars?" Merrill hissed. "You think you can drop your sword and win a fight because of your name? I'll name all my bastards after you."

Leo was done ducking and sidestepping. Merrill moved forward with a blow that Leo caught in midair with his bare left hand. The blade did its worst as the Bloody Rose pulled Merrill closer, not bothering to even wince from the pain. As Merrill struggled to free his sword, Leo landed a right hook that disfigured his nose.

With what might he had left, Merrill twisted and pulled frantically to free his sword from Leo's grasp. The Bloody Rose tugged on the sword, pulling Merrill close enough to clench. He grabbed Merrill by the mullet and pulled his head back to expose the neck. His teeth sank into Merrill's jugular and tore a chunk of bloody flesh before he pushed Merrill to the ground.

Merrill's hands worked to stop blood that poured from the hole in his throat. Leo spit flesh from his mouth onto him as Merrill struggled in a panic to fill the void in his neck.

The Bloody Rose watched his work until the loss of blood drained the life out of ol' Merrill. Leo knew his hands and arms should hurt. The Netche Brew covered the pain like a warm blanket as he stood over Merrill with a sour mouthful of the dead bastard's blood.

It was quiet. Too quiet. Women stood covering their mouths as men diverted their eyes quickly away from the Bloody Rose's deadly glare. The rage slowly subsided and familiar faces came into view. They all shared the same reluctant demeanor as if a monster stood in their presence.

Juan approached cautiously and handed Leo his sword. He leaned in with a hushed voice. "Leo, if you can hear me in there, maybe we should go for a ride and get some air."

* * *

Leo woke to the sound of chainmail rustling towards his door.

"Sir, we've got visitors from the west. Looks like the Priest's Council if I can tell a sword from shield," Sgt. Jaxon Griffon said, peeking into Juan and Leo's cottage.

"On my way." Juan slung the bastard sword over his back. He'd almost made it to the door when Leo got to his feet.

"What'd I miss? And where the fuck are my weapons?" he growled, looking around. It wasn't a big cottage and it didn't take a university master to realize his arms had been confiscated.

"Relax," Juan said. "Bruce has them right outside. After you nearly bit a man's head off, folks got nervous. It eased a lot of minds to separate you from them at least until you'd slept off whatever it was that possessed you last night."

Leo palmed his face. "Fuck my life," he cursed, realizing it wasn't just a bad dream after all.

"Don't beat yourself up too much, though. That crazy shit quelled a riot. Nonetheless, Nestin prohibited all outside alcohol from the camp until further notice and they're rationing what's left of the wine. Might want to wash that blood from your face before we go welcome the Priest's Council, though. Can't wait to hear what they're calling you now."

The sun was blinding but after the Frostbite, Leo had little to complain about the weather. Natalie and Bruce stood outside the hut clad in armor. *On watch, perhaps? Did I create such a spectacle that I had to be disarmed and guarded?* Whether they were protecting the people from him or the Bloody Rose from the people, he didn't ask. He didn't much care, really. A man can't maintain order in a killing unit without a healthy dose of fear every now and again.

"Your weapons, sir," Bruce said, handing Leo his hatchet and sword.

The "sir" caught Leo off guard, and even Bruce was surprised it came out of his own mouth. Nobody saw fit in making an issue of it. They soldiered on like the camp hadn't buried a stack of dismembered corpses their commander had left behind during the night.

Mandy caught his eye. She was also in full armor and after last night Leo didn't wonder why. Her face was hard and cast a chill, but crumbled when her eyes met his. For a moment it looked as if she was about to embrace him, but that notion died in the womb.

"Thank you," she said, extending a dirtied hand. Least she could do was help bury the fuckers last night, but not before she'd stomped a few of their heads to mush and watched Bruce and Edger piss on what was left. "Next time it'll be me who does the killing."

Natalie cut the tension in half. "Better get some water down. Unless it's blood you drink now." She tossed a water skin at Leo's chest. "The Reds were spotted marching this way. Won't be long till we get to test the strength of Edger's wall."

At Town Square, Nestin and Abigail welcomed the Priest's Council. Strangely, they were accompanied by a dozen Drago Smiths, each wearing dragon-scaled armor. Leo realized something was amiss when he counted two fewer priests gathered around, his brother nowhere in sight.

"Where's Jewel?" Leo asked of the silent, violet-robed crowd.

Bishop Isabelle was the first to speak. Leo paled when he saw her carrying the High Priest's golden staff. "Well met, Commander," she said, gliding forward as if floating on air until she stood before him. "The Kiman Empire has put the sword to Veronia and the Church alike. Jewel and Michael allowed themselves to be taken captive so the rest of us were able to flee the Shield."

The thought of his brother, a priest no less, taken prisoner by the Red Fucking Army boiled his blood. The urge to kill a man came upon him like an addiction he couldn't shake. Trion hurried the Priest's Council out of Leo's reach lest the Bloody Rose fill the need to open a few more throats.

"Easy now, Leo," came Juan's subtle voice of reason. He sounded more and more like Jaminez all the time. "We'll get them back, you know we will."

"Shouldn't have left his side," Trion said guiltily.

"Commander," a priest said, escaping Trion's grasp. A new addition to the council? One Leo didn't recognize. "The sacrifice your brother has made is one of biblical proportions."

"Who are you?" Leo asked.

"My name is Dondarion, a newly-elected bishop of the High Priest's Council. And this is Bishop Joshua." He pointed to another priest Leo didn't recognize. "Together we've been the Keepers of King Solomon's golden shields. Biblical relics that have the power to shield us from a storm that may already be heading our way."

Leo didn't know what in the hell Dondarion was talking about, but the priest sounded sure enough about it. "Keepers of shields? What's that got to do with anything? Where's my brother?"

Two Drago Smiths Leo recognized as Val and Mortis carried a wooden box forward and set it between Dondarion and Leo. Jonas looked twice his size in dragon armor. He hefted the lid from the box and stepped back.

Leo's curiosity got the best of him. His first realization was that a shield rested in the box. Not just an ordinary shield, but one of solid gold. Runes covered its face, which reminded Leo of the ones on his hatchet. At its center lay a budded cross. He tried to make sense of the other etchings that surrounded it but the carvings tired his eyes and made his head spin.

He staggered defensively away. "Sorcery?"

"Sorcery has limits, divine intervention does not," Dondarion replied. "This is a gift from God. A shield to protect against troubled times," he continued, leading Isabelle forward by the hand. "We've a lot to explain and little time to do so, Commander. You want your brother back, as do we. But first it was your brother's wish to appoint you as the Shield of Veronia and Guardian of the Church."

Either he was still half-drunk or the golden shield began to light the day. Leo wasn't the only one looking for answers as many of the crowd dispersed in fear.

"Kneel before the Shield!" came the mighty roar of Jonas. A command that consumed everyone within earshot. Before Leo knew it, only Brother Dondarion was left standing.

"Leo Rosewood, the Guardian Church has selected you the Shield of Veronia," Dondarion shouted, then bent at the waist and lifted the shield from the box like a loving father hefting a child. The priest took a knee across from Leo and stretched the shield towards him. "Take this divine instrument and rise a soldier of God's mortal army and Shield of Veronia."

Leo took hold of the shield and slid his left arm through the forearm straps. To his surprise the straps of many colors cinched firmly around his arm. The shield burst forth with a glow that lit up the day once again. What drained his energy before now filled him as if he'd sucked it from those standing nearby. His reluctance faded away. Something about the shield put missing pieces into place and Leo felt whole again.

"Veronia!" Leo bellowed, lifting the shield to the sky.

Tamore greeted their new Shield with a cheer heard for miles. So loud was their roar it gave pause to the massive Red Army who were just hours away from Tamore.

***

"What is the meaning of this?" yelled Jewel, voice hoarse from being ignored. Michael's unconscious form lay in the center of a candlelit pentagram the Light Priest had methodically erected just before night had fallen upon the shield. The sight of Berinon producing a dagger from his robe sent Jewel into an uproar.

Try as he might, he could do little to escape his iron shackles. Every time he tried standing, a chain running from his leg shackles to alternating hands was yanked by his goalers, sending him to the cobbled courtyard he'd stood so proudly upon not long ago.

As the pentagram took shape, General Agnen lost himself in the crowd. Jewel had heard all the stories of Agnen's past. An ever-present thorn in Veronia's side, but at least the Gorronian didn't revel in blasphemy like the others. *Or perhaps he fears the sorcery?*

Abaddon shed his crimson cloak for a solid black jerkin like the Kotian wore. Lyle silently directed Berinon about the pentagram.

"You really don't know about Nicholi or the Twelve, do you?" Abaddon asked. "Two decades in the Priest's Council and Nicholi never aged. That doesn't seem odd to you?"

Well, now that you mention it. He tried smothering

his ignorance with a question. "The Twelve?"

"Yes, the Twelve." Abaddon drew the hood of his cloak, his eyes glowing in the darkness. "Perhaps the Mozzaroth is a more familiar term. Your friend there is among the Twelve, as is Master Lyle and I."

Jewel gasped in awe. "Demon spawns!"

Evil laughter escaped Abaddon's hood. "Demon spawn, is it? Such a typical response. I expected more from a High Priest. Frances must have been more tightlipped than I'd thought."

"We're nearly ready, Master Abaddon," called Berinon, doing nothing to mask his excitement. The Light Priest knelt just outside the pentagram, a dagger resting atop his massive Book of Light. His white robes were a stark contrast to Lyle, who looked a mere shadow of a man lurking over Michael.

A human sacrifice! The realization bit hard, like a shark feasting upon injured prey. Berinon wasted no time seizing the moment with an uneven smile.

"You white-robed weasel," Jewel spat. He rushed headlong at the Light Priest, making only a few strides before his chain was yanked and his feet gave out from under him. Jewel kicked and flailed as they dragged him farther away from the pentagram.

No one enjoyed the dragging more than Berinon who left the pentagram to twist the knife. "God loves nothing more than the blood offering of a righteous man. Theodore was generous with his, although he'd nearly bled out by the time I got to him. But Frances…"

Berinon laughed. "Frances lingered long enough to watch his cup runneth over the mercy seat."

"Berinon!" Abaddon scolded until the Light Priest scurried back to the pentagram like a whipped pup.

"My apologies, sir," Berinon said, hiding beneath the hood of his robe as if it were a shield against Abaddon's wrath.

"The next time you try that will be your last," Abaddon threatened. A threat Jewel had no intention of testing. "Lyle, if you are ready let us begin." He slid the stolen ring from his finger and carefully handed it to Lyle, taking care not to step into the pentagram.

Berinon stood outside it next to Abaddon. "Let us kneel."

The Red soldiers clanked to their knees, forming a half circle. Agnen wasn't the only soldier showing visible signs of discomfort as he reluctantly knelt ahead of his men just beside Jewel, careful not to turn his back on the shackled priest. Many of the Reds refused to cast their eyes on the pentagram. Others quietly dismissed themselves to the beach.

Berinon carefully handed Lyle the ceremonial dagger. Its blade was etched with symbols Jewel couldn't make out. Lyle attached the ring onto the end of the dagger's grip. The Kotian withdrew a summoning orb from within his jerkin. Stars in orbit circled within it, casting blue and white enchanted light.

Lyle's face and hands were blistered and whelped with burns that looked bad enough to kill any other man. Jewel didn't know how he was still standing. Michael put up a valiant fight but didn't stand a chance two against one.

At the sight of the orb, Abaddon knelt, leaving only Lyle standing. Inside the circle Michael's star-patterned tattoos came alight. It did little to improve his unconscious state. The fight he'd given Lyle and Abaddon left him burnt-out and on the brink of death.

"Ring of Solomon, I summon your power!" Lyle's voice was like thunder. A roaring water that made Jewel shudder. It was the first time he'd heard the Kotian speak and now he realized why.

"Heavenly Father, I, Lyle, One of the Twelve and Keeper of the Zodiac, bearer of Pollux, granted the ability to conjure and summon all things lesser than you, call upon your grace to relinquish the power reserved only for the ring-bearing starborn." He raised his dagger in the air, eyes fixed steadily on the orb in front of him.

"Here, oh Lord, is the ring of Solomon. By the blood of Nicholi, instill within it the power of dominion over all things summoned henceforth."

Lyle diverted his stare from the orbit onto Michael's exposed chest. Lightning struck the dagger as the conjurer drove it towards the human sacrifice, knocking Lyle off his feet. It was some time before Lyle regained his composure enough to pick up the dagger. The runes on the golden ring shifted as if awakened.

"Your ring," Lyle said, removing it from the dagger and handing it to Abaddon.

Abaddon slid the ring upon his finger just as before, only this time the ring was alive. So much so that his knees buckled. When he rose his eyes were like fire.

"Well done, Lyle. It appears we didn't need the blood of Nicholi after all." Abaddon looked up to the stars like an eagle surveying his dominion below. Orion's Belt began to loosen around the giant in the sky. "Berinon, make me another pentagram."

ABOUT THE AUTHOR

Daniel L Welch is a fantasy/fiction author. After serving in the United States Marine Corps, he began working at his local Sheriff's Office where he is now assigned to the Criminal Investigations Division. Daniel graduated from American Public University with a Bachelor's degree in Criminal Justice.

"Tears of Blood" is Daniel's first novel in "The Veronian Archives" series. He currently lives in Claremore, Oklahoma where he continues to serve his community and write gritty fantasy novels. To learn more about his upcoming books, visit his website at www.daniellwelch.com.